THE BITCH

Dedication & Acknowledgements

As always, first and foremost, I dedicate this book to my readers. Without readers, writing is like having sex with yourself. The feedback you get for your performance is ultimately flawed.

I also owe a tremendous debt to my friend Cort McMeel, who has sadly passed away. Cort read this book several years ago and immediately began to champion it. He went out of his way to get it in front of all the publishers he could, telling every agent and editor he was able to that they needed to either represent or publish it. He took it upon himself to write letters, pigeonhole the literary gatekeepers in bars and other writerly environs, and do everything in his power to persuade them of its value. He was delighted to learn, just before his death, that Jon Bassoff of New Pulp Press was going to publish it, as he had the same tremendous admiration and respect for what Jon was doing in literature that I have.

A special thanks have to go to my friend Michelle Lutz, R.N., who, when I was casting about for a disease to give Jake's wife Paris in the story, came up with preeclampsia and educated me as to the nuances of the condition and how it could work in the plot. If not for Michelle, I probably would have given her leprosy or shingles or something equally stupid, but her suggestion worked out perfectly. Thanks, Michelle!

I'd also like to acknowledge a group of people who rarely appear in book acknowledgements—my brothers and sisters who've been behind bars and are trying their best to stay out and just become regular straights on the bricks. I think my fellow ex-cons will recognize Jake and will be empathetic to his struggle to do just that. They, more than anyone, will understand the choices he makes.

And finally, I'd like to dedicate this book to my wife Mary who's presently upstairs in our home—which we refer to as The Crime Scene—and to the greatest kids a guy could ever hope for: Mike, Sienna and Britney. They've always been there for me, even when I was at my most obnoxious.

Praise for *The Bitch*

"*The Bitch* is the kind of raw crime fiction that's right up my alley, like sandpaper for the brain. Edgerton has got the chops. Mad chops. Gonna make us all ashamed of our puny efforts one day."

—Anthony Neil Smith, bestselling author of *Choke on Your Lies, Psychomatic, Hogdoggin', Yellow Medicine, The Drummer, To the Devil, My Regards,* and others.

"*The Bitch* is a vicious barnstormer of a novel, a noir roller-coaster that won't let you unbuckle until that final three-word smackdown. Les Edgerton is Eddie Bunker's pulpy cousin and Eugene Izzi's soul brother, and with a spiritual family like that, you can't go wrong. Pick it up immediately."

—Ray Banks, internationally bestselling author of *Dead Money, Beast of Burden, The Big Blind. Saturday's Child, Donkey Punch, No More Heroes* and others.

"Every crime novelist remembers how his breath was literally taken away when he first started to read the early novels of Elmore Leonard. Les Edgerton has used the time he served in prison well. Years from now many future crime writers will also remember discovering him. His first crime novel, but not his first published book, *The Bitch* is a realistic crime noir kind of novel that reminds me of *Unknown Man 89, La Brava, Stick,* and *The Killer Inside Me*."

—Joseph Trigoboff, author of *The Bone Orchard* and *The Shooting Gallery.*

"*The Bitch* is superb. Edgerton's hard, pitch-perfect prose and relentless plot provide a one-two knockout punch of crime novel perfection...the real bitch of *The Bitch* is that I tried to buy this priceless work and publish it under a new imprint and I couldn't afford the damn thing. Now it's gold in someone else's pocket."

—Cortright McMeel, author of *Short*, founding editor and publisher of Murdaland Magazine: Crime Fiction for the 21st Century and Noir Nation: International Journal of Crime Fiction.

"Imagine, if you will, Les Edgerton, Dashiell Hammett and Raymond Chandler sipping straight whiskey while swapping lies in the back booth of the Linebacker bar as the "noir" legends welcome Edgerton into the brotherhood of broken dreams. With *The Bitch*, Edgerton earns his way into this special literary brotherhood. No, The Bitch isn't a wild woman, but prison slang for "ha-BITCH-ual criminal." This is a taut tale of double-cross, death, diamonds and destruction as Jake Bishop fights to protect all he holds dear—his freedom, his pregnant wife, and his teen-age brother—by holding The Bitch at bay when trapped into one last job. Sam Spade and Phillip Marlowe could learn a thing or two from this hairdresser."

—Bob Stewart, author of *Remorse,* a True Crime Book of the Month selection, *Hidden Evil*, and others.

"I liked *The Bitch* so much that I wanted to publish it. But we lost out and New Pulp Press got a hell of a book. *The Bitch* is a dark crime fiction story that never once pulls a punch or ducks behind some bullshit like 'happy endings' or 'closure.' *The Bitch* isn't afraid to stay dark until the very end."

—Brian Lindenmuth, editor/publisher of Snubnose Press and Spinetingler Magazine.

"Les Edgerton. I just read his newest hard-boiled effort, *The Bitch*, and I realized I didn't once breathe through the entire thing. Okay, that's an exaggeration, but it is one of the most fun, dangerous, if not pyromanic literary performances of the past year (word up is that parts of it are taken from Les's own life. Holy crap, this guy shouldn't be alive!). Like Les's previous bestselling nonfiction effort on writing, *Hooked*, this novel is a sure bet."

—Vincent Zandri author of *The Remains, The Innocent, Moonlight Falls* and *The Concrete Pearl*.

"Les Edgerton's brilliantly hardboiled *The Bitch* is the tense and hard hitting story of Jake Bishop, a reformed ex-con whose dark past drags him back into a life of crime like an umbilical cord tied tight around his neck."

—Paul D. Brazill, author of *13 Shots of Noir*.

"The satisfying stink of criminal authenticity wafts up from the pages of *The Bitch*. It reads like the diary of an ex-con who can write—somebody with literary skills but no damn sense for staying out of trouble. Maybe that was Les Edgerton as a young man before life beat some sense into him. If you're wondering why Goodreads Listopia for classic noir fiction included *The Bitch* in its top fifty books of all time, alongside Mickey Spillane and David Goodis, the answer is simple: It deserves to be there."

—Anonymous-9, author of *Hard Bite*

Foreword

As a writer, I want to be like Les Edgerton when I grow up. I want to be that raw, that honest, that fearless. I want to craft voices that chill your blood while fascinating you at the same time. I want to write crime fiction that makes you all cringe.

I want all that.

Just without the "actually went to jail" part.

Les has told me for a long time that he loves my work, and I've told him for a long time that I love his. I can see how some readers might look at hard-candy shell of our books and say, "Oh yeah, those two, very similar writers." But crack through the surface and you can taste the differences. I write about the things that scare me, and I use language that amps up that fear. It's all special effects, like the sudden scary music in a horror film. You will feel what I'm trying to get you to feel because I'm pushing your buttons. But Les, he's the raw "found film" footage. No special effects. What he's got to tell you, he delivers straight. The matter of fact-ness makes his work even more frightening. No violin stabs to convince you it's just for fun. Nope.

He does it in *The Bitch*. Opens right up with a scene of parental abuse, no filters. A father whose punishment is worse than the crime. We see, right before our eyes, the instant a soul turned bad. Can't unsee that, can you?

He does it in *The Rapist*, letting this charming voice lull you into engagement. How can you help but listen to a guy telling you a story this way? The whole time he's talking, he's also getting into your head, directing your nightmares. You know it, too, but you don't want to stop listening. You can't. He's got you.

There is fearlessness in these books, and I don't mean the macho, quip-tossing, roaming army dude sort of fearlessness, because that shit is just compensation. The danger in those other types of thrillers is cartoonish. It never rings true. It's all Hollywood bling, where Les is bringing you the documentary. He's not worried about his characters looking tough. He's not concerned with giving you a superhero in denim. What you get when you read Les Edgerton is the unedited footage of how awful people can be to one another, usually over not-so-large sums of money. The fearlessness comes from letting you see it, mostly without judgment. Here's what happened, take it or leave it.

Les ain't Instagram. Les is the real deal Polaroid camera.

In *The Bitch*, we're listening to Jake tell his story. He's settled into a nice life after prison, but of course it doesn't take long for the past to catch up with him. And maybe his present is a good excuse to embrace it, too. Regardless, from the first pages, he's got you. You're going to keep buying him drinks way past last call, whatever it takes to finish the story. He'll talk about his younger brother. He'll talk about what's been happening to his wife lately, how weird she's acting. He'll talk to you about "Spitball". He'll even talk to you about cutting hair if you'd like. And about how it feels to fall off the wagon.

Square in the eye, too, the whole time. Go ahead and look away if you can.

After he's hooked you, the feeling of dread builds. Talking about the jeweler, real slimeball, trying to blackmail him. Talking about the lies he has to tell to those closest to him.

You get a feeling in the pit of your stomach when you hear this. It's never a question of if the lies will fall apart, but when. You're already grinding your teeth. Jake's wife thinks he's cheating on her. Problem is that the truth would be even worse. He doesn't have a chance, right?

Noir is like that. We realize there's going to be a bad fall. The reason we keep reading is to see how bad. We will peek between the fingers covering our eyes. We will curl up in our seats, trying to keep the acid from gnawing too hard.

No need to spoil the rest (Hint: get a big tub of Tums, eat 'em like candy), but if you're hoping for a happy ending… well, "happy" is in the eye of the beholder, right?

Les Edgerton just keeps getting better at this. He keeps raising the stakes. I can't read one chapter—no, one page—without learning something new to steal for my own bag of tricks.

So if this is your first Les Edgerton novel, congrats. You've got a lot of feeling bad ahead of you. Glorious badness. Enjoy.

—Anthony Neil Smith, Sept. 2013

THE BITCH

Les Edgerton

Prologue

When I was 11, my father walked into his bedroom and caught me stuffing several of the coins he collected and kept in a sock into my pockets. Most of them were foreign coins he'd picked up overseas during World War II and I have no idea how I planned to spend English half-pence or German kroners or if I even planned to spend them at all. I just wanted them because I thought I could take them without getting caught. After he put his belt away, my father made me take four of the smallest coins and swallow them.

"You want them, you've got them," he said. "You need to remember this. A Bishop doesn't steal. None of the Bishops have ever been thieves."

My mother came up while I choked them down and stood there, tears dripping slowly and quietly down her cheeks. She didn't say a word. My father was the king of his castle and she was just a slightly higher placed vassal than my sister and me.

She cried but not this tough, 11-year-old criminal. I came close, but I choked down my tears along with the coins once I saw her begin to weep. I glimpsed in that instant my future if I wept, that I'd become as weak as she had. That I didn't break down made my father angrier than my theft.

"I ought to make you eat them all," he said.

"I'd like some salt then," I said. "And a glass of water." I knew what saying that would bring and instead of being fearful, I felt a power like never before surge through me. He could hurt my flesh but he could never dominate me as he had the other members of my family. The knowledge I gained in that instant was my earliest reward for being a thief.

He sighed and undid his belt again.

When the coins came out, a day later, I reached into the stool and mushed the turds with my fingers, extracting them one by one. I took the bar of my father's Lava he used every day after work and held it under the tap until the dried swirls of his oil and grime were rinsed off and the bar shining clean and then scrubbed the coins with it. For an hour I scoured them until they gleamed and shone a dull, lucent silver and copper. He never asked what happened to them and I have them to this day.

The first murder is the hardest. No matter how many more you might commit, it's the first one that always appears at night in your dreams.

That doesn't mean the next one is all that easy. Just *easier*. Like they say, it's all relative.

The funny thing about *thinking* about doing a crime is that once the thought enters your brain it's all over. You might as well write that baby down in the logbook of your life, because it's as sure as rain in Seattle going to happen. And if you talk about it to another human being, then that landslide is already halfway down the mountain. Like a train wreck, once the engine goes off the track, the rest of the cars are going to follow.

I have no excuses. My mother, after all, prophesied daily the bad end she was convinced I took aim at. From the time I could zip up my own trousers, my mother used to say pretty much the same thing when she weighed in against sin on my behalf. A daily battle she fought for my soul. A battle we both knew she'd lose.

"If you have a sinful thought, Jacob, in God's eyes it's the same as committing the sin," she'd say. She'd show me in the Bible where it said that. "See?" she'd say, her cheeks brightly flushed with Divine Evidence. "You think something bad, son, you're going straight to Hell. You don't even have to do it. All you have to do is think it." *Wasn't much I could do about that,* I wanted to tell her, but didn't. I'd joined the other side a long time ago, maybe as far back as birth. That original sin thing.

The day she died, her last words still tried to reach my poor, black soul. "Jakey," she said, her voice barely audible against the whoosh of the respirator and the other machines the ghouls in white, starched uniforms had hooked her up to, keeping her burned body alive. "Promise me you'll be a good boy. Promise me you'll try to find God." Thirty-two years old, her confused, dying, fucked-up mind saw instead this kid with mittens on a string. Part of her mind had already gone on ahead to where her body would follow.

What do you do in a situation like that? You promise, that's what you do. It's your mother. She's dying. It's easy to promise. I've made a lot of promises in my life. Keeping them, though...

Chapter 1

It all began with a phone call. The other stylists had already left for the day, but I'd had trouble with my last client's color, trying different shades while she bitched at me the whole time. It kept coming up the wrong hue of red, but I'd finally gotten it to where she liked it and now I was alone in the salon, putting my tools away, including the vent brush I'd thrown against the wall the minute she left. I called my wife Paris to ask if she needed me to pick anything up from the store on the way home. These days I knew if she wanted anything, it likely wouldn't be milk and bread. Seven and a half month pregnancy-activated hormones desired more exotic foodstuffs, although she hadn't yet requested pickles. Just about everything else, though... Not today. She said she'd probably just throw up anything I brought and then she excused herself to go present another offering to the porcelain goddess, not forgetting to mention that she loved me, hated my sperm before she clicked off. I was headed for the door when it rang again. I should have let it go.

"Tangerine Z Hair Designs," I said, picking up. "This is Jake."

My memory failed me utterly for at least a full ten seconds before I recognized the voice blathering on the other end of the line. Then, it hit me. Walker Joy. A guy I'd spent every day of my last two years in Pendleton with. My-ex cellmate.

"Walker? Walker Joy?"

The voice on the other end paused, then started up again,

with that rapid-fire patter I should have recognized right off the bat. "Well, who the hell'd you think it was, asshole? A bill collector?" He snorted, pissed I hadn't recognized him. He still had the criminal mindset. Lifelong criminals have a way of approaching relationships that's different from straights. Because they get separated from members of their society for years at a time, when they do hook up again, it's always as if they'd only been away for a day or two.

The moment I recognized Walker's voice, a picture of those gray walls of Pendleton came up sharply in my mind and I felt the moisture on the palms of my hands.

"God damn, Walker," I said. "How the hell long's it been? Three years? Four? Damn. It's four years, Walker."

Four years. The end of my second stretch and the last time I meant to ever spend behind bars.

The first of the two times they cut me loose from the joint I strutted out—young and cocky, this *badass*—and I broke the oldest rule of prison. The rule that says if you *look* back you'll *be* back. I looked back. Walked out the front gate, took about twenty steps to the flagpole in front, turned square around, a big-ass smirk on my kisser. Looked defiantly at the fourteen-foot-thick concrete walls of Pendleton Reformatory, outlined against the lighter shade of slate of the winter Indiana sky that particular day.

The second time I smartened up. The second time, I pulled my collar up around my ears, hunkered down into my state-issue seersucker jacket and marched resolutely out the front gate, through the parking lot slush, out to the road that led to the highway, over the railroad track, and down to the bus stop out on Highway 38. Never looked back time one. Didn't even use my peripheral vision to glance to the side.

The first time I possessed the immortality of youth.

The second—and last—time I'd found out Pendleton wasn't a place I could ever go back to. And live. Something happened during that last stretch that shot that mortality bullshit all to hell.

The last time I'd seen Walker Joy. Or even thought of him. I saw him in my mind's eye, sitting on his bunk, opening the package of Oreos I'd given him as a going-away present.

A lot of water under that four-year-old dam.

"I'll be late," I told Paris over the phone a minute later. "I got a call from an old friend. I'm going to buy him a beer. You and Bobby go ahead and eat without me. I may be late." Bobby being my kid brother who lives with us.

I got off the phone quickly, before she could question me about who the "friend" was.

A gust of icy wind blasted me the second I stepped outside. I hunched down into my jacket and shivered. Dirty snow lay everywhere in mounds that resembled volcanic ash, and a gray-yellow haze lay in the air that the December sun struggled bravely to break through. The Notre Dame campus lay just up the street, and there must have been a pep rally for the Irish football team as traffic in front of the Tangerine seemed to be a bumper-to-bumper mass of traffic all heading north toward the school, tires hissing in the black snow melt, only a few cars passing by in the opposite lanes. Just as I opened the door to my white Lumina, a bank of dingy clouds passed over and the temperature dropped another couple of degrees, matching the feeling I'd had inside ever since I'd recognized Walker's voice.

Half an hour after Walker had reentered my world via Ma Bell, we were sitting in the Boat Club bar near Howard Park. Sitting in a booth, my old cellmate knocked back shots of peppermint schnapps while I sipped on a ginger ale. A few feet away, the local hustlers worked the pool table and each other.

"So, Walker. How long you been out?" I asked. I was the only one I knew who called Walker by his given name. Most folks called him Spitball. He got that from his face. It looked just like one of those little glops we used to throw at each other back in high school. His features sort of scrunched all around in this ball that passed for his face. He was also hairless as a three-minute poached egg and had all these folds of skin where his hair used to be, which at a distance looked like a Dudley Do-Right pompadour.

One thing I'd forgotten about Walker came back to me the second I sat down. His smell. He always smelled like the woods do after a week of steady rain. I always thought it was because he didn't shower much—I hardly remembered him in the showers back in the joint. Some people do that—don't bathe much—don't end up with B.O., but more like that odor he always carried. After the initial sniff, I didn't notice it much after that.

I owed Walker. He'd saved my life one night back there in the joint. One really bad night I'd tried for years to forget but which crept back in the form of nightmares even at this far remove.

"Couple of months," he said, sucking on the shot I'd just bought him. I'd guessed as much. He still had on his black prison issue shoes and a shirt that had gone out of style about ten years ago. Even before we were cellmates, back here on the downtown streets I knew Walker, and he'd never had the kind of wardrobe would be featured in *GQ*. Only difference between what he wore in the joint and out here on the bricks was his shirts. On the outside, he favored flannel shirts in the winter, the kind lumberjacks and goat-ropers wore, and in warmer seasons he usually had on a black T-shirt. Jeans, both seasons. He wore his winter getup now. A red flannel shirt straight from J.C. Penney's winter clearance sale.

"Get laid yet?"

He laughed. "First night. That be the ugliest girl I'm ever going to fuck for the rest of my life." I laughed at that. I knew what he meant. First day out of the joint, a guy'd fuck a snake if he could get somebody to hold it. The bar gets raised for the second piece of ass. Although... it was hard to imagine Walker being picky, with the face he had to go around in public behind.

"Well, you going to tell me what this is all about?" I said. "You sounded pretty desperate on the phone. You need some money?"

I figured I might lay fifty bucks on him, maybe even a C-note. I couldn't go much more than that, not with the plans Paris and I had. In less than a month, I meant to open my own hairstyling salon. Right after New Year's Day. Paris volunteered to be the receptionist until we got on our feet. She'd already put in for a month's vacation from the insurance company she clerked for. We figured a month would be enough time to have our feet on the ground to where we could afford to hire a regular receptionist. Optimists. Paris says we're the "glass is half-full" types, and laughs when she says that, but I see the bit of squint that comes into her eyes and know she sees the air in the top of the glass more than I do.

"Naw, man. I'm good. In fact, I'm going to come into a pretty good chunk of change real soon." He paused, looked away from me to stare at the guys shooting pool. "What I need is a favor."

A favor... I thought about something cute I heard someone say one time. "A favor," he said, "is a French word for 'let me fuck you.'"

Walker looked away when he said that; gave me a funny feeling.

We shared a history, Walker and me. Even before my last bit. Clear back to my first stretch, almost twelve years before. We weren't cellies that first time, but we buddied up during my last sentence. Cellmates over in J Cellblock first and then over in D Dorm. They called Pendleton a reformatory, which sounds like a reform school for juvies, but it wasn't. What it was, was one of Indiana's two maximum security prisons. Back then, convicted felons under the age of thirty went to Pendleton, over thirty they were sent up to the prison in Michigan City. Same kind of convicts both places. Rapists, armed robbers, burglars. Murderers.

Walker did armed robberies and I plied the fine art of burglary, those years. The second-degree kind of burglar, guys who went into businesses after the closed sign appeared in the window and the lights went off. Bars, mostly. First-degree burglars were the idiots who broke into houses. House-creepers. Idiots, because first of all, there was never anything in houses to steal except somebody's fucked-up stereo or a TV you'd get a hernia trying to carry, and secondly, because Indiana judges frothed at the mouth over scum who broke into other folk's houses.

Walker specialized in supermarkets, department stores. A cut above your ordinary street bandit. He looked down his nose at 7-11's, liquor stores. "Chump change artists," he called them. "Handkerchief-head jobs."

What saved his butt from longer stretches when he got popped was that Walker never had any shells in his gun when he held up a place. Judges looked favorably on stuff like that. Plus, Walker had this Sorrowful Jones air about him that always got to magistrates. He had a look he could put on, standing there in the docket, that just screamed contrition. Judges ate that crap up.

We'd hooked up in Quarantine way back then, the isolation cellblock they put you in before you got cut loose into population. Print you, photograph you for the prison records, send you to the shrink and assign you a counselor. Give you tests, figure out if you should work in the laundry or the metal shop or learn the two prison ways to cook beans, depending on what you told them you saw in the ink blots.

"I'm in a jam, Jake. Some serious shit. The thing is, I can get out of it. But I need your help. I've got a job lined up."

Even if I didn't see the begging in his eyes, I would've heard it in his voice. I should have hung up on him back at the shop earlier. Where this train was heading, I knew I didn't want to ride along.

"I'm out of the life, Walker. There's some good stuff about to happen. I'm not going to screw it up. I've been straight for four years, my friend."

"You owe me, Jake."

There was that. He was right. If it wasn't for Walker Joy I wouldn't even be sitting here now. Anywhere else, for that matter. I'd have embalming fluid instead of O negative in my veins.

"It's a house, Jake. And I know for sure the owner's going to be out of town."

"Are you crazy?" I said. "A house? A *house*, Walker?"

I drained the last of my ginger ale, tried to get the waitress's eye and succeeded. I held up two fingers.

"It's a piece of cake, Jake. The guy doesn't even have a decent burglar alarm. And, it's kind of a business, actually."

Plainly, he'd skipped past the thinking stage. The avalanche had begun and I was already part of the snow and ice. I could feel it in my bones.

Chapter 2

A "piece of cake" is what got me busted both times I got sent up. They're all sure things *before* you pull the job.

I sighed. "Walker, I got to explain something to you. I've had two falls, brother. You know what that means."

He knew what it meant all right. The Bitch. Three strikes and you're out. Ha-*bitch*-ual criminal. One more pop and I knew the judge would be peering down at me over his wire-frames and saying, "Jacob Bishop, I hereby sentence you to life imprisonment. Have a nice day, loser." Just the thought made my balls shrivel up and the back of my neck ache.

"Fuck, man," he said. "Don't you think I know that? I'm in the same boat as you are. But, Jake, this job is really a lock. And the payoff's something like you and I never thought we'd ever have. I'm talking serious fucking money, pal." He paused for effect. "How does a hundred grand apiece sound to you, Jake? Maybe more."

It sounded like a fairy tale to me and that's what I told him.

"I'm flattered you thought of me, Walker," I said, forcing up a smile. "But I'm going to have to pass. This deal's that good then you shouldn't have much trouble finding a partner. Hell . . . " I nodded toward the pool table and bar. "I'll bet you could find six guys in here right now would go in with you. For a lot less, too. Maybe for even what you'll actually get."

I put my hands on the table and pushed myself up.

"Sorry, Walker. Like I said, I appreciate the offer, but I'm in a different place than I used to be. I've been here a long time and I like where I'm at. I want to wish you luck though."

I was more than in a "different place." I was on an entirely different planet than the one I was on the last time Walker and I had communed together.

Four years ago, I'd gotten on that Greyhound smoking north and not only had I not looked back at Pendleton that time, I hadn't looked back on any of the rest of my past either.

Since then, I'd gone through several jobs, each one better than the last one, and now I was working in the toniest salon in town. Cutting hair hadn't been my dream in third grade—it was a trade I'd learned in the joint.

It was weird how I'd landed this gig. Two and a half years ago, I'd just lost my second job since getting out—only lasted a week at the first. The boss, Jim Nance, died and the shop was going to be sold for taxes. As I walked out the funeral door after paying my respects to Jim's family and wondering what I was going to do for work, a man walked up to me and introduced himself. Though he wouldn't have had to. I recognized him. Big Daddy Koontz. Whoever'd given him the nickname "Big Daddy" hadn't displayed a lot of imagination—the guy *was* big. Huge. Not tall-big. Wide-big. Whenever I saw him, I always thought about that old Bill Cosby character, Fat Albert. That was Big Daddy—a white Fat Albert. His voice even sounded like Fat Albert's: deep and husky. A cartoon voice. And he hadn't walked up. He'd waddled up, gaberdined-thighs slapping each other with the same sound someone makes when acting out the "Hand Jive" song. Big Daddy also owned the hottest shop in town. Make that *salon*. The Tangerine Z. He offered me a job.

I guess I had an even better reputation than I'd thought.

The first *day* on the job, I earned more than I had in my best *week* working for Jim, and I'd thought that serious money. But the Tangerine Z just plain cooked.

Then I did something just for the hell of it. I signed up for a class at the Indiana University regional campus over on Greenlawn Avenue, on the St. Joe River bank. IUSB. A survey course in Contemporary English Lit. They had us read books by Vonnegut, Brautigan, and Ray Bradbury, the sci-fi writer. Mid-term, I booked an A in the class, surprised to find college that easy. A major success in my bag, I took two classes the next semester. Sociology 101 and another lit course. Intro to Shakespeare. Paris came into my life in the soc class. She walked in the first day and sat two seats from me in the same row. I took one look at the longest, slimmest legs I'd ever seen, and I'd just about gotten my breath back from that, when I caught a gander of her face. She was a natural blonde with brown eyes. One fucking striking combination. Much later in our relationship, after we'd hit the sheets and done the horizontal bop, she told me it was the rarest hair-eye combination there was.

"Naw," I said. "I've seen lots of blondes with brown eyes."

"No, you haven't," she said. "Not natural blondes, anyway. Check it out." She paused a second and gave me a smile that wasn't really a smile. "On second thought, *don't* check it out. Just take my word for it."

I thought about it, and a minute later admitted she was right. None of the ones I'd known were natural blondes. They were all brunettes, blonde from a bottle. It was a combination you couldn't match, chemically.

"I guess you're the real deal, aincha?" I said. "I guess this isn't Miss Clairol down here, is it?"

Way before we got to that stage, though, I didn't even think she'd go out with me. It took three more class sessions before I got up the nerve to approach her. Mister Smoothy here didn't act like Mister Smoothy—instead of one of the clever and dazzling lines I usually came up with when I tried to get next to a babe, as soon as I'd said hi to her, my brain went into freeze mode and I found myself stammering like some pimpled geek in his first encounter with a person of the opposite gender and wearing longer hair. I'd meant to ask her out to the Kiss concert next Friday, but that plan vanished from my mind and I ended up asking her if she'd let me buy her a Coke instead, like one of the characters in an Archie comic book. Mister Smoothy transformed into Mister Lame Doofus. She must have been having a slow week, guy-wise, because, amazingly, she said, "Sure," and five minutes later we were walking to the student union, exchanging horoscope signs and all that other bullshit you do when you meet some-one in college, even when you don't believe in it.

Two hours later, we were still sitting across from each other at one of the booths and we hadn't yet stopped talking. We talked like alternating machine guns, like we'd known each other all our lives, and then I blurted out something in the same instant it came bubbling up in my mind, but before I'd processed it. She must have thought she'd found herself sitting with a moron.

"Willie Mays," I said.

"Excuse me?"

"Willie Mays." I tried to explain. And not very well. "When I was a kid, I was a baseball freak. A Giants' fan. And Willie Mays was my hero."

"Yeah?" she said, her eyebrows snapping into Ronald McDonald arches. "That's truly fascinating, but what does it have to do with New Orleans?" That's what we'd been talking about before I injected the Mays' bit into the conversation—cities we'd like to live in.

I tried to form sentences that would make sense.

"Willie Mays was electric. Pure electricity."

"Okay," she said, the golden arches vanishing, her mouth twisting over to the side in a wise-guy smirk. "That's also a pretty spine-tingling piece of information, but I'm still lost here as to what the electric Willie Mays has to do with New Orleans exactly."

Her attitude pissed me off.

"Look," I said, feeling my face begin to burn. "I'm trying to explain something here."

"I'm sorry," she said, and by the way her mouth relaxed, I knew she meant it.

"Okay," I went on. "This is kind of hard to explain, especially to a girl, but whenever I watched the Giants on TV and Mays stepped to the plate, I always got the feeling that something dramatic was about to happen. Something big. A home run. Especially in a situation like the bottom of the ninth, score tied, two outs—that kind of shit. Last chance time. O.K. Corral time. Willie Mays was about… possibilities. Heroic possibilities."

I shut up. I'd never tried to articulate what I felt when I saw the Say Hey Kid step up to the plate with lumber in his hand, but that was it. *Possibilities.* Electricity.

I tried again to put into words what I felt at those times. "The camera couldn't keep its eye off Willie Mays," I continued. "In the field, at bat, hell…even sitting in the dugout. Wherever he stood on the field, whatever he did, when that camera panned to him, my heart stopped for a second and then began beating, but faster. My hands would sweat and I'd find myself holding my breath."

"Wow," Paris said, letting the word out softly. "This Mays dude was some kind of guy, wasn't he? But—"

"What does he have to do with New Orleans? Nothing. Nothing at all. But he does have something to do with *you.* Me. Let me finish, see if I can get this right."

I had the feeling that whatever I said would be important and that I'd better get it right.

"I've watched sports all my life," I began, slowly, trying to get my thoughts formulated before I spoke. "There have been lots of great players. Hank Aaron, O.J. Simpson, Ken Griffey, Jr.… fuck, Man O' War." I didn't know if she knew who those names were, but it didn't matter. I knew she grasped that they were great athletes. "The thing is, I never felt the way about any of those guys that I did about Mays. Mays was just bigger than life, just pure-d adrenalin. You just knew something magical and heart-stopping was going to happen. The only other guy who did that for me was Gale Sayers for the Bears. You knew every time he touched the football a touchdown was possible, even probable. But even Sayers didn't do for me what Mays did, although he came close."

I paused, watched her face closely to see if she was getting this, understanding.

"My whole body chemistry changed when I saw Willie stride to the plate," I said. "I've never been affected by another human being like I was with Willie Mays."

I paused again and Paris did the right thing. She didn't say a word. If she'd spoken just then, I don't know if I could have said what I did next. Somehow, it would have been ruined.

"And I never thought I would be again," I said, my voice lowering as I said it, so softly I wasn't sure she could hear me. "Until I met you, Paris Meecham. When I see you walk into class, I get that same feeling I did when I saw Willie come out of the dugout with his bat in his hand." I stopped, looked over at her. "Pretty corny, huh?"

"Thank you," she said, finally. Then, "I think I want you to come home with me, Jake."

It turned out she had her own apartment.

It also turned out that six months after that, I proposed to her down at her folks' cottage on Chapman Lake. Her parents, Gloria and Jerrol were elated. Paris had been a miracle baby for them, born when Gloria was in her mid-40s and Jerrol was already 55. We were married a week later and the next week Jerrol took an early retirement. That was two years ago.

Every time we see one of her girlfriends they all say the same thing, right away. "You're still on your honeymoon, girl."

I wish that was true and in some ways it is, but not entirely. We've been having some problems lately.

I could have foreseen those problems if I'd paid attention to what Paris said that day two and a half years ago when we finally left the student union and were driving over to her apartment in her car.

"What did you mean," she said, with a seemingly innocent smile, "when you said, 'This is kind of hard to explain, especially to a *girl*'?"

Chapter 3

My parents' house burned down and both of them died of smoke inhalation. The clothes dryer in the basement caught fire. Where my brother Bobby usually slept. That night though, he'd sacked out on a couch on the sun porch. Never woke up through the whole thing. A fireman found him and carried him out. In fact, Mom had been drying Bobby's clothes. She put in a load just before she and Dad went to bed. Caused by the vent clogged with lint. Happens all the time, I guess.

Bobby took it a lot worse than I did. Hell, I barely knew Mom and Dad. I don't mean I didn't love them; I did, but most of the past ten-fifteen years had been spent either in prison or in other states and there hadn't been much contact other than the occasional phone call on holidays. Bobby, on the other hand, was just a kid, had never been away from home. Besides, as it turned out, he was carrying around a serious shitload of guilt about how they died, but I didn't learn about that until a lot later.

I had a sitdown with Paris. She was terrific. Sure, she said, we can let him have the other bedroom upstairs. We probably won't even know he's here, half the time, she figured.

Before that, I barely knew my little brother. Not that we disliked each other—we just didn't know each other well enough at that time to have formed likes or dislikes. I don't think he was all that red-hot to move in with his brother and sister-in-law, but he didn't seem motivated about too much of anything. He just kind of went into a shell. I figured it was grief over our parents and eventually he'd shake out of it, get on with his life.

He shook out of it all right. Before the accident, he always seemed to me to be a pretty normal kid. Never any serious trouble, except once he'd gotten caught shoplifting when he was fifteen, but that wasn't really even his fault. He'd just been with a kid who was snatching and grabbing, and he knew what the kid was doing but thought if he didn't take anything himself, he was all right. He learned a legal lesson. About being an accessory to a crime. No big deal that time. I sat him down and gave him a righteous talking-to. He seemed to understand the seriousness of the situation, and by the look on his face while I was giving him my personalized version of *Scared Straight,* I knew I'd gotten through. Turned out, he did some community service and the court wiped his record clean.

Before the accident, Bobby'd been on the John Adams High School baseball team. A pretty fair pitcher and he also played shortstop and some first base. After our parents died, he just up and quit the team. His grades went south, too.

I had a few talks with the vice-principal and his counselor, and we all agreed his behavior to be pretty much what you'd expect, considering.

"He'll come out of it," Mr. Black, the counselor said. "This is normal. His parents just died. He seems to feel guilty about that. Probably because it was his clothes your mother was drying."

That made sense to me. I kept meaning to talk to him about that, explain how it wasn't his fault, but somehow I hadn't gotten around to it yet.

Then, just a month ago, he got popped again. A much more serious bust this time. He was riding shotgun in a brand-new Mustang his buddy Johnny Nicks was driving. The problem was, it wasn't Nicks' car. It belonged to a woman over on North Michigan Avenue who had just bought it. It still had dealer's plates on. The shoplifting thing was a misdemeanor, but this was a bona fide felony. And Bobby wasn't just along for the ride on this one. He was the one who actually broke the window and hotwired it.

We were dealing with that now. Paris wasn't too happy about all this. Her insurance company happened to be the carrier on the woman's car and she vocalized loud and often how embarrassed all this made her. She'd even suggested maybe Bobby should think about moving out, maybe get hold of a distant cousin we had in Louisiana, our only living relative. We'd had some discussions. Arguments.

Along about then she started some weird shit. Started going to the library, bringing home all these New Age books. Fruitloop shit. Started staring out the window at night, up at the stars, searching for aliens. Began talking crap about her "past lives" and going to this place out in the mall that sold crystals, little pop-up pyramids you could set in up in your living room and crawl into, weird shit like that. I tried to keep my mouth shut, some of the hooey she started to spout, biting my tongue when I wanted to crack on her.

"This is how those morons who followed Jimmy Jones got started," I'd say to her, but she couldn't see the connection. "You went to college," I said. "You sat in class and learned there isn't a single, solitary, scientific scrap of proof that there's life anywhere in the universe and now you believe there are little Alfs from another galaxy down here checking out our cattle and implanting trailer-park women with Farrah Fawcett hairstyles with their sperm? Paris..." Conversations in the living room became spooky at times, the things she came up with.

Other than that, my old life had been regulated to history. Until now.

•   •   •

"Sit down a minute, Jake," Walker was saying, across from me. "I need to explain some things to you. You owe me that much. I'm calling in my marker." He twisted his hands together as he spoke. "I'm in a real bad jam here, Jakey."

I sat back down. "Go ahead," I said. "You got twenty minutes."

It took half again that much time for Walker to lay out his situation, but I didn't leave like I should have.

Seems like he'd lined up a job as a runner for a local jewelry store owner who dabbled in black market gems on the side, mostly diamonds. A guy named Sydney Spencer. I knew Spencer. Tweedy little scumbag. The guy came in the salon. Fucked around with all the girls, trying to get them to go out with him, but as far as I knew none of them had. I'd even been in his store on South Michigan Street once when we were looking for Paris's engagement ring. Heftier prices than we'd seen anywhere else. Which hadn't made sense. His store lay smack between two strip clubs in one of the worst areas in town. Sold a lot of Zircon and diamonds with flaws you could see with the naked eye to fat, drunk Romeos who'd just fell in love with girls named Holly Hooter and Venus Vulva, I'd bet.

"I've been taking stuff up to Chicago for him," Walker explained. "Made three trips with no problems. Last week, some shit happened."

"Some shit" was a carjack in Gary, Indiana. He'd gotten off the toll road before he hit the Windy and somehow made a wrong turn, ended up on a back street. Walker admitted he might have been doing a little toot and his reflexes might have been off a tad. "Man! I'd just stopped at a red light and there they were! Seven, eight mothers. I'da seen 'em coming, I'da just run the light. I spaced for a minute, I guess."

They'd thrown Walker out of the car—"Lucky they didn't

cut my fucking throat"—and there he stood, carless and weaponless. On foot in the hood. "I got lucky," he said, a bitter snort erupting on the word "lucky". "A black-and-white came by, took me to the bus station. I had a few bucks in my shoe they didn't get. Asshole cops said they'd put it on the sheet, but I might as well kiss my car goodbye. I didn't mention the merchandise in the trunk."

Sydney Spencer's merchandise. An assortment of hot diamonds worth roughly $100,000.

Which upset Sydney considerably, according to Walker.

"I'm a dead man, Jake," Walker said, and I had no reason to doubt him. "I don't come up with $100,000 by next Friday you can come put poesies on my grave. If there's a body to bury. I think Spencer uses guys who favor quicklime."

"Damn, Walker." What else could I say? I felt for him, but it was his problem, way I saw it. I was out of the life. Walker was just going to have to figure a way out of his mess his own self. I couldn't see where he had the right to ask for my help in this kind of deal. To his credit, he said as much.

"I know, I know," he said, lifting his hands. He spread his fingers on the table, flexed them. "If it was just you and me, believe me, I'd understand, Jake. But..." he hesitated. "There's more to it than that. Spencer knows about you. I guess he really wants you in on this job. He thinks you're the best B&E guy on the planet. I..." he looked away. "I kinda built you up."

"How's that, Walker?" I said. A funny feeling grabbed me deep in the gut.

"I guess...I guess maybe I talked about you. One time, up in his office, just shooting the shit. You know how that stuff goes. Telling war stories."

Fuck. I could feel the spot in my stomach that always ached when I was tense. "What kind of war stories, Walker?"

He shined me a weak grin, waved his hand like shooing a fly away or something equally trifling.

"You know. Jobs you pulled. Stuff like that. That one in Argos. Remember that? A fucking classic, dude!"

Sure. I remembered. I'd gone into every single store in that dinky little town one night, years ago. Nine places. A couple, I'd gone back into twice. The drug store and the town bar. Made out like a downtown hooker on New Year's Eve. The Barney Fife of Argos must have taken the night off, been at his bowling team banquet. I just roamed around all night, breaking into places like I owned the burg.

"You told him about Argos?" This was unbelievable. "Thanks, you dimwit. In case you didn't know it, I'm out of the outlaw game these days, Walker. I really need this kind of publicity, you know. This Spencer guy, he comes in the salon. He's got a big mouth. They find out I did time…" I gave him a hard look. "You know all about big mouths, don't you, Walker." Pissed wasn't a strong enough word for what I felt at this.

"I'm sorry, Jake." Sincerity dripped from his voice. "I…uh…I also might have mentioned something about the Clark station."

I could only stare in disbelief at what he said.

"Why would you tell anybody about that?" I said, finally. That sonofabitch! He couldn't begin to come up with a good excuse for telling anyone that, not even if he was the dumbest shithead who ever lived. Not even Paris knew about the Clark station incident.

An incident that happened a long time ago. If I hadn't been a lot younger and a lot more foolish, I'd never told Walker about it. The minute I had, I knew I'd made a mistake.

Years ago, right after my first bust and out on bond, I drifted, scuffling, barely making ends meet. The burglaries I pulled at that time seemed to all end up in a sack of quarters and a couple of bottles of Wild Turkey. I hit the sauce those days, regular as church, so I didn't much mind not getting a lot of cash on a job, so long as I scored enough whiskey. Besides, I knew my luck would change.

One night, down to my last two bucks, and on the way to the apartment I shared with my current girlfriend, my car ran out of gas. I tried to nurse it home on fumes, figuring I'd borrow a few bucks from Wendy and get gas in the morning. I cut it a bit too close and it died on me two blocks from the apartment. Fortunately, it quit running right in front of a Clark gas station. I slammed the door, kicked the side of the car—a dented-up, sad-looking Ford Fairlane—and walked up to the station. We were in the middle of one of South Bend's famous snowstorms—we got the lake effect off Lake Michigan and never had just snow showers but always blizzards of epic proportions, like one of those Jack London's characters kept getting lost in. Ol' Buck would have felt at home in this one. The snow reached halfway to my knees already, and you could barely see your hand in front of you for the white stuff that was falling. Inside, a guy in coveralls and a greasy Cubs' baseball cap counted the money in the till.

"I need a few bucks worth of gas," I said.

The asshole didn't even look up. "Sorry, pal," he said. "I'm closed. Already turned the pumps off."

Well, fuck me, I thought. "So just unlock them. What's that take? Twenty seconds?"

He looked up—snarly little motherfucker—and said, "It'll fuck up my books. Can't open them again till the morning." I spotted a half-gone bottle of Southern Comfort behind him on the shelf peeking out from behind a stack of 10W40's. You could also smell it as soon as he opened his mouth. I started to crack on him, then thought better of it. Just turned and left.

I pushed the car all the way home, cussing with every step. Luckily, there was enough ice under the snow I could do that, but I was a whipped puppy by the time I cranked it onto my street, just off Lincolnway West. I just pushed it into the first space available, three doors down from our duplex apartment. Instead of going home, I got inside the

Ford, out of the wind, and fired up a Camel. I smoked it all the way down and by the time I put it out, I was hotter than the cigarette had been.

I popped the trunk, grabbed the jack handle and walked back to the Clark station. I spotted the guy right away. Sitting in a rust bucket of a red pickup truck just off to the side. Freezing-ass cold and this turkey had the window down, his legs sticking out. I could see him raise up as I approached and slug down a belt from the bottle and disappear below the window. Drunk on his ass.

I snuck up—not hard with the snow falling in thick, wet flakes—grabbed the door handle and whipped it open. He came halfway out with it, his back bent in two, scrabbling to regain his balance, his eyes wide. I just reached over, grabbed him by the ear and clocked him across the back of the neck, near the shoulder. "Umpf!" he said, falling down into the snow on his knees. He reached a hand up to massage his neck where I'd nailed him and as he did that, I clipped him across the back of the skull. He fell face down in the snow. I reached in his back pocket, and he had a billfold stuffed as full as you could get it. The receipts from his shift, I figured. Looked like at least six-eight hundred. I figured later he was probably supposed to lock it up in the safe for the owner, but maybe was going to take out a little loan for the evening. Maybe he'd already cooked the books to cover a ten or twenty he planned to cop. Too bad. I took the billfold, and then, just to be mean, grabbed the bottle of Southern Comfort that I spotted on the truck floor.

No big deal, and I never got busted for it, but it amounted to strong-arm robbery, a felony that carried a ten and a quarter sentence. And the statute of limitations didn't expire soon on that variety of crime. Not to mention The Bitch I'd draw if I got popped on it.

Stupid!

Walker kept yapping. "Hey, Jake, I'm sorry, but it just came out. We were talking about grudge-fucks and I said, let me tell you about a buddy of mine who got the ultimate grudge-fuck. I thought he'd get a hernia, way he laughed. I didn't see no harm."

He had such a hang-dog look, my mad died down a little. Only thing… if the Man ever found out about that little incident, that'd be all she wrote. I didn't think the statute of limitations had run out yet on a strong-arm robbery that had just happened six and a half years ago.

"Walker, you're a dumb shit," is all I said.

We sat there in silence for a bit.

"He's gonna use that shit against me, isn't he?" I said at last, fixing Walker with the dirtiest look I could muster up. "What we call… what is it we call that shit, Walker? Blackmail? Yeah, that's what we call it." I slugged down the rest of my ginger ale and slammed it down on the table so hard the ice cubes jumped.

"Jake, I'm—"

"Sorry?" I said. "You bet your ass you're sorry. A more sorry sonofabitch I've never met." I sighed. One thing I learned a long time ago is that you can't look back and play "what-if" games. Best thing to do is roll with the punches, figure out a way to keep your ribs from being broken in the fall. I rubbed my temples to forestall the headache I could feel coming on.

I thought of something. "You didn't tell him about…" I didn't even want to say it.

He knew what I was talking about. "Oh, man, Jake. No way."

That was good. We shared a secret that even Paris didn't know about. If he'd told Spencer that… well, I didn't even want to think about that. I didn't even want to think what I'd have to do if *that* ever got out into the world. The look on his face told me he was telling the truth about that and I softened a bit.

"Tell me some more about this job," I said. I held up my hand and crocked my finger for the waitress, and when she came over I came within a millimeter of ordering something with alcohol in it—at this point, staying sober seemed like the wrong thing to do—but I ended up pointing at my ginger ale and indicating a refill of that instead. Not the best time to be falling off the wagon. I had a feeling I'd need all of my wits about me with this Spencer character. It looked like he had me by the short hairs at the present moment, and I needed to figure out a way to change that. I needed to meet the guy, face-to-face, see how far he intended on taking his little squeeze play. Maybe I worried too much about nothing.

Yeah...

Chapter 4

I drove toward home, wondering what in the hell what story I could cook up to lay on Paris.

We'd rented a house on Twykenham Drive a year and a half back, a street that used to be the classiest in South Bend twenty-thirty years before, but had steadily deteriorated, at least around our neighborhood out north, out by Notre Dame and Big Daddy's salon. At the south end, five or six miles away, it still retained a lot of its former grandeur, the homes still valued at high-six figures and up into the millions, but as you traveled north the homes got smaller and less expensive, especially after you crossed Lincolnway East and Mishawaka Avenue, until you got to our neighborhood where they were mostly three-bedroom ranches and little bungalows in need of paint jobs or new siding. We were in one of the brick ranches with a fenced-in backyard and no trees. The other houses on the block were all exactly thirty feet from the curb, but ours was set back from the street an extra twenty feet. When I said something about it, Paris said that was a plus. I'd be able to find it even if I was drunk. I didn't bring up the fact that my drinking days were over. What sold us—sold *her*—on the place was the living room. No sooner had we followed the professor who owned it into the house to look it over than she began squealing, "This is exactly like the living room in the house I grew up in!" She turned and looked up at me. "Please, Jake? This is a magical room. A magical house. I guarantee it." What could I say? We signed the lease about ten minutes later.

Not the worst neighborhood, but not what most South Benders thought of when the name Twykenham Drive came up, either.

In less than thirty days, we'd be opening our salon and I just knew we'd make a lot of money fast and then we'd be able to buy our own place.

I parked the car and waved at our next-door neighbor to the north, a guy whose name I'd been told but forgotten. Out hauling his trash cans to the curb, which reminded me of that and I'd better get our own out before Paris jumped my case again.

Paris sat cross-legged in shorts on the living room's magical couch—what I'd taken to calling it for our inside joke—a copy of People Magazine in her lap, and on the TV Robert Stack stood in this old building, yapping in that irritating drone of his something about Confederate ghosts.

"Sorry I'm late, hon. I'll get the trash out," I said.

"You can do that later. Your supper's in the oven warming," she said, slipping her legs off the couch and tossing the magazine onto the coffee table. "Eat first. You want me to fix it?"

"Naw, naw," I said, waving her back down. "You relax. I can get it."

"So," she said, wandering into the kitchen while I fetched out a plate with meat loaf, green beans and mashed potatoes from the oven where it warmed. "Who's this friend you saw?"

I took the plate over to the table, grabbed some silverware and a can of Barq's root beer from the fridge and sat down.

"Would you bring me the ketchup?" I asked, realizing I'd forgotten to get it, but mostly buying a few seconds to figure out how to answer her question. What the hell should I tell her, I wondered? That an ex-cellmate wanted me to help him out on a burglary and that they'd slap the Bitch on me if we were caught and so maybe we shouldn't have signed the lease just yet on our shop building and would she remember to bring cigarettes when she came to see me on visiting days?

So, no, I couldn't tell Paris the truth. I definitely couldn't go there.Just then the front door opened and Bobby walked in. Talk about being saved by the bell.

"Where the hell have you been!"

I winced at the vehemence in Paris's voice. I knew she and Bobby weren't getting along these days, but she appeared to be more than just pissed-off. I figured I better step into this. Calm the waters, see what that burr up under her saddle looked like, if it could be removed. Hormones, I bet. I knew she wasn't nuts about Bobby's recent difficulties with the law, but she hadn't been *that* fried over it.

"Take it easy, honey," I said. "It's not that late. It's only—"

"Ten-thirty!" She was shaking with fury, which completely caught me off guard. Christ! He was a teenager. Ten-thirty was pretty early for a kid his age. I started to say something, but she started up, eyes blazing. "I waited for an hour before I ate, Bobby. You told me you'd be home right after school. First, your brother calls me at the last minute, tells me he's not going to be home, and then you don't show up at all. I went to a lot of trouble to cook this, you know."

She walked away to go stand at the window, her back to us. Bobby just stood there, a dazed look on his face.

"Bobby," I said, standing up. "Where were you? If you were supposed to be here for supper, why—"

"Out," he said, curtly, with that teenaged wiseass attitude I saw everywhere these days. "I was out, that's all. Jesus! A guy can't hang with his buds?" The red crept up from his neck into his buzz cut he still kept from his jock days and the startled look in his eyes mutated to one of anger. "I can't do anything right around here. Who wants her lousy meat loaf anyway?

It tastes like shit. Give her one of Mom's recipes, why don't you? I'm tired of everything being burned."

"Watch your mouth, Bobby," I said, sharply, but he ignored me, turned on his heel and started toward the stairs.

"Just get off my back," he said, his voice coming from the stairs as he clumped up. "I'm going to bed."

I walked over to Paris, slipped my arm around her waist and turned her to me. Tears were brimming in her eyes.

"There, baby," I said, caressing her hair with my hand, pulling her into me to hug her. "He's just a kid. He probably just forgot the time. Probably got wrapped up in some conversation over what rock group's the best or who has the biggest tits in his class. You know how teenagers are. I'll go up and talk to him. I'm not going to let him talk to you like that. He needs a swift kick in the ass is what he needs. He needs to apologize to you." I tried a smile on her. "And that crack about your cooking? Hell, he *loves* your cooking. He eats twice as much as either of us. And I think it's fantastic, so who cares? Look. I'll go talk to him right now." I pulled away, looked down at her. "Straighten him right up."

She looked up, the mad still there. You could almost see the sparks flying from her eyes and they weren't the brown they normally were, but almost black. "Like hell," she said. "I told him specifically this morning to be here on time. And what's he do?"

Chapter 5

"Bobby, that was some shit downstairs, you know."

He was lying across his bed, earphones on, thumbing through one of his X-Men comics. He didn't even look up.

"Take that damn thing off!" I roared, snatching the headphones and ripping them from his head. He scuttled up on the bed, his eyes large. "Now," I said, my voice calmer. "Maybe you can hear me, participate in this little chit-chat we're gonna have."

He started to say something and I held up my hand like a traffic cop. "Save it. You just listen."

I read him the riot act. Told him I wasn't going to put up with him treating Paris that way. The whole time, he just stared at me with that kind of half-mad, half-scared look kids get when adults get in their face. I knew that look. I'd had it myself when I was a kid, more than once. It suddenly dawned on me that I was giving the same lecture Dad had given me when I sassed Mom. I softened up.

"Look, Bobby," I said. I saw the surprise in his eyes when I shifted gears. Hell, he wasn't a bad kid. He was my brother, for Christ's sake, and here I was leaning on him like he'd committed a capital crime. He'd lost his parents and all he had was one asswipe brother coming down on him and a sister-in-law who spent half her time playing a Ouija board. "Just try harder to be nice to Paris. She does a lot of things for you, you know. I know you're going through some tough times, but you don't need to take shit out on her. You might remember she's the one suggested you move in with us. She tries hard, you know."

The anger went right out of his eyes.

"I know, Jake. Shit." He turned aside and I thought I saw moisture in his eyes. He looked back up and I saw he'd gotten it under control. "It's just a bad day, is all. I got a detention today."

"What for?"

"Bullshit. Randy Ames called me a jailbird and I clocked him."

I couldn't help it. I laughed.

"I hope you nailed him good," I said.

A big smile spread over his face. "I don't think I broke his nose, but it sure bled like it was."

I put on my serious "parent" face. "Well, that shit bites. I know. Been there, heard that. But," I leaned over, put my arm around him and squeezed, then pushed him away playfully, "… you've got to control yourself when dudes do stuff like that. They know they can get your goat, you're gonna be in a million fights. And you're the one who's going to get in trouble."

"I know, I know."

I got up, stretched. "Hey, if you want, there's still some meatloaf left. Put a lot of ketchup on it, it's not too bad."

We both laughed and he got up. "Yeah. I could eat some, I guess."

We went back downstairs and he walked over to Paris, still sitting at the table, and gave her a quick hug and apologized.

"You suppose I could have some of that meat loaf?" he said, looking down at her. She waved her hand at the oven. She was still mad, I could see, but she'd calm down. Bobby cut off a hunk from the pan and slathered it with ketchup, and once he began devouring it in huge bites, her lips relaxed from the straight line they'd been in.

Later, Paris microwaved some popcorn and we all sat in the living room and watched a rerun of Cheers.

I got lucky. She forgot to follow up her question about who I'd seen earlier in the evening.

And, sure enough. I had that nightmare that night. The one where I was back in Pendleton, locked in my cell. The midnight train was passing by, blowing its whistle, and in the tier above me, someone was sobbing great, wracking sobs.

I woke up in the middle of that shit and spent the rest of the night sleeping in fits and starts.

Thanks a helluva lot, Walker.

Chapter 6

I was in the middle of a haircut the next morning when our receptionist Jessica came over to tell me I had a phone call.

"Get a name and number and I'll call them back," I said.

"It's that Spencer guy who comes in here," she said, wrinkling her nose in distaste. Last time he'd been in, he'd offered to take her to Acapulco and she'd sniffed, said, "I've already been with a really ugly guy, but thanks and good luck on your Mission Impossible," and just walked away. She didn't turn away at what I told her, but stood there, an "I know you'd like to hit me" grin on her face and said, "Spencer says you'd be glad to take his call." I can't begin to describe the tone of voice she delivered that news with, except it was plain she was burning with curiosity as to why he was asking for me.

"Okay," I said. "I'm sorry, Sandra," I said to the girl in the chair. "This won't take a minute."

I opted for the phone in the back room.

"Yeah?"

"Jake!" The voice was booming.

"Yeah."

"We need to meet."

I tried a bluff. "Spencer, we have nothing to meet about."

He chuckled. "I think we do. Didn't our mutual friend talk to you?"

"So what?"

"So what, is that maybe he mentioned a little gas station

incident to you? Something happened a while back? Something I don't think you want the cops to know about?"

Fuck. This slimeball wasn't playing. I couldn't think of anything to say. I ended up agreeing to meet him after work. Paris wasn't going to be any too happy about me coming home late two nights in a row. I didn't have a clue how I was going to explain this to her.

"You think you got me by the short hairs, don't you? Screw you and the horse you rode in on."

"How 'bout the Boat Club?" he said, in this drippy sweet voice, acting as if I hadn't just told him to get fucked. "Walker's coming with me. He suggested that might be a good place, one you feel comfortable at."

I couldn't see any way out of this.

I waited a few seconds and listened to him breathe. Finally, I caved. "You're scum, Spencer. You know that, don't you. Okay, I'll sit down with you just so I can explain to you why you've got the wrong guy in mind for this crap. But not the Boat Club. I'll meet you at the Linebacker. At six. For half an hour. That's all." The Linebacker was just across the street from the Tangerine Z. I didn't want the people in the Boat Club to see me there two nights in a row, especially with those two. Being seen anywhere in public with those two was already a mistake, I knew, but what could I do? At least, at the Linebacker, nobody would think it odd me being in there. Even though I didn't drink any more, I ate lunch there quite a bit and nobody would look twice if I showed up there after work. If I "happened" to run into Spencer there, nobody'd think twice about that either, since he got his hair cut at our place.

"Great!" he said, his voice booming again. "I'll look forward to it, Jake."

"Don't," I said. "You might want to think this through some more, asshole. I don't like being threatened." I slammed the phone down, startling Jessica who was just coming through the door with a coffee cup in her hand.

"Spencer want you to cut his hair?" she said, as I brushed by her. I gave her a dirty look. "You don't seem his type," she called out behind me. I heard her giggle and my blood pressure rose even higher than it already was.

I finished Sandra's hair, working almost in complete silence. Usually, I dried her hair myself after I cut it, but today I called Keith, one of the assistants, over to do it for me.

"Book me out for the rest of the day," I said to Jessica on my way out.

"You've got a full book!" she wailed. "And Mrs. Doherty's coming in. What am I supposed to say to her? She'll have a cow. She—"

"Tell her I'm sick," I said, curtly. "All of them. Deal with it."

I was lucky Big Daddy was gone. He was the kind of boss who didn't take kindly to his stylists taking off like that in the middle of the day, especially with a full slate of appointments. I'd deal with him tomorrow. Right now I just needed to get someplace, figure this mess out.

I started for my car, then changed my mind, walked across the street to the Linebacker.

When the bartender walked over, I said, "Jack and water, Tommy. Make it a good color."

Chapter 7

I don't know why I did that. I think it shocked Tommy more than it did me. He knew I was a recovering alcoholic. He stared at me for the longest moment, started to say something, then shrugged and poured the drink. He placed it before me and said, "Want me to run a tab, Jake?" I nodded, staring at him defiantly, daring him to say something. He averted his eyes, walked back down to the other end and began drying glasses from the wet sink.

It was too early in the day for any but the hardcore drinkers, maybe half a dozen, mostly older guys, scattered here and there throughout the bar, sipping whiskey in solitary. The Linebacker was an old-time sports bar. None of that chrome and fern bullshit. Just signed pictures of Notre Dame football players tacked up on the walls, ranging all the way back to Rockne's time. A couple of photos of basketball players like Austin Carr, Sid Catlett and Collis Jones from the Johnny Jordan era and Kelly Tripuka from Digger's time. Nothing from the John McLeod regime. An old-time bar, just the kind I always favored back in my serious drinking days. Fake oak paneling yellowed by decades of cigarette and cigar smoke, the stench of stale beer and ammonia, a juke box with nothing newer than the Rolling Stones and a scratchy copy of Knute Rockne's famous "Gipper" speech that got played at least ten times a day, more on football weekends. A place where you wouldn't wear your Michigan or Purdue sweatshirt in, not unless you had a death wish or you were as big as a house and bad as a rabid Rottweiler. Even if you were, you'd still be in trouble. A lot of Irish ex-nose tackles hung out there.

I closed my hands around the glass, feeling its wet coolness, and stared at the amber liquid. All kinds of thoughts swirled up in my brain, but I cut them off at the pass. "Here's looking at you, keed," I said out loud, and gulped it down in one long drink.

Nothing happened. A meteor didn't crash into the bar, my head didn't fall off, a burning bush didn't appear and start to talk. I didn't feel a thing, even after all that abstinence. Not even the slightest buzz.

"Again," I said, staring straight ahead, knowing Tommy was paying close attention at the other end. I doubted if I was the first guy to ever fall off the wagon in his presence, but I'm sure it aroused at least a morbid curiosity in him.

"Sure, Jake," he said, putting down his towel and walking back down. "Old ice?"

I was back home. If I was going to come crashing down from the back of the wagon, at least I was in the hands of a pro. The young punk bartenders you get nowadays always think they're doing you a favor by giving you new ice each drink. The major leaguers always ask. They know the value of old ice.

I cracked a smile and nodded. "Just add new," I said. "And keep 'em coming." I looked down the bar. "How about one of those eggs?"

At eleven, three waitresses arrived, did a double-take when they saw me and what I was drinking—all of them came in the Tangerine and knew me—and at noon the joint filled up and Tommy brought me a tuna fish sandwich and my fourth drink. When the rush died down and all the secretaries and cellular phone salesmen had left for their appointed rounds, I found I had the place to myself. Tommy must have sensed

I wasn't in the mood for conversation as he stayed mostly down at his end of the bar, coming over only to pour me a new drink.

At four-thirty, the regulars started coming in, and in an hour the place was rocking, the juke box blaring and good-natured arguments raging all over the place about the game last week, which N.D. had lost to Michigan State. At six o'clock precisely, I was pulling out another twenty from my pocket to pay for my eleventh drink when Walker and Spencer walked in, a big sleazy grin on the jeweler's face, my old cellmate's face a study in gloom, most likely for my benefit.

I still hadn't copped a buzz. Remarkable.

A booth at the far end emptied out just then and I inclined my head toward it. I picked up my drink and wove my way through the drinkers. Spencer started to slide in next to me, but I didn't move.

"Sit across from me," I said. "I want to keep my eye on you. Besides, I just had these pants dry-cleaned and I don't want grease spots on them." I looked at Walker, standing behind him. "You can sit here, Spitball," I said, moving over. He knotted his brow. I'd never ever called him Spitball before. He got the message.

"Spitball, eh?" Spencer let out a high-pitched giggle and slid in on the other side. "That's a perfect name. You didn't tell me that's what guys called you, Walker. I like it. Spitball. It fits you, you know."

Walker eased into the space beside me. I could tell he was fuming, but he didn't say a word.

"That a drink?" he said. "Thought you didn't drink any more, Jakey."

I ignored him, stared at the man across from me, got right to it. "What's on your mind, Spencer? You got some idea you're gonna blackmail me? You might want to think that over, motherfucker." At first, I'd planned to just act pissed, try selling the slimeball a wolf ticket, watch him back down from his threat. But here it was, this punk sitting across from me, telling Walker he was going to snitch me out, get me sent up for something I'd done a long time ago, and I saw I wasn't going to have to play at being mad at all.

"I ought to cut your balls out right here, Spencer." I leaned forward across the table until I could smell his stinking garlic breath. "You make your little phone call, Spencer. Tell you what's going to happen. They may believe you or they may tell you to get lost with this bullshit. That stuff happened years ago. I wouldn't make book the cops even still give a shit about some asshole gas station alkie. You haven't thought this through, I don't believe. You don't even know if the guy's even still around. He might be dead for all you know. You know, the more I think about it, the more I'm pretty sure the cops aren't going to be all that interested in your little story should you go to them with it. You ever see a cop wasn't lazy, Spencer? You're talking about a lot of paperwork, lot of work looking up some ancient history stuff. Then, somebody's gotta try and find this guy. Without a victim, what can they do? You know—" something occurred to me and I went with it— "I might even look for this guy myself. I might even find him first. He might disappear. Where's your case then, greaseball? He disappears, it's all bullshit. *You're* bullshit."

I wondered if he could feel the hatred that was churning up inside. I had to hand Spencer one thing. He was a hell of a poker player. If he was scared, he sure didn't show it. Just kept staring at me with those bland little pale-blue peepers buried deep in his porker face, no emotion at all in them.

"Jake, I—"

"Shut up." I turned to Walker, gave him a look, and turned back to the jeweler. It was amazing how the alcohol I'd consumed had made my head clearer. I don't know if I'd have thought of all this if I'd been sober. At least that's what I was thinking. The other thing I was thinking is that it would sure feel nice to reach over and bust Spencer in the chops. I took another swallow of my drink and leaned back. I smiled. I was on a roll.

"Spencer, I don't think you thought all this through, did you? For instance, I don't think you thought about what might happen if you told the cops your little story and they didn't fucking care. I don't think you thought about what I might be feeling should that happen. I been out of this outlaw game a long time, but some things are coming back to me. Like what you do to snitches. You might want to give that some thought."

I caught Tommy's eye at the bar and gave him a nod. He grabbed one of the waitresses and pointed her toward our table.

"You done?" Spencer said.

I couldn't fucking believe it. Here I'd just laid out the possibilities for Spencer's future and he was acting like I'd just given him the weather forecast for the next day. He really was an ignorant fat punk. And arrogant.

"Tell him I'm for real, Walker." I stared at the jeweler, and if I was mad before, now I was smoking. The near-dozen drinks I'd consumed were only adding fuel to the fire banking inside my gut. It was all I could do to not reach over and bitch-slap this motherfucker. What I really wanted to do was have him by the throat, a pig-sticker at his belly. I knew then why I'd started to drink earlier. All I could see in my mind's eye was my old cell at Pendleton, and all I could think of was that this cocksucker was threatening to send me back there to die.

"Jake..." I turned, saw the most helpless, abject look on Walker's kisser. The look I gave him withered him completely. "Jake..." he began again, "...there's more." He looked across at Spencer, silently pleading with his eyes to help him out. I almost felt sorry for him. Almost. That look on his face—that broke-dick-dog look—was designed to inspire sympathy in me but that's the last thing it was generating.

A thought occurred to me. Had Walker lied about not telling Spencer our secret?

The waitress, a youngish woman named Becky, appeared. I'd done her hair a couple of times. "Hi, Jake," she said. I nodded briefly at her.

"Everybody," Spencer said, swirling his finger around. "Put it on my tab." She smiled again at me and left, probably wondering why I didn't shine her one back.

Spencer leaned back, completely relaxed.

"Jake, I don't want to see you back in the joint. I really don't."

I turned my head, stared out over the bar.

"I want you for a particular reason."

I turned back, looked at him. "Yeah? What's that, Spencer? You like my looks? Maybe what you really want is to suck my main vein."

He smiled. "Three reasons, actually. One, you're the best. Everybody knows you could get in and out of a place and not even disturb the dust on the floor."

I *had* been good, damn good. He was right there. Only thing he was forgetting was that had been a long time ago. And the reason I'd been good was that I had burglar's nerves. Which meant no nerves at all. That wasn't true anymore. I knew what was at stake now. Freedom. When you're twenty, freedom's just a word...like they say in that song. At thirty-two, you know what freedom actually is. Life. I didn't say anything, just sat there and listened, see what kind of jive he'd throw at me.

"That's reason number one." The drinks arrived and this time I managed to force up a smile at the waitress.

"Thanks, Becky," I said, lifting up my glass in a kind of a toast. She grinned and bounced off on her rounds.

Spencer sipped his own drink, a martini, and resumed

talking. "Reason number two is that you've got more at stake than anyone else I know. I know that because I know what you've done in the past four years since you got out. Pendleton isn't a place you ever want to see again, is it, Jake?"

The question didn't require an answer.

"So what's your reason number three?" I said, an edge to my voice. The booze was finally starting to affect me, and the feeling I was getting was mostly negative. It began to filter through that I'd made a mistake in taking that first drink.

"Reason number three is..." he paused, his voice growing softer with each word. "...is that the guy you robbed at that Clark station was my Uncle John."

That got my attention.

"*What* you say?" He had to be putting me on!

"Truth. He's my mother's brother. I grant you, he's not much. But he's my uncle. It wasn't until your friend Walker here was telling me the story of your little escapade that I realized who it was you'd attacked. That's when I knew I was going to have you pull this job. Kind of a little get-even thing, you might say."

Now he was openly beaming and I thought...hell...I didn't know what to think. The clarity I'd thought I was operating under from the drinks just vanished. I tried to act stoic, not let him see my confusion.

"Uncle John almost died, Bishop. But he didn't. He still lives around here, too. Over in Mishawaka. In Belgian town. He still remembers that day. In fact..." he leaned over again, his eyes glittery. "...we *all* still remember that day. Almost killed my mother. I don't give a fuck much about Uncle John, but my mother..."

He picked up his glass and drained it, smacking his lips.

"Ahh. That's good." He wiped his sleeve across his mouth. "So you see, I don't think it'd be much trouble finding him, and I don't think it'd be much of a job at all for the police.

In fact, I think they'd get a big kick out of someone handing them a case like this, all tied up and neatly packaged."

The fucker had me. If what he was saying was true, he had me cold. As I stared at him, my brain trying to function, I realized what he was handing me was no bullshit. He hadn't made it up. One thing I can do is read people and I read him loud and clear. It really was his uncle whose head I'd dented that day long ago. Now that I thought about it, I could remember the guy—what he looked like—and he had the same sunken pale blue eyes Spencer was staring across the table at me at this very moment with. I'd bet his mom had the same pasty orbs.

Shit.

Only good thing was Walker hadn't told him about the other thing. I hoped.

Spencer wasn't done. He'd have been a great basketball player if he'd been a foot taller and eighty pounds lighter. He had that killer instinct. Celtics player, like Larry Bird. When you got the Lakers down, put your foot on their throat, finish 'em off.

"In case that doesn't convince you, Bishop, there's something else."

"Yeah? What's that?" I was trying to act nonchalant, like what he'd said hadn't just been the biggest bombshell of my life, but he and I both knew that's all it was—an act. My mad just kind of disappeared and in its place came a feeling of utter hopelessness. I was going to do what this fuck wanted, like it or not. The train had started down the mountain.

"You got a brother. Bobby, isn't it? Yes. Bobby Bishop. Nice young kid, from what I hear."

The mad returned. In the form of a buzz in my ears. I started to get up, come across the table, but my legs turned to jelly and I slumped back into the booth. I was drunk and I vaguely realized it. Some fucking hardcase I was. The one time I needed to be sober and here I was, half an inch from passing out.

"Leave my bruth...bruth..." I was slurring my words now, the battle for sobriety lost.

Spencer's grin was truly evil. "Leave your brother out of this?" He chuckled. "Sorry, pal. Your brother's my ace card. You see, I know about his bust. I know about his probation, all that. But what you don't know is this. Last week, I got robbed. It's the neighborhood. Happens all the time, but this holdup happened at a very good time. The day after your friend Walker and I talked, and the day after I knew I wanted you for this job. It was kids pulled the job. They didn't get much—" he laughed loudly—"although the cops and my insurance company think they did. But what's really cool about all this is that the description I gave the cops could fit just about any teenager in town."

He gave me this look and I knew what it meant. And he knew I knew what it meant. He shook his head in a satisfied way.

"I knew you were no dummy, Jake." He was back to my first name now, a sign that in his mind we were already partners on this deal. "About any time I want, I can go down to the police station, go through the mug books and guess what?" He turned, waved his hand at Tommy, made that swirling motion again and turned back, a broad grin on his face. "It could turn out it was your brother held up my store."

I never wanted to kill anyone in my life as much as I wanted to kill that cockroach at that instant. Messing with me was one thing, but messing with my little brother was something else. If it'd been just me and him, alone, out in the country someplace, there was no doubt in my mind what I'd've done that moment.

"They might not convict him on that, you understand." He was clearly enjoying his little drama. "But I think they'd revoke his probation, very least that happened, situation like that. What's the sentence for auto theft? One to ten? Yeah, that's it. One to ten. Usually get your parole in two. Unless you fuck up. I think I know enough guys down there can see to it he fucks up."

He moved his slimy ass over to the end of the booth and stood up. "I'm going to the john, boys. When I get back, I'll lay out the details. You'll both want to pay close attention to that. You might want to switch to coffee, Jake, clear your head. You look like your eyeballs are bleeding."

The only way to describe what I felt when Sidney Spencer left the booth was... stunned.

Walker started to say something. His voice was strained and his eyes were begging. "Jake, I'm sorry. I—"

"Shut up," I said. "Just shut the fuck up, you simple fuck."

Chapter 8

Spencer decided we ought to all take a ride up to Niles where the guy he wanted to rob lived. I couldn't think of any way out of it, so I climbed in the front of his Mercedes SL—white with white interior, natch—with him, and Walker Joy got in the back, sitting as far away from me as he could get on the other side, behind Spencer. My head felt like the street he turned out onto looked: wet, black and slushy. I tried to get some kind of plan together, but nothing came to me. Spencer had me by the balls, and he and I both knew it. When this was over, I was going to kill Walker, I decided. At least bust him up. I sure didn't owe him this much. What I'd do to Spencer, I didn't know, but something. He wasn't going to use me like this and just skate.

The jeweler headed over to Highway 31 and turned north toward Michigan at the corner by the Notre Dame golf course. Settling into the flow of the traffic, he began bragging. Typical of a shit like him.

"It might surprise you to know," he began, "that I'm one of the biggest diamond dealers in the state."

Like . . . big deal, I thought—this is Indiana, not New York—but I kept that observation to myself. Let the asshole talk. Maybe he'd say something I could use. Let a guy talk long enough, he usually reveals a weakness. Although what his could be I didn't have a clue. Or how it could possibly help me out of the mess I was sliding into.

He slipped in a CD of some guy singing opera. It wasn't a regular opera, just the arias from several of them. His "Best of Fat Guys Singing" or something collection. One even sounded familiar.

In about ten minutes, we were crossing the Indiana-Michigan line and five minutes later Spencer was hanging a left onto a two-lane county road. The snow piles were leaner here. Michigan was farther north, but Niles didn't get the lake effect off Lake Michigan like we did in the St. Joe valley. South Bend got exactly the same weather Chicago did, for the same reason. Blow all that shit south from Canada and dump it on the other side of the lake.

Soon, we were traveling down another road, and the houses thinned out even more. Half a mile between each residence where we were driving now. Hundred-year-old farmhouses mostly, big old white two-story suckers, a falling-down unpainted barn behind some of them. This sure didn't look like the kind of neighborhood you'd find the kind of score Walker'd talked about in. I said as much.

Spencer and Walker both laughed. It didn't bother me so much when the jeweler did, but it irritated the hell out of me that Walker found anything funny. I turned and shot him a look that wiped the grin off his face. "Yeah," I said. "Cracks me up too, Spitball."

"Let me explain the setup," Spencer said, slowing down as he talked, his eyes searching the countryside to the right of the road. We were passing by a regular Oregon forest, seemed. For the past two miles, all that had been on either side was trees. It was lucky he slowed down just then, as a four-point buck ran suddenly out in front of us, crossing the road from one woods to the other. The whitetail was so close that if Spencer had been driving just a little faster or if he hadn't had half-decent reflexes, the damn thing would have been sitting in the front seat with us.

"Christ!" Spencer yelled, hitting the brakes and slewing on the ice before he got the car under control. A "Sonuvabitch!" came from Walker in the back seat. The deer stopped, safely across, glared at us a long second and then bounded into the trees and disappeared. Spencer shoved the transmission in park and reached inside his suit coat—a suit I'd bet cost more than I made in a month—and pulled out a pack of Salem's. I noticed his hands tremble slightly as he lighted his cigarette with the most beautiful lighter I'd ever seen in my life. Solid gold—you could tell it was the soft type, more carats—and his initials were outlined by diamonds.

I liked it that the near-collision with the deer had unnerved him. He wasn't as tough as he appeared. That was the kind of information I could use. A weakness.

"Through there," he said, his voice back to normal. He inclined his head in the direction the deer had disappeared toward. I hadn't seen it at first, but there it was. An ordinary, nondescript brick-and-frame ranch house, just part of the front door and a window barely visible through the trees. Then I saw the road that led to it, maybe fifty feet in front of us. Actually, you couldn't see the road, but there was a mailbox and I figured it would be safe to assume a driveway led to it from the house.

"That's the guy?" I said. "Fucker's in the boonies, isn't he?"

"That's right, Jake," Walker piped up from the back, practically the first he'd spoken since we left South Bend. There was real excitement in his voice and I knew why. He figured the layout of the place would prove to me how easy this job would be, appeal to my burglar's instincts. What he didn't realize was that I didn't have any burglar instincts these days.

Or did I?

The longer I stared at that house—or at least what I could see of it—and the more I remembered the isolation we'd just passed through, the more confident I felt about the chances of getting away with this. Even with a burglar alarm, we had to be at least eight-ten miles from Niles, and unless there was a county mountie in the area, we'd have plenty of time to get in, get the stuff and back out and on our way. That was supposing the worst—that the guy even had a burglar alarm or, if so, one I couldn't circumvent. Which was unlikely. I started to feel a bit better about the whole deal. If I was going to have to participate in this heist, at least it looked doable. Not that I was fully committed to joining in—I was still trying to figure a way out of it.

"Has to be done Sunday," Spencer said, hitting the window button and flicking his cigarette out. The rush of cold air felt good and I hit my own window, letting the window partway down and inhaling the brisk country air.

"*Sunday?* You've got to be kidding me." Three days from now. "I need more time than that." I looked over. "That is, if I even do this. I haven't said I would, you know."

Maybe it was time for a bluff.

"You know," I said, twisting around to look at the both of them. "I wonder how long it'd be before they found your body out here in the sticks, Sidney. You think about that? You know, if you were to disappear out here, seems like that'd clear up both my problem and my friend Walker here's problem at the same time." I had no doubt that if I put my mind to it, I could take a guy like Spencer.

Fucker just laughed, this soft little burst of air that was more like a snort. "You won't do that, Jake."

"Oh yeah? Why not, fucker? You think I can't whip your ass whenever I want to?" Asshole was making me mad. Madder. "You think I can't just reach over, snap your fat-ass neck like a fucking twig?"

"Oh," he said, grinning widely. "No doubt. No doubt at all, my friend. But you won't."

"Why's that? I'd say I've got good enough reason to, don't you?"

He reached over for the shifter, slipped it into drive. "You won't because you can't, Jake. I read you like a book. You're a burglar, not a killer. You were a killer, you wouldn't be owing your friend Walker here this favor, now would you?"

He was right. I slumped back, the wind out of my sails. If I could actually take a human life that easily, I wouldn't be sitting here in the first place. Walker wouldn't have had reason one to call in this favor and someone else would be sitting where I was. No, I was in it now. Up to my neck in it. The train had started down the mountainside. Even the guy singing opera quit at that precise moment. Spencer leaned forward, removed the tape, put his foot to the gas, and we went by the house.

"I know everything about you, Jake. I do my research."

"What the hell does this guy have that you want so bad?" I said.

I didn't get it. Sure, at one time I'd been one of the best burglars in the business. But if Spencer had done all this research, he'd know that I'd been out of the loop for years now. Burglary's like anything else. It changes. There's new tricks, new ways to do a job. Why me and why not somebody else? Why didn't Walker just go in and do the job himself? If what he said was true, that getting in would be a piece of cake, why was getting me to pull the job so important? I asked those questions out loud, and Spencer thought for a moment, and began talking as he drove.

"Good questions, Jake. Good questions. Now you're thinking right. First of all, I've already told you why I want you for this job. I don't care how long you've been away from it, there's still nobody better around here at breaking and entering. I know. I know all the players. Believe me, you could be out of the business for ten years and you'd still be better than the jokers we got around these days. Second, it's personal. I figure you owe me something for what you did to my mother's brother. Bet you didn't know you scrambled his brains, did you? Well, you did. Guy's practically a vegetable."

He took his gaze from the road, looked over for a second and smiled before he looked back. I couldn't see any warmth in his eyes.

"Every single day, my mother goes over to his house, gets him dressed and plants him in front of the TV. She fixes all his meals. You know what he likes? Tombstone Pizzas. Out of the box, microwaved. It's all he'll eat. That's what I call him. Uncle Tombstone."

He snickered and Walker started to do the same in the back seat, until Spencer turned around, fixed him with a glare and Walker just turned his head to stare at the passing rural vista, his face scrunching and turning red.

"So there's that," Spencer went on. "Then, there's the canary yellow."

"Excuse me?" He lost me. "Canary yellow? You want me to steal a bird? What, this guy owns the original Tweety or something?"

This time Walker laughed out loud and Spencer didn't chastise him. "Tell him what a canary yellow is, Walker," he said.

"It's a diamond, Jake. It's got this yellow color to it."

"I thought diamonds with yellow in them weren't worth much," I said, remembering some of the stuff I'd learned when Paris and I'd been shopping for her engagement ring. "Yellow diamonds are the cheap ones, aren't they?" This didn't make sense.

"Different kind of yellow, Jake. This particular kind of diamond has a brilliant yellow color to it. Diamonds come in all colors. Canary yellows—*perfect* canary yellows like our Mr. Calvin here owns—are worth a lot. He's also got a mocha I want very badly. A mocha's—"

I interrupted. "Brown, right? A brown diamond? Coffee-colored?"

"You're pretty quick, Jake," Spencer said. "That's right. Also rare. Mr. Calvin has a lot of rare gems."

"Calvin a jeweler too?"

Walker chimed in. "Naw. He's a designer. Makes these rings and crap for rich bitches."

"Walker's right," Spencer said, nodding. "He's one of the best. Gets clients from all over the country. I send him customers myself."

We were coming back into South Bend and it was so cloudy it looked like night, even though the official sunset was two hours away.

"That's how you know what he's got, I take it?"

"You *are* quick, Jake," Spencer said, admiration in his voice. "Exactly right. He's using the canary for a client I sent him, matter-of-fact. Indianapolis lady."

The picture was shifting into focus.

"So. What you're telling me is that you're robbing a fellow businessman. Kind of a partner. That about it?" I glanced back at Walker to see if he was getting this. There was nothing but misery on my ex-cellmate's face. I guess I'd feel the same way, I was him. Sitting in a car with a guy who was squeezing him by the balls for a major fuckup and with another guy, a *friend*, he'd forced into a scheme that might end up in a life sentence in the joint for that friend. I guess I might have a frown on my own face if I was in his situation. It made me feel sorry for him in one instant and in the next I was feeling disgust for myself for feeling that way about him. Still...

"Drop me off at the Linebacker," I said, abruptly.

"Don't you think you ought to lay off the sauce a little?" Spencer said.

"Don't you think you ought to lay off your mouth a little, Sidney?" Fucker. "You know, I'm really getting tired of you.

I was you, I wouldn't be so goddamn sure I won't just cap your punk ass, Spencer. The idea has come up in my mind. You know what happens when you get an idea like that, don't you, Spencer? It just kind of worries at you until you do something about it."

"Yeah, well, I guess," he said, thumbing through a pile of CDs on the seat between us. One wolf ticket unsold.

"This has got to be done Sunday," he said, abandoning his search for something to play. "Calvin's a Bear's fan. Takes his little honey to all the games. They play Minnesota this week. He won't miss that one. Sometimes, he goes up Saturday morning and stays over in a hotel. Lets his honey do some shopping."

Sunday. Fuck me.

We were at the Linebacker. Spencer pulled into the parking lot, nearly hitting a guy and gal exiting from behind a row of cars. The man grabbed the woman at the last second and yanked her to him. As Spencer's Mercedes swerved past him, he reached out and pounded his fist on windshield, right in front of Spencer, who blanched as he braked. His face went bloodless from the near miss.

I opened the door. Behind me, I could see the guy coming up. He was a large sucker, looked like he'd played some football for the university up the road. Looked also like he was carrying a load. At least ten beers, I'd estimate. "Looks like you got a visitor, Spencer," I said. "Hope you got some shit on him. Otherwise, you might want to vacate these premises. Be seein' ya."

I slammed the door shut. The guy was about fifteen feet away and walking toward Spencer's side of the car with what I could only describe as a major hard-on.

"Guy picked me up hitchin'," I shouted to the guy. "Faggot tried to put a move on me. I made him stop here, let me out, but I think he's pissed. Him and his boyfriend…" I jerked my thumb toward Walker sitting in the backseat, staring out, "...said they were going to pick up an N.D. student here, get him to give them a blow job. I'd be careful, I was you."

That stopped the guy in his tracks, but only for a second. I could see the red rise from his neck as he moved again toward the car and this time he was running.

I don't know what happened after that. I turned and walked across the street to the Tangerine where my own car was parked. When I pulled out onto South Bend Avenue, I could see Spencer hadn't taken my advice and left. He was dangling off his feet, up against his car. Dangling, on account of the big guy had him by the lapels of his Botany 500 topcoat and was discussing something with some heat. I could just see the top of Walker's head as he emerged from the back seat. He didn't look too joyful, and I laughed at the thought. Joyful...Joy. Walker Joy. Have some fun, kids, I thought, chuckling, then turned onto Twykenham and sobered up almost immediately.

What was I going to tell Paris?

Chapter 9

Paris was already asleep when I went home and I wasn't about to wake her and try to explain where I'd been. There was a plate of cold pork chops in the fridge, which I polished off with one of her Budweisers. After washing the dish, I grabbed a blanket from the hall closet and crashed on the downstairs sofa. The last thing I wanted was a wide-awake Paris asking me why I'd been out this late.

Or smell the booze on me.

I scrambled awake in the morning, a loud crash upstairs in our bathroom the cause. The wall clock read six o'clock and I could see by the sun it was morning. My head was throbbing.

I opened the bathroom door. Bits of yellow plastic lay everywhere. On the sink, the floor, even a large piece caught in one of the shower curtain hooks. Paris was standing there, a brush in one hand, her hair messy and wet.

"Your dryer explode?" I said, trying a smile on her.

I didn't get one back.

"I threw it," she said, matter-of-factly. "You just get in?" I was still in my clothes from yesterday.

"Oh . . . no. I got in a little late and figured you needed your sleep. I crashed on the couch downstairs."

"That was big of you."

I didn't say anything, just stepped into the bathroom and began collecting pieces of yellow dryer. I felt her eyes lasering on me.

"Was she good?"

I stood up. "Huh?"

Her eyes were small and bright and dark like they get sometimes with little yellow flecks, and I could see the slightest tremble to her bottom lip. I didn't get what she was saying at first, and then I realized she thought I'd been out with another woman.

"Oh, baby!" I came toward her, tried to put my arms around her. She twisted away.

"Well?" Her lip had quit trembling. She was just plain old-fashioned pissed-off now.

I laughed. Which was absolutely the worst thing I could've done.

She slapped me. Hard. My ear was on fire. Which didn't do much for my hangover. She raised her other hand to slap me again, and I caught both her wrists in my hands. I wasn't laughing now.

"Baby, baby. Calm down."

"Screw you, you son-of-a-bitch," was her response. "You're seeing some whore, aren't you? Tell me the truth, Jake."

What the hell was I going to do? The truth was the last thing I could tell her.

"I'm up against something," I said, finally, letting go of her hands. "Sweetheart, I just can't tell you. I wish I could, but I can't. It's something from my past and that's all I can say. You'll just have to trust me on this. When it's all over, I'll tell you all about it, but I'm going to have to ask you to trust me on this. Believe me, it's not a woman."

I didn't know what else to say to her.

She must have believed me. Her eyes lost their narrowness, and the hard line her lips had taken relaxed.

"Okay, Jake," she said after a little silence, during which her eyes darted back and forth, searching my face. "I guess

I have no choice. This has something to do with when you were in prison, doesn't it?"

I nodded. "Don't ask me anything else," I pleaded.

She turned back to the mirror and began yanking at her wet hair with the vent brush.

I was already turned and going out the door when I heard, "You go to jail, don't expect me to visit. Don't expect me to wait on you, either. It won't happen."

I went downstairs and turned on the TV and watched *Good Morning America* until she came down, dressed for work.

"You'll be home tonight?" she said, her hand on the door.

"I think so," I said. "Probably. Hey, maybe we can go out."

She slammed the door behind her.

"Or not," I said to the door. Jesus.

It was a lousy day at the Tangerine. Three cancellations in a row, and half an hour before my next client was due, the boss came out of his office and motioned for me to come over.

"We need to have a conversation, Jake," he said.

"Sure, Big Daddy," I said, chipper-like, stepping behind him into his office. I was smiling, but not on the inside. Big Daddy Koontz never talked to anyone unless he was pissed about something. I felt like the aging baseball star probably feels when his batting average has gone to south of the Mendoza line and his manager calls him into his office and there's a bright-eyed rookie already sitting there avoiding eye contact.

"Close the door," he said and went over to sit behind his desk. I took a seat in the chair in front of it, and Big Daddy pushed the button on the intercom. "Jessica, bring in Jake's appointment book." That done, he eased his massive bulk back into the chair, raised his pudgy arms, and clasped his hands behind his head. And smiled.

Fuck.

Big Daddy never smiled. Not unless you were a wealthy client...which I wasn't.

"Heard some stuff about you, Jake," he began.

Great. It wasn't about me fucking midget ballerinas in the back room, I knew. I hadn't done that in a while. Well, never. I tried to guess what sort of crap it was he'd heard that prompted this meeting. My guess was he was going to ream me out for leaving early yesterday and cancelling my appointments.

Jessica came in and placed my appointment book on Big Daddy's desk. Not a good sign. On the way out, she surreptitiously slipped me a thumbs up and then crossed her fingers and bit her lower lip, pantomiming the universal charade of, "Hang in there, champ! Good luck! ...Except you're fucked..."

I winked at her as she swung her hips out the door then turned a serious face to Big Daddy who was staring at my book.

"You not happy here, Jake?" he began.

What do you say to that?

"Hell, yes, I'm positively sappy with happiness. Why? This about yesterday? I wasn't feeling good." This sounded lame, even to me.

He closed the book, leaned back and folded his hands in his lap.

"That's funny. I heard you were leaving us."

Shit. I should've known he'd find out. So that was it. I was almost relieved.

"How—"

"I find that out?" He cleared his throat. "David told me."

I knew instantly who he was talking about. David Jerna, the beauty supply salesman from Fashion Lines. Jerna was the one I was buying my equipment from.

Then, he surprised me.

"Jake, lots of my stylists have left to open up their own place. Remember Dixie? We even gave her a party."

I started to feel a glimmer of hope. I really needed this job for the next three weeks until we opened. It wasn't like I had all the money in the world.

"Yeah," I said. I leaned forward, tried to look like the hapless, but innocent young boy who'd just got caught with his hand in his mom's cookie jar. "She got drunk and threw up on her best customer."

He laughed and I followed suit.

"That *was* funny, wasn't it?" His smile disappeared. "The point is, she told me she was leaving and I was fine with that. Nothing wrong with someone trying to better themselves. Hell…I left the guy I was working for. Left on good terms."

"Look, Big Daddy," I started. "I'm sorry I didn't tell you. I just thought—"

"I know what you thought, Jake. However, that's not the problem here."

It wasn't? Well, then, what the hell?

"The problem is, I got a phone call this morning."

I didn't have a clue what he was talking about. I didn't say anything, just kept my mouth shut and waited.

"It was from a customer. Know what this person told me?"

He didn't wait. It wasn't a question he expected an answer to.

"I was told you were an ex-con, Jake."

What do you say to something like that. I hadn't told him—I hadn't told anybody. It isn't something you broadcast. But, hell, I'd worked for the guy for over two years now. Wasn't it obvious I wasn't a criminal? I didn't know what to say.

He went on. "I made some calls. Looks like this person was telling me the truth. Jake, I've got a name in the community. A reputation. Do you know what something like this can do to business once it gets out? The mayor's wife comes in here. Father Joyce comes in here." Joyce was the guy who ran all the Notre Dame sports stuff. Big shot.

I sighed. "Well, hell. What do you want me to say?"

His smile had completely gone.

"How about 'goodbye.'"

Chapter 10

"What're you doing home?"

She startled me. I must have dozed off. I slipped my legs off the couch, sat up and rubbed my eyes, clearing the fuzziness.

"Oh, hi, honey."

She walked over, picked up the magazines that were strewed all over the coffee table, and began to put them in piles.

"Have a no-show?"

"I wish!" I laughed, trying to set her up, make her see I wasn't concerned at all. "We're going to have to put the shop in a bit early, looks like."

Paris slowly stood up. She folded her arms and stared at me. "You got fired, didn't you?" Without waiting for my answer, she turned, walked over to the picture window and stared out. "Big Daddy caught you fooling around with that little receptionist, didn't he?"

I got up, went over to stand beside her. I put my arm around her, felt her tense up, but she didn't move away.

"He found out we were putting in a salon."

She twisted free of my arm and stepped back. The look she had on her face was best described as grim, and her eyes darted here and there as she searched my face.

"That's it? You're telling me the truth?"

She must have seen it in my eyes because her own features softened and her chin trembled the slightest bit.

"Oh, Jake!"

She stepped toward me and I took her in my arms and she buried her face in my chest. A torrent of muffled words erupted.

"Jake...baby...I've been so...worried. The way you're acting. I thought... I was sure—"

I gently pushed her back, smoothed back the hair from her forehead. "That I was seeing somebody else?"

She swallowed, looked down. "Yes."

"Oh, Paris!" I reached for her hand, turned, and we exited the bathroom and went down the stairs, hand-in-hand, her following. I led us over to the couch and sat down, pulling her down beside me and slipping my arm around her again.

"I'm not seeing anyone, sweetheart, but I am in kind of a fix right now."

"Your job?" she said. "That isn't that big of a deal. We're opening in less than a month. This will just give you more time to get ready. It'll be tight but we can do it."

I felt like crap. I hadn't lied to her—exactly. I just hadn't told her all of it. Did that constitute a lie? I didn't want to pursue that argument in my mind.

"Yeah, you're right. But, I'm talking about something else. I'm talking about the reason I've been late coming home the past couple of nights."

I was going to have to be careful. If Paris had the slightest inkling there was the chance I'd be involved in a crime, she'd be upstairs in a nanosecond, packing her bags. Right from the very start, she'd made it clear that if we ever ceased being totally honest with each other, I needed to color her gone.

"I got a call from Walker Joy," I finally said.

"Walker Joy? Where do I know that name from?"

Her brow twisted as she thought, and before I could say anything, she said, "Walker Joy! He was your cellmate!"

I nodded.

Her face darkened.

"What the hell does he want? Money, I'll bet. You just tell him to get out and work for his same as we do. I'll be damned if I'm going to give some scummy ex-convict any of our hard-earned money!"

Her face was contorted into a rage I hadn't seen before. I felt my own cheeks flush. It was like she was calling *me* the "scummy ex-convict."

If I'd had any idea of telling her before what Walker Joy's game was, that decided it for me. I'd never seen that look on her face before and it did something inside. One of those little *ticks* in life's movie that occurs, and you're aware something important has changed but you don't want to look to square at it at the moment so you let it go. In the back of your mind, you know full well that later on you're going to look back at that and see that's where all the shit started, but you're still optimistic at this point… and you don't. All that—or rather, the *gist* of all that—went through my mind, and I said, not looking directly at her but off to the side toward the front window where a grainy sun was struggling to shine through greasy clouds, "No, it's nothing like that."

I felt my story coming together as I told it. I was surprised to find out how easy the first lie to my wife came out. The first lie if I didn't count the lie of omission I'd committed just a minute before. The realization gave me the same feeling as an inner ear infection does. Off-balance and queasy. It didn't stop me though.

"Well, actually he did hit me up for a loan, but I turned him down."

Paris stared at me as if to say, *I knew it*, and I went on.

"What I did do was agree to help him out on this job."

"Job?" The storm clouds began to roll in again over her features.

"Not what you're thinking. A *real* job. Legitimate."

I couldn't believe I was doing this. This was the first time I'd deliberately lied to my wife. The first stone had broken loose with Walker's phone call and already it had kicked up a bigger rock. The avalanche was starting down that mountain, and I didn't even bother to see if there was anything to grab onto.

"He's my friend, Paris. He saved my life once. If it wasn't for Walker Joy I wouldn't be here today. I didn't see any way I could refuse him. If somebody I'd known a month had come to me and asked the same favor, I'd do it."

She didn't say anything, just waited to see what I was going to say next. With a look on her face I wasn't crazy about. I ignored it, went on.

"What it is…" I made it up as I talked. "He got a job remodeling this hunting cabin up on the other side of Niles, and he found this old barn they'll let him have the lumber from if he'll just take it. I'm going to help him tear it down and haul it up there."

For a guy who'd never lied to his wife, I was amazed at how good I was at it.

Thing is, she bought it. It was that easy.

I embellished it a bit, telling her how if Walker didn't make some honest money, I knew him and what would happen. He'd be out pulling a stickup and be back in Pendleton in a week. I was saving him, I told her, just like he'd saved me that time back in the joint. I could see she was reluctant at first to buy that, but she seemed to come to some kind of judgment in her mind and she nodded. "I guess I can understand that kind of debt, Jake."

She reached over, put her hand on my arm. "Okay. I guess you have to do this. Nothing else, right?"

I looked into her eyes and never blinked once. "I won't even go out for a beer with him. Besides, this is a chance to make a few extra bucks and we need that now. With the…" I hesitated. "…stuff at the Tangerine and all."

That satisfied her, and later, after getting a pizza delivered and watching some TV, we went up to bed and made love. She made the first move, sliding her hand under the cover. At first, I couldn't get hard and that bothered me as I'd never had trouble like that before, but then she lowered her head and that was all I needed.

Afterward, she gave me a quick peck on the lips, turned her back to me and fell asleep almost immediately.

I didn't.

I lay on my back staring at the ceiling, thinking about the road I'd started down in our relationship. Once, I reached over to wake her, going so far as to place my hand on her shoulder to give her a little shake, but I changed my mind and withdrew it.

Too late, though.

"Whatzit?" she murmured, shifting slightly, straightening out her legs from her curled-up position to touch mine.

"Nothing," I said. "Go back to sleep. I love you."

"Me, too," she said, her voice muffled by her pillow.

Downstairs, I heard the front door open and close. Bobby. I glanced over at the clock on the dresser. Ten past twelve.

I was going to have to have a talk with the little shithead.

I wondered who it was who had called Big Daddy and snitched on me. I had an idea who it might be.

Chapter 11

Paris had already left for work when I finally woke up. I must have been really tired as I hadn't heard her leave our bed or take her shower. The digital numbers on the clock read nine thirty-five, and through the window I could see there wasn't a cloud in the sky. A beautiful day. Maybe my luck was going to change.

Half an hour later, showered, shaved, teeth brushed, and dressed, I opened the door, took one step out and returned inside. It was downright balmy out there. I hung up the full-length leather coat I'd had on in the front closet and grabbed my Notre Dame jacket. It had to be sixty degrees out there, maybe even warmer. Half the snow had already melted, and brown patches of grass stuck through the disappearing white in the front yard. Only the slush-covered piles at the curb looked the same as they had.

I had my hand on the door getting ready to go back out when the phone rang.

It was some lady from Adams High School, the assistant principal, she said. Calling to see if Bobby was sick. Seems he hadn't shown up for his classes. I covered for him, telling the woman that yeah, he was in bed with a bad cold but he should be back tomorrow.

That little sonuvabitch!

As soon as I hung up the phone, I rushed upstairs to his room.

Gone.

The bed wasn't even made.

Little peckerwood!

I thought about looking for him, but knew I wouldn't have a clue where to begin. Probably at one of his buddy's houses, maybe driving around drinking flavored vodka. Doing the same stuff I had in high school. I caught him, I was going to ream him a new asshole. Thinking that made me laugh out loud. I was becoming Dad.

I'd deal with it later, I thought. Sooner or later, he'd come home, if for nothing else to get something to eat. Right now, I had other, more pressing matters to attend to than chasing all over town trying to find my brother.

I jumped in the car and headed over to Highway 31. My plan was to go back up to Niles, do my own casing of this job.

Half an hour later, I was turning off the highway onto the road Spencer had taken the day before. Out in the country, the snow was still piled high on the fields, and the glare was so brilliant I had to slip on sunglasses, and even then I had to squint a bit.

The house was easy to find. On the way, I'd come up with what I thought was a half-decent plan to let me take a good look at the situation. I'd just knock at the door and when the guy answered it, I'd tell him I was a hunter and wanted to get permission to go after bunnies on his place. It was a bit risky. Next week, after he was robbed, he might recall our meeting and be able to pick me out of a mug shot book, but I was wearing sunglasses and had a scarf and stocking hat to throw on before I knocked on his door. He wouldn't get that good a look, I figured. At least not good enough to make a solid I.D. if it came to that. Chances were, after the heist went down, he wouldn't even connect the two events.

I started to turn in the driveway and then thought twice about it and braked. Asshole hadn't plowed it out since the last snow, and even though it was melting, I could see a drift a few feet away that I wasn't positive the bald skins on the Lumina could navigate. Paris had wanted to buy new snow tires last week, but I'd nixed that, wanting to save every nickel we had for the new shop.

Actually, that made it better. I pulled forward a bit, just past the drive and off the road as far as I dared. There didn't seem to be much traffic, and what stray car or two that might come by had plenty of room to go around. I'd just walk up to the house and he wouldn't see my car.

I put on the scarf and stocking hat, pulling the hat down clear over my eyebrows and adjusted the scarf so that it covered the lower part of my face right up to my bottom lip. A quick glance in the rearview mirror told me that with my sunglasses on he wouldn't be able to give any kind of description at all.

When I stepped out, I was surprised at the crispness of the air. With the sun beating down so brightly, I guess I thought it was going to be warm out. It might have been in the open, but here with all these trees, it was flat cold.

What had Spencer said the guy's name was? Calvin. That was it. I couldn't remember if that was his first or last name. Snow covered the mailbox and I knocked it off.

Calvin must have been his first name. "C. Brewer" was the name on the box.

I walked toward the house. As soon as I got to the drift, I was glad I hadn't decided to drive up. It was clear up to my knees and under was pure ice. I'd've been stuck there a week.

I could see a lamp shining on a small table through the drapes when I peeked into the picture window, shading the sun from the glass reflection with my hand, but when I pressed the doorbell, I could hear it clearly in the house, but nothing else. I pressed it again and again, nothing.

It was beginning to snow and the sun had gone behind a cloud. Through a break in the trees that surrounded the house, I could see a dark bank of thunderclouds scudding my way. Other than a pair of squirrels who were chasing each other in an oak tree at the side of the house and chattering insanely at each other, there was no sound.

This was great. The guy wasn't home. I could case the place and take my time. If he showed up, I'd just use my "hunting permission" story. I started around the east end of the house.

Ten minutes later, I knew all I needed to know.

There wasn't any alarm system. None at all. The guy had stickers on two of the back windows that informed the house was protected by ADT Systems, but I looked for the lead-in wire from the power pole and there wasn't any. That wasn't uncommon. Lots of people bought those stickers on the black market and put them up, and for the average burglar, that was enough to make them walk away.

What it meant was this guy was a cheapo. Probably depended on the fact that hardly anybody knew what he did and all he had to worry about was kids breaking in. I'd bet the new salon that inside he had a clunky old safe, probably bolted to the floor, and he felt perfectly secure with that, knowing that even if some juvenile delinquents broke in or even a more seasoned burglar, they'd make a stab at getting it open and would quit at that, knowing there was no way they could get the thing loose and carried away before somebody came.

It was obvious he wasn't too worried about a real pro.

I decided to call Spitball and Spencer, let them know what I'd found out. Maybe they'd see they didn't need me after all. Anybody with a screwdriver could break into this place with relative ease. I didn't really think Spencer would buy that, since he wanted me to do the job for his own personal revenge, but it was worth a shot. If he wouldn't let me off the hook, at least I knew this was going to be pretty simple and easy. I was feeling a lot better about everything walking back up the driveway to the road and my car. Until I was maybe twenty feet from the road.

There was a car parked on the road just behind mine. And it wasn't just any car. It wasn't say, this Brewer guy's car. It wasn't even a county mountie's car.

It was worse.

It was Paris's Escort.

And she was sitting in it.

Chapter 12

Pissed.

That was easy to see.

But what in the hell was she doing here?

"Hi, honey," was all I could think of to say.

She flipped the cigarette she was smoking out the window and past my head, almost hitting my nose.

"'Hi, honey?' Even for you that's pretty lame, Jake." She lit another cigarette. "What's her name? *Honey.*"

So that was it. She still thought I was cheating on her.

She took another puff on the cigarette, flipped the almost-new butt past my nose again, even closer this time, and shoved open the door. I jumped back just in time to avoid being hit. She swung her legs out. "Let's go meet your friend, Jake."

Jesus, could this get any more fucked?

"Paris, get back in the car. There's no one home and there's no girl."

Besides having to worry about my marriage dissolving before my eyes, it suddenly occurred to me that Calvin Brewer might choose this time to return home. I had no doubt that if he pulled up right now that Paris would be in his face, demanding to meet the wife he didn't have and detailing how I was screwing her.

I had to get her out of here.

"Look. Get back in your car and follow me. I'll find a coffee shop, we'll have a latte and I'll tell you the whole deal.

There's no woman, but there is something I haven't told you. I promise to tell you everything."

She just stood there, arms folded, her eyes lasering me into shreds.

"Trust me for this one time, honey," I pleaded. "If the guy who lives here comes back, I'm in serious trouble. Christ Almighty, let's just go. I give you my word I'll tell you everything. I—"

Shit. I could see a car coming behind Paris. It was a ways back, but it'd be here soon. It might just be a passerby, but it might be Brewer, too.

"C'mon," I said, brusquely, grabbing her arm and forcing her toward the driver's seat. "Don't fuck around. Let's go. You want to see me go back to the joint? You don't get in that car right now and follow me the hell out of here there's a good chance that can happen."

She must have believed me. She still had her pissed-off look on—even more so—but she climbed back behind the wheel, slammed the door and started the engine and yelled out the window, "This better be good, Jake. It isn't, I'm coming right back here and meet whoever lives in that house."

I ran to my car, started it and hit the gas. The wheels slued a bit in the snow, then found traction. In the rearview mirror I saw Paris pull out behind me. The car I'd seen coming up the road was still coming and was about the equivalent of a couple of city blocks away.

And it was Brewer. Probably. Most likely. I didn't have a clue what the guy looked like, and the car was so far back I couldn't tell if a man or a woman was driving it or if there was even more than one person in the vehicle. I watched as the car got to the driveway of the house I'd just been at and turned into it. Paris must have been watching as well. She flicked her lights on and off at me. In case I missed seeing it, I guessed.

She admitted as much, sitting across from me at a back table in the coffee shop I'd spotted driving through Niles earlier.

"I wanted to be sure you saw your little girlfriend," she said.

"Paris," I said and reached across the table to take her hand, only to watch her jerk it back into her lap and turn her head to glare in the direction of the front window.

It was as if she'd slapped me. I didn't know what I was going to say. The truth, I supposed. I'd wrestled with the problem all the way into Niles, and the only thing I could come up with was to simply tell her the whole story and hope she'd understand.

And not leave me.

It was sinking in just how much I loved my wife. Not that I hadn't realized it all along, but now, at the prospect that she might pack her bags and leave our life together, I was close to panic. What would I do without her? She was my whole life.

I hadn't known how I was going to tell her and I started out clumsily, my heart thumping and my hands sweating, but then I settled down and just laid it all out for her. Walker's first call, the meeting with Spencer, the drive up to this guy Brewer's house. I told her about the Clark station incident and tried to ignore the look of shock that passed over her features when I told her how I'd hit the guy with a tire iron. I told her everything. Almost everything. I kept out the one event I'd never tell her.

She'd never asked any of the details of the crimes I'd committed, and I'd never volunteered any information, but I could see by the varying looks on her face that she was reassessing the way she'd looked at me. It wasn't that she didn't know about my criminal past; it was more that I think that before now it had been an abstract notion on her part. Maybe she'd even romanticized what I'd been before we met. What was certain was that whatever image she'd held of me before we'd sat down in the coffee shop was swiftly being edited and refocused in her mind. When we left this place, our relationship would be profoundly different from what it had been before we entered. I looked around at the assemblage of ordinary characters who were sitting at the other tables and booths and thought it mildly humorous that a man's life could be undergoing a major, cataclysmic upheaval ten feet away and they could be totally oblivious to the event, laughing and gossiping over their cappuccinos and lattes.

I finished, finally, and waited for her response. Not once during my recitation of what had gone down the past couple of days had she interrupted. Once, she had started to say something but had changed her mind, waving her hand as though chasing a swarm of gnats, indicating for me to hurry up, get it all out.

Now she knew the whole story. I waited for her to say something, anything, but she just kept staring at me. After what seemed like at least five minutes but was only probably a minute or even less, I opened my mouth, but she did that gnat-waving thing again. I had the weirdest thought that she was chasing her own thoughts of murder and mayhem away.

"You're really in it, aren't you?" she said.

Her words were flat in tone, but I thought I could detect a spark of compassion in her eyes, which never left mine. Actually, her gaze was disconcerting, and I was the first to look away.

"I really am," I kind of mumbled.

"If you get caught and they find out I knew about it before-hand, I can be arrested as an accessory, can't I?"

Of all the reactions I had considered she might have, this wasn't among them.

"Well, yeah, but—"

Again, the gnat-waving gesture... More like swatting a bee this time, more urgent, a gesture that said she regretted what she'd said.

"I'm sorry, Jake."

I could tell she really was by the contrite look that flashed over her face and the way she averted her gaze for a brief second and then looked back, a wan smile on her lips. This time, it was she who reached over and put her hand over mine and gave it a squeeze. A glimmer of hope for *us* shot through me.

"It's just that…" she started and then tailed off.

"It's just that you saw yourself in a six by ten cell? I've seen myself in that same cell. Pretty chilling, huh?"

That cell was all I'd been seeing myself in since Walker had laid down what he wanted.

I turned my hand over and cupped hers tenderly.

"It's all right, sweetheart. But don't worry. I'd never do anything to get you sent up. No matter what."

She was quiet for a moment.

She cleared her throat and began to talk. I became aware I had been holding my breath.

Chapter 13

"You're going to do this, regardless of what I say, aren't you?" she began. "Or do."

I considered my answer carefully. The truth, Jake, I told myself. Just stick to the truth and don't cop any deuces. Be a man.

I plunged in.

"I have no choice, baby," I said. "Spencer's not fucking around here."

"Asshole!"

"I agree. But, asshole or not, he's got all the cards. I don't do this for him he's going to set Bobby up. Not only that, he'll make sure the cops know about that little incident with his uncle." I sighed. "He's got all the aces, Paris, and I'm sitting here with a broken straight." I let out a hollow laugh. "I'm fucked, plain and simple."

I could see the wheels going round as she pondered the situation.

"Yes," she said, at last. "I do believe he's got you by the curlies as you guys would say."

In spite of myself, I had to grin. And then, miraculously, she smiled herself. It was brief and she reverted to her dead-serious look immediately, but it was enough to make me think there was maybe some hope.

"There's maybe something good here," I said, trying to capitalize on that quick grin and the promise behind it.

Close the deal. "This isn't going to be the hardest job I've ever pulled. In fact, it looks downright simple. We should be in and out in half an hour, and the guy's going to be in Chicago. If we get away with this, we'll be set for life. Our kids can go to Harvard."

That was the truth. Now that I'd admitted out loud that I had no choice but to participate in Spencer's plan, I began to see the positives in the situation. I was eager to communicate them to Paris, get her to see what my share of the take would mean to us. This could work—really work. I tried to keep the growing excitement from creeping into my voice.

"He's talking—"

"A lot of money. I got that part, Jake. We don't need money. I've got a good job and you're about to open a salon and it's going to be a success. Don't try to snow me, Jake. I'm trying to figure this out, and a con job by you is only going to make me go the opposite direction than I think you want me to."

The tingle of excitement I'd had a moment ago faded. It looked like I was back to trying to make a sale. I didn't know if I had it in me, though. Truth was, there wasn't much more I could see to say to paint the picture any different than it was.

"There's something else," she said after a silence that seemed to be endless. "Your Spencer guy. What makes you think this is going to be the end of it with him? I mean, let's just say you do pull this off. He's still got the same cards. What keeps him from making you do this again? And again?"

She had a point. Something along those lines had already occurred to me, but I'd preferred to jam the thought in the back of my mind, not consider it.

"I don't know. Nothing, I guess. Except… honor among thieves?" That was such a ludicrous statement I had to laugh at it myself. "Yeah," I continued, not looking at her, but guessing I knew what her reaction was. "I guess that's kind of a stupid thing to say, isn't it?"

She didn't reply, for which I was grateful. At this point I appreciated any small favor like letting me cling to the little bit of dignity I still owned.

Paris then said something which made me love her even more.

"We'll just have to deal with that if and when it becomes an issue."

I stared at her.

"We?"

"I'm thinking."

Her eyes were luminous, huge moons.

"I'm scared, Jake."

She wasn't the only one.

Chapter 14

Outside the coffee shop, the wind had gotten teeth, spitting out a few isolated snowflakes and the sun had disappeared behind a bank of nasty-looking almost-black clouds. I pulled my collar up and put my arm around Paris while we walked toward our cars. I couldn't tell if she was stiff because of the cold, her pregnancy, or because of our situation. I decided to blame it on the chill.

"What now?" I asked, opening the door to her Toyota for her.

"Let's go home," she said. She slid in and looked up at me. "Home?"

"I want to feel safe. Mostly, I want to be away from…" She waved her hand in a general direction, indicating downtown Niles, Michigan. "…here."

I knew what she was referring to. Calvin Brewer's house and the break-in I was going to perform on that residence just a few miles away from where we were standing. The crime that was about to change our lives and our relationship irrevocably, no matter how it turned out.

Once home, Paris did something that completely surprised me. I went into the living room and switched on the TV and sat down to watch CNN, idly thinking that there were some chores I needed to get at for the new salon. Check on our supply order, see if the styling chairs I'd ordered had come in yet. See a printer and get announcements made to send to clients. Nothing pressing—I had more than three weeks before we opened and most everything had been done—but just sitting around would drive me nuts, I knew. At least if I did some work it'd keep my mind off Sunday. Paris had disappeared upstairs, and I'd kind of forgotten she was even home when I heard a stair step creak and looked up and here she came down the staircase.

In a negligee.

Thunderstruck would be the word I'd use to describe the feeling that swept over me.

"You want to have sex?" I sputtered.

By way of answer, she turned to go back up the staircase, twisted her head in my direction and nodded solemnly. When she turned, her red negligee—my favorite!—twisted up and exposed the side of her ass. She wasn't wearing any panties. She began to walk back the way she'd just come. All I saw was those long, long legs going away, and I was instantly hard.

And following her up the stairs.

I knew why she wanted to have sex. She was acting exactly like I used to when I was robbing places as my career of choice. The specter of jail looms and with it the fact that if you get busted, sex as you know if it is going to be seriously curtailed.

I closed the door behind me and began shucking my clothes. Paris was already in bed, the covers pulled up around her chin and she wasn't smiling. This was going to be deadly serious.

I dropped my pants and shirt and got in bed. I reached for her, and her arms went around my neck, and I moved into the curve of her body. I felt the smoothness of her legs against mine and her breasts pressed into my chest. I barely felt her tummy, but for some reason, that turned me on as much as anything. Our mouths opened and met and her tongue was sweet and electric, her breath hot. I was so hard I thought I might come before I even entered her. I bent my head and took a nipple into my mouth, lightly tonguing it the way she liked. She moaned and arched her back to give me more of her breast and I took as much of it as I could into my mouth, sucking as if I were a new-born babe, reaching at the same time for her other breast, which I cupped with the palm of my hand, and began gently squeezing the nipple. Her breasts were half-again as large as before she got pregnant and swollen with milk. Her panting grew quicker, interspersed with little moans. One of her hands was at the back of my head, her fingers twisting my hair and pushing me into her breast, and her other hand was squeezing my ass.

And then…

We both shot straight up in bed.

Somebody was downstairs.

I turned over to reach under the bed for the Louisville Slugger I kept there.

"Bobby," Paris said.

Whoever it was took the steps two at a time and clomped into Bobby's room. Almost instantly, the stereo switched on, booming out the sounds of Limp Biscuit.

"Bobby," I said, sighing and rolling the bat back under the bed. I swung my legs over the side.

"Where are you going?" Paris whispered.

"What do you mean?" I said. "Bobby's home. We can't—"

Before I could finish my sentence, she reached over and grabbed me by my hair and jerked me toward her.

I yelped.

"Listen, Buster," she said in a low growl, her face inches from mine and an angry red. "This is my house and if I want to get fucked in my own house, I'm going to get fucked. I don't care if that's the fucking Pope down the hall."

I had to laugh and that got her tickled and she giggled. And reached down for my cock which had begun to shrink a bit. Reversed that.

I tossed the covers back and slid over and down until my

nose was buried in her muff. She moaned a low, guttural moan when my tongue found her clit and began flicking at it in small, rapid movements. She reached down, pulled my hair, forcing my face harder up against her. The smell of her sex filled my nostrils, her pubic hair sweet and tickly against my nose, and… the music stopped.

Silence from Bobby's room.

I raised my head a couple of inches and looked at Paris. She angled her head and gave me a fierce glare as if to say, "Don't you dare stop, mister."

"But, baby… my brother's home. He'll hear."

"You're talking, aren't you. Why are you talking? The kind of talking you're doing isn't turning me on, you know." I looked at her face and didn't recognize her.

I went back down on her. She pulled me up, guided me into her.

The silence coming from Bobby's room filled the house. The normal sounds of an old house settling, creaks as floorboards shifted downstairs, a burst of sleet against the kitchen window—you could hear them all. Which heightened every sound we made as we made love. Paris, panting louder than I'd ever heard her, giving sharp intakes of voluble breath with every thrust… only *thrust* wasn't the right word… as I strained with my utmost to remain as silent as I was able to. Every moan she made, every groan of bedsprings, sounded magnified in my ears, and the more I concentrated on suppressing any sound of our sex only made her obviously bent on making more and louder sounds. She was cursing. Paris never cursed, at least not like this. I opened my eyes and glimpsed her face and what I saw was pure rage. It should easily have been the best sex I'd ever experienced, but it wasn't. It was the worst. It was *savage*. That's the only way I can describe it. From her responses, I knew she was in a place she hadn't been before, at least not with me—but I don't think "sweet" was a way she would have described the way she was feeling. She was almost raping me. She had me by my hair, one hand on each side of my head, and she was forcing it back so fiercely I thought my neck would break, all the while pulling me tight into her with her legs. The oddest thing was, the more she clawed at me, the more she uttered animal moans, the more terrible the act became for me…and the more passive I became. She was making me her "boy-toy", and for the first time ever, I had the feeling of being completely controlled by my partner. It was frightening, and all I could focus on was trying to come as quickly as I could, the exact opposite of what I usually tried to do.

It was…scary.

The longer it went on, the more vocal and loud Paris became, the more I wanted it to end. Just get it over with. I knew what was happening. She'd had a vision of everything slipping away, of us slipping away. The baby, the business, the house…She was fighting to keep it all. I knew how she felt because that was how I felt as well. Only…we went about dealing with our frustration in different ways.

This was…I guess…Danielle Steel-quality sex. For Paris, anyway. For me, well, for me it was more like what I'd always thought at least some women experienced. I was making love to my wife—trying to—and she was *fucking* me and then she came, an explosion of curses rent from her lips, and she pulled me so close to her I couldn't breathe, wrapped her legs around me, dug her heels into the middle of my back and squeezed so hard I couldn't draw air in. I didn't dare move until she was done and then, finally, she was, and she loosed her arms and I gulped down air.

I hadn't come.

It didn't seem to matter to her. I doubt she even knew I was there for that brief moment when release came for her. Or before.

I finally got my breath and leaned over and kissed her on her wet brow.

She looked at me and whatever was in her eyes wasn't love. "You bastard," she whispered. Then...something in her eyes changed and the look was gone. She looked confused for a second or two and then she smiled, weakly. "I'm sorry," she said. "I—"

I put my finger on her lips. "Shh," I said. "I know. It's all right."

She smiled thinly again, then turned her back on me and curled up. I rolled over on my back, our thighs touching, the sweat on my chest and forehead cooling. Her breathing got more and more measured and soon she was snoring lightly.

After a while, I slid my hand over. With the backs of my fingers I barely touched the cool skin of the back of her thigh just below the curve of her butt. When her skin warmed, I moved it just a little, seeking another cool part. I didn't think about what had just happened between us. I just wanted to touch her leg, feel her silkiness.

I realized what I was doing. I was creating and storing up a memory.

My cell in Pendleton came up in my mind and I was back there, lying on my bunk on a Sunday afternoon. Any Sunday afternoon. I could *feel* the prison all around me. I could feel how I felt back then. This I would remember. The touch of her leg. The coolness and firmness and smoothness of her thigh. *This* I could feel *inside*. The sex I'd forget. I knew that. Not this. If it was meant to be that I got caught, got sent back up for life, I knew that this would be the memory I'd draw on. The feel of her thigh on the backs of my fingers, feathery and cool.

I must have fallen asleep.

There was a banging on the door. We both jumped.

"Hey! You guys done in there?"

Bobby.

"I'll kill him," Paris said. She struggled to sit up, rubbing her eyes.

I held up my hand. "No," I said. "*I* will."

I found my clothes and began putting them on. Paris watched me.

"I want my home back again," she said. "I want Bobby out of here."

I just looked at her. I understood how she felt, but there was no way I was telling my poor, little, sad-assed brother to leave. Although, if I ever would have considered that, this was the time. But, no; as mad as I was at him at the moment, there was no way I was kicking him out. I didn't say so to Paris, just nodded at her and said merely, "I'm going to talk to him."

Halfway to Bobby's room, the doorbell rang.

"Shit," I said, out loud.

I opened the door to two suits.

"We don't own the house," I said. "Not interested in aluminum siding. Or anything else. And I have a religion. I believe in reincarnation. I'm coming back as Marilyn Monroe's bra." I started to close the door in their face, when one of them, the shorter, burlier of the two, stepped toward me and put his foot in the door, preventing me from closing it.

"Hey, asshole," I said, thinking—man! I've heard of salesmen with this kind of nerve—when the man reached in his suit jacket and brought out a shield.

I was losing my touch. I should have recognized the cheap suits. If not that, the four-door blue sedan I'd glimpsed parked out front should have told me who these guys were. Aluminum siding and insurance salesmen usually drove Cadillacs, not Chevy Caprices.

"Police," he said. "We got a warrant for Robert Bishop."

Chapter 15

What the hell was this?

Which is what I said to the lead cop, a skinny little guy with a lantern jaw, which looked like he'd borrowed from the Man of Steel as it certainly didn't fit the rest of his physique.

"It's simple, man," he said, a slight sneer crossing his kisser. I had a feeling from his attitude he probably knew about me and my past.

He did.

"You understand warrants, don'tcha? You're the brother, right? Jacob Bishop? The B&E expert?" He turned his head to grin at his partner, a beefy Polack-looking dufus with a flattop and part of his lunch plainly visible on his clip-on tie. He took a glance at the paper in his hand. "Pendleton inmate number four nine oh two eight?"

"What's the charge?" I said, moving forward slightly to block his way into the house.

"Who's there?" I turned my head to see Paris at the top of the stairs, and that was all the leverage Lantern Jaw needed. He shoved past me and walked toward the staircase. I didn't even try to stop the other guy as he eased around me and into the house.

"You the wife?"

Lantern Jaw to Paris. It made me mad to see this little creep even talking to my wife, much less calling her "the wife." I took a step toward him and grabbed his shoulder and spun him around.

"That's none of your business," I said. I'd forgotten his beefy partner, who clamped a giant paw into my own shoulder from behind. I shook loose and gave him a dirty look.

"You said you had a warrant. You're supposed to show it to me before you come into my house and play tough guy. You flunk that class at the academy? That the day you're seeing if your dick is half as big as your snubnose?"

The skinny one laughed. "You jailhouse lawyers know your shit, don'tcha, Bishop? Here." He shoved the paper at me and waited for me to look it over. I didn't have to look at it to know it was real.

"Where's Robert Bishop?"

"He's at school," I answered. I didn't think that would satisfy him, but I wanted to make this as hard as possible on the pair of Dick Tracy's. What was going on in my mind was what in the hell had Bobby done now?

"Already been there, Bishop. We know he's here. You want to go get him or should we?"

"What's the warrant for?"

Upstairs, I heard the music go back on in Bobby's room. Paris had crept halfway down the stairs during our exchange, and I looked at her and she just shook her head as if to say, *What a dummy your brother is.*

I had to agree. Not dumb—it was obvious he didn't know who was downstairs—but man, did he have bad timing!

The smaller man just grinned.

"He's been identified as the perp in an armed robbery. Spencer's Jewelry Store, over on South Michigan. The owner I.D.'d him from the mug shots. You wanna go get him now? Or we can." He shined his beefy partner a grin, making it plain which option he preferred.

Damn! Sydney'd turned him in. But why?

There wasn't much to say or do at this point. I nodded to Paris, and she went back up the steps, and in a couple of seconds we heard the music stop, and a minute later here they both came.

"Don't worry, Bobby," I said while they were cuffing him and reading him his rights. "I'll get you out. Just sit tight and don't talk to anyone."

"Jake," he said, the most pitiful look on a human being I think I'd ever seen. "I don't know what the heck they're talking about. I didn't do this. They got the wrong guy."

My heart reached out to my little brother, standing there, hands cuffed behind him, looking as forlorn as a dog just got spayed. For a brief moment, I thought about just cold-cocking that little bastard of a detective and yelling at Bobby to make a break for it. Get us both shot, I figured, and even if he were to get away, it'd only be a matter of time before they'd nail him again. And, with me sitting in jail for helping him escape, well… the Bitch for sure.

Before the detectives and Bobby were out of sight, I was grabbing my coat and hunting for my car keys.

"Paris," I said. "Get dressed and get down to the jail, see what Bobby's bail is. Get him out of there."

Backing my car out of the drive I could hear Paris yelling something at me, but what it was I didn't have a clue. I could guess though. She'd seen the murder in my eyes. She'd do as I asked, though, then sit and worry that I was doing something crazy.

Like killing Sydney Spencer.

Chapter 16

I burst through the heavy glass door of Spencer's Jewelry, loaded for bear, and there that fat-ass Sydney stood, behind a counter. Waiting on a customer, some old lady in a black mink coat bent over the counter, drooling over the diamonds. His eyes opened wide at the sight of me and then narrowed and his face split into a smirk.

"Excuse me," he said to the mark. He hurried around the counter toward me.

"You're dead, you son-of-a-bitch," I said. Out of the corner of my eye I couldn't help but see the old woman gasp and put her hand to her mouth.

Spencer stopped, turned his obese back to me and said to the lady, "Mrs. Culver, it might be better if you were to come back a bit later. This gentleman and I have some business."

He turned back to me and said, "Take it easy, Jake. I've been expecting you. Don't worry about your brother. He's going to be all right. He'll be out bright and early Monday morning, back in his room reading his Playboys."

The only thing that kept me from walking over and breaking his jaw and then get serious about tearing him into small pieces, was that a bit of good sense struggled through the rage behind my eyes. That rich bitch would scream, the cops would come, and I'd be in the same bullpen as Bobby. And I wasn't sure if Paris would bail me out, considering. Wouldn't matter if she did. I'd be fucked, regardless. That fucking Bitch colored every move I made. I was sick of it.

The woman left as quickly as her arthritic knees would carry her through the door. She scurried past me like a creaky mouse around the cat. Behind her, Spencer called, "Don't worry, dear lady. I'm all right. My tall friend and I just have a small personal disagreement to work out. Come back later this afternoon and I've got something to show you I think you'll absolutely adore."

Once the door closed behind her, Spencer walked over to it, turned the lock and flipped the Open/Closed sign. He pulled the shade and turned to face me.

"Jake, Jake. I can see you're all wrought up. It's Bobby, isn't it? I take it the gendarmes picked him up?"

"You know they did, you bastard. You're the one turned him in. What the hell for? You knew I was going to do your fucking job."

"I know you were, Jake. I know you *are*. I just wanted a little insurance policy."

"Insurance? I'm gonna give you some insurance, you fat fuck." I stepped toward him, fist balled up and drawn back.

He put up his hand like a traffic cop. "Hold on. This is the deal. You pull this job Sunday like a good boy and I go down to the station and tell them I made a mistake. I just remembered the boy who held me up had a big mole on his left cheek. All these teenagers look alike. Your brother just looked like the culprit but fortunately, I remembered that mole."

He had me. He knew it and I knew it. I stared at him the longest while, neither of us saying anything. I was the first to break the silence.

"Okay, you fuck. I'm gonna do your lousy job. The second I'm out of there and you've got your stuff, you hike your fat ass down to the station and get Bobby cut loose. Not Monday. Sunday. You don't and…" I let the threat hang in the air.

"I know, I know," he said, airily. "You'll cut my nuts out or something." He laughed. "Don't let your elephant mouth overload your hummingbird ass, my friend."

I just looked at him and slowly his smile faded.

"Go on," he said, at last. "Get the hell out of my place. I've got a business to run here. You just be at the house tomorrow morning, eight sharp. I just had a little chit-chat with my friend Calvin and he tells me he's going to Chicago early, let his little girlfriend do some Christmas shopping on Michigan Street. Should be leaving about right now, in fact. And be sure your pal Walker shows up sober." His words were tough, but his delivery wasn't. I knew from the timber of his voice, he'd seen what was in my heart and it scared him.

It should have.

Chapter 17

More bad news. It just kept coming. If my life was a football game, God should have called a penalty for piling on. He didn't seem to be anywhere on the field.

Paris was there when I entered the police station. She was sitting on the bench in front of the day sergeant's desk and jumped up when I came through the door.

"It's no good, Jake," she said. "His bond hearing won't be until Monday."

"I'd get your brother a good lawyer," the sergeant on duty said, when I asked him if what Paris had told me was true. "Although, it won't do much good until his hearing. F. Lee Bailey probably couldn't get him out till then. Sorry." The guy could have been an asshole but he seemed half-decent.

He was right and I knew it. They could keep him for up to forty-eight hours before he could post bond. I asked if we could see him.

The sergeant was hesitant. "I don't know. Visiting hours aren't until this afternoon."

Paris stepped up. "Officer, we're his only family. His parents were both killed last year. There's been a mistake—Bobby couldn't have done this crime. I already told you, he was home with us that day. This is a poor, scared teenager who doesn't understand any of this and is just frightened to death." She was oozing charm, and for a minute I thought she was going to turn on the waterworks as well. I watched her work the guy, almost distracted from the anger I was feeling for Spencer, in amazement at the sales job she was performing. She even poked out her belly more than usual.

It worked. He gave us ten minutes.

He called another policeman in the back room and had him escort us to the day room, and five minutes later another cop brought Bobby in, leg shackles and all.

"Oh, Jake," he said, hopping to a chair across the table where Paris and I sat. "I don't get this. I didn't rob any store." He looked close to tears.

I nodded. "I know you didn't, Bobby. Don't worry. We're going to get you out of here."

His face brightened, then fell when I told him I'd keep trying, but it looked like I couldn't get him out until after his arraignment on Monday.

"Hey, guy," I said, trying to cheer him up. "Relax. You get three squares a day in here. And no pop. Keeping off the Pepsi for a couple of days is going to do wonder for your zits!"

My feeble attempt to lighten his mood failed to even get the trace of a smile.

He leaned forward, lowering his voice so the cop standing guard in the corner couldn't hear him. "Jake, there's a guy in the bullpen who says he's gonna..." He stopped, looked at Paris, reddened. "...make me do...things. This is a big guy, Jake. Whaddo I do? I can't fight this guy. He makes two of me."

All the teenaged bravado I was used to seeing my little brother cloaked in these days just disappeared. His shoulders slumped and he looked... *small*. It dawned on me that he was just a kid. A scared kid. I was livid, but I tried not to show how I felt. I was also scared for my brother, and I really tried not to show that.

"It'll be all right, Bobby. Ask the turnkey to put you in safekeeping. Hell, *I'll* ask him."

I twisted in my chair to face the guard. "Hey, partner. Who do I see to request safekeeping for my brother? Some queen's putting the moves on him." I could see Bobby redden out of the corner of my eye and knew I'd embarrassed him, but to hell with that.

"I'll ask the captain," he said. "But I don't think we have a cell open just now. There's just the one single we use and there's already a dude in there."

I fought the urge to get up, go over, put my hands on this guy's neck and insist forcibly that he get my kid brother out of that damned bullpen.

I smiled, instead, made my voice calm. "Well, hey, try willya? My brother's just a kid. You know how it is in there. They really shouldn't have him in there in the first place."

The cop nodded. "Yeah. I wouldn't want my brother in there. I'll see what I can do. The guy that's in isolation now's scheduled to leave for Pendleton this afternoon. Papers should come down any minute. Soon as he leaves, I'll see what I can do to get the kid here transferred."

I thanked him. "That sounds good. Appreciate it. In the meantime, do me a favor, will you? Keep an eye on the pen? Ask the turnkey to keep a watch?"

"Sure," he said. "You got it."

I turned back to Bobby and grinned and he seemed to relax a bit. Paris reached over and placed her hand over Bobby's manacled hands.

"Just keep to yourself," she said. "Don't act like you usually do."

That got a weak smile from Bobby and a laugh from me.

"You mean, don't be a smartass?" he said.

"That's exactly what I mean," she said.

"She's giving you good advice," I chimed in. "When you're in the joint, become invisible. Just stay away from the guy until they get you fixed up with another cell."

The guard came over, tapped Bobby on the shoulder. "Time's up, kid. I got to take you back."

He let us say our goodbyes. Paris hugged Bobby and lifted up on her toes to plant a kiss on his cheek. I stepped up and put my arms around him and gave him a squeeze. I whispered in his ear, "Bobby, if it comes down to it, go for the eyes. Don't do any of that John Wayne bullshit like in the movies. Just go for the eyes and forget everything else. Don't be bitch-slapping the guy or trying some stupid kind of boxing moves. Use your fingers and gouge the eyes. You get his eyes, it's all over. You got me?"

He nodded, his eyes wide. "The eyes…"

"Yeah," I said. "The eyes. This guy's been here a while, right?"

"Yes. I think."

"Good. That means he's sober. This was a guy just thrown in here, drunk or high, that's a different story. You can't hurt some guys like that. A guy that's sober though, that's a guy feels pain. Something happens, he comes after you, just get one thought in your head. You're going to do everything you can to gouge out his eyes."

"Oh, God," he said. "Jake…"

He didn't finish his sentence. I watched him as the turnkey led him away, and all I could do was shake my own head. He turned just before they rounded the corner, and I gave a little wave and a weak-ass thumb's up.

On the way out to the parking lot, Paris said, "You're really going to do it, aren't you? Rob that guy."

"He's my brother, honey. What choice do I have?"

She thought about that a moment, then nodded her head. We stopped and looked at each other. Police cars were coming and going and one coming in the lot slowed as the driver looked at us for a few seconds before pulling away and parking down the row. Probably thought we were getting ready to have a brouhaha, the way we were looking at each other, wild-eyed as we both were. Maybe the officer thought Paris was a whore and I was her pimp. I could see him out of the corner of my eye, just sitting in his cruiser, eying us.

Forget you, I thought.

"Then I'm going with you," she said.

That was insane and I told her so. "No, you're not. Are you crazy? If we get caught—not that we will…" I hastily added, "…then you're in prison for sure. If anybody's going to end up in the joint, it's going to be me. Not you. Don't even think about arguing about this, Paris."

If I had to, I'd tie her up and lock her in the basement. I think she sensed I was considering something like that, for she started to say something, then changed her mind and reached up, kissed me on the cheek, and walked to her car and was quickly gone. To work, I assumed.

Going out of the lot, I passed the officer still sitting in his car and felt a bit of satisfaction when slush sprayed from my tires onto his rear window. He was just getting out of his car when I turned out of the lot. I waved and then thought, what a dumb thing that was to do. But he didn't jump back in his car, and I put him out of mind. There were more important things to think about.

Like finding Walker Joy.

I had an idea about the job we were going to pull, and it depended on finding him pronto.

I was really worried about Bobby. Sure, the guard had said he'd try to get him transferred to a secure cell, but I knew the way things worked in jail. He might do what he said and he might not. I couldn't count on him. No, it was up to me. I had to do what Spencer wanted and get his fat ass down to the jail right away and get Bobby out. And before Monday. If Bobby didn't get put in safekeeping then Monday'd be too late to save his ass. Literally. My only hope was that Bobby could get through tonight okay, in the event they left him in the bullpen.

For a minute back in the day room, I'd considered doing something to get thrown in the bullpen with Bobby. Take a poke at the guard, maybe. I decided against it, knowing that would blow the deal with Spencer, and while I might be able to protect Bobby over the weekend, I had no doubt Spencer would carry out his threat and Bobby would end up with some serious time. Once that happened, the only way I could protect him was to get busted myself for something serious and hope they sent us both to the same place.

Bad idea, I'd decided. Bad, *bad* idea. No, Bobby was just going to have to make it through the night until I could spring him in the morning. And maybe they would move him and soon.

That fucking Bitch really did color everything I did. Or didn't do.

I got lucky for a change. Walker was in the first place I looked. Sitting way in the back at the Boat Club. So far back I almost missed him. I'd walked in at the front, glanced around the bar and tables and was ready to walk back out, try another place, when he sat up and I saw the top of his head over the booth edge. Sitting by himself, he must have been slumped down and I'd just assumed no one was occupying the booth.

I went on back and took a seat opposite him.

Looking at him, it occurred to me that this might not be the greatest idea I'd had all day. Asshole looked three sheets into the wind. Fuck it. All I needed him for was to point out the diamond we were supposed to get. As far out in the boonies as the guy's house was, it didn't much matter if Walker was roaring drunk, stumbling into every piece of furniture in the place.

"Walker, there's been a change in plans."

"Hah?" There wasn't much white showing in his eyes. Lots of little red blood vessels that looked like they were about ready to pop. Shit.

"We're going in tonight. Just as soon as I get you sobered up."

My announcement was met by my former cellmate with what could only be described as a stricken look. Kind of the look I imagine a political prisoner might have when the warden comes to his cell to inform him he'll be facing a firing squad in the ayem.

"Tonight? You crazy? The guy'll be home. Did Sydney—"

"Spencer ain't got a fucking thing to do with this. Don't even bring up that asshole's name. You know what he did?"

I told him.

"Jake, I'm sorry, man." He put his head in his hands.

"Yeah, you said that before. You're going to be even sorrier when this is over."

He started to reach for his drink, but I pushed it to the far end of the table.

"No more, Spitball. I want you sober."

"But, Jake," he said, looking up, a plaintive look—probably the winner he gave judges—plastered on his kisser. "What if Brewer's there?"

"Then we won't go in. We'll wait. But, there's a good chance he won't be. Spencer said the guy goes up early to Chitown sometimes."

That seemed to ease his stress.

Something else occurred to him. "Why you gotta call me Spitball?" he said, a plaintive tone to his voice. "You never did that before, Jake."

I almost felt sorry for him. He knew full well why I'd begun using the name he hated. Christ. After all this crap he'd gotten me into, on top of all that, he wanted me to like him! I saw the weakness in him I'd never noticed before. That worried me. Somebody with a softness is somebody who will turn on you eventually.

"I'll call you whatever you want if you do your job right," was my answer. "Just don't fuck this up… Walker."

That got a grin and I had to turn away momentarily at the sight of his obsequy. This was a far cry from the man who'd saved my life that day so many years ago.

"How'd you ever get mixed up with this guy, anyway?" I asked. "Spit—Walker, if you'd needed a job, you should have come to me. I know a lot of people. I could have helped you."

And I did. Working in a salon like the Tangerine brought you into contact with hundreds of people, many of them wealthy, with their own businesses. I'd connected up more than one person with another client for employment.

"Ah, Jake," he said, reaching for the glass I'd shoved aside. "I'm an outlaw. I don't pretend to be anything else. Don't make me you." I frowned at him, but let him retrieve the drink. He slugged the rest of it down hurriedly, as if he thought I'd take it away from him again. The whiskey seemed to revive him, give him back his confidence. "Aah," he said, patting his potbelly. "That hits the spot."

Seeing him swill down his booze made me want a drink myself in the worst way. For a second, the urge was overpowering and then I fought it off. I'd fallen off the wagon yesterday, but there was too much at stake to get weak right now. After this was over, maybe I'd go on a week's bender, get it out of my system. I didn't even want to think about the bullshit I was feeding myself and drove the thought out of my mind.

Walker slid back down a bit until he was sitting on his spine. "Jake, there was no way I was going to ask you for help. I knew you was a straight John."

What a load of horseshit. "Right. That's why you got me mixed up in this mess."

He straightened up a bit, looked at me with what passed

for an earnest look, and said, "I didn't mean for you to be. You've got to believe that. I just got carried away, talking about you. How'd I know the guy you conked that time was Spencer's uncle?"

He had a point. Still, he shouldn't have been jacking his jaw like he had. He knew I'd told him that story in confidence.

Looking at the man who'd been my cellmate for years, I felt a deep sadness. This was a man who'd not only saved my life when another inmate had approached me "with lovin' on his mind"—had gone after Toles—but had been a friend, day in and day out, in the worst of all possible situations, a state prison. We'd shared laughs together and we'd shared tears together. There was a bond between us that was the bond that existed between brothers. Stronger.

At least, there had been. That had been shattered and that was what I felt an incredible sadness over. The one thing you never did was threaten a man's family by your actions. And this is exactly what Walker "Spitball" Joy had done by his.

I'd do this job for him, but after that I'd never see him again. I think he understood that and was feeling some of the same emotions I was. We'd been close for so long that I felt as if I could almost read his thoughts, and I think he had the same sensibilities toward me.

The only decent thing he'd done was not tell Spencer about that other thing.

I ordered Walker a coffee, black, and he could see from the look in my eyes that he'd better drink it. I ordered one for myself as well. Once it arrived and he started sipping on it, I told him to sit tight and I'd be back in a minute.

Paris answered on the first ring. Must have been waiting right by the phone, lord knows what was going on in her mind.

"I'm at the Boat Club," I told her. "Just wanted to let you know I won't be coming home right away and not to worry. I'll be a little late. Maybe around ten, eleven."

"You're going to pull this job now, aren't you?" she said, her voice flat.

"No, no baby," I said, hurriedly. "Not on your life. Tomorrow night. I'm sticking with the plan. No, the thing is, I've got Walker here and I'm sobering him up. We're just going to go out in a bit and get the tools I need. We may drive by the guy's place. Just to check it out."

The last thing I wanted was for her to think we were going in tonight. Even though we were. Besides Bobby and the fix he was in, Paris was the other reason I'd decided to do this thing early. I'd be in and out before she knew it and that way wouldn't have to worry about her maybe showing up like she'd threatened. The last thing I needed was some amateur walking around and jumping or even screaming at every little noise like the house settling or something. Or if somehow we got busted. There was no way I was going to have my wife there for that, even if I was a thousand percent sure nothing was going to go wrong.

Walking back to the table, it struck me that I'd just lied to my wife again. A week before, the thought of misleading Paris in any way was something I couldn't have imagined; now, it was becoming a normal thing. I sighed, told myself after this was all over, it would be like it was before. No matter what, I wasn't going to lie to her ever again after this thing was done.

I honestly believed that.

When I sat down across from him, the first thing Walker did was start whining. "Why we gonna go tonight? Spencer said Saturday's when we go. The guy's probably there, Jake."

"Shut the fuck up, Spitball. We're going in tonight and that's that. I'm in charge of this program, not you. Spencer just told me the guy's maybe already left. If he's on the up and up, everything's going to be fine. We'll get in and out and get your punk-ass friend his stuff and I'll get my brother out tomorrow morning. Finish your coffee. We've got some things to pick up."

The look he gave me didn't thrill me. What he said next didn't either.

"Fuck you, Jake. I'm not going tonight. Tomorrow is when Spencer said to do it. He knows what he's doing. I'm not gonna do it tonight."

I could only stare at him in disbelief. The motherfucker had got me into this mess, put my family in danger, put me at risk to get The Bitch... and now he was saying... I leaned forward, put my face right up in his, two inches away. I could smell the stink of his breath.

"Say what, Spitball? I think I misheard you. You want to repeat that?"

He said it again, dully, refusing to meet my eyes.

"I'm not going tonight. We're gonna get caught, we go in tonight."

I didn't say anything for a long moment, just stared at his chickenshit face, resisting the overwhelming urge to just reach over and bitch-slap his ugly, wrinkled face.

Chapter 18

Extremely stupid!

That's what I was, all right.

That word—*stupid*—and all its synonyms kept running through my head during the entire drive up to Niles and then out in the country.

To Calvin's house.

Alone. Partnerless.

In broad daylight.

But… it was raining. And lightning. And almost dark, what with the thunderclouds. It was coming down so hard, visibility was maybe fifteen, twenty feet. Turning the snow into ice.

Actually, this was better than night. With all the crashing and booming the thunder was making, I wouldn't have to worry about making noise. And it was bad enough weather no one was out cruising around. I figured any cops or sheriffs would do what cops do best—find a warm doughnut shop to wait out the storm in.

When I came to the house, I didn't stop to check out the lay of the land, see if anyone was home. Just rolled up the guy's driveway and around to the back where my car couldn't be seen. More luck. If Calvin was home, he was carless.

Getting in was even easier than I'd figured it would be. Which was extremely lucky, being as part of my stupidity was not following my original plan and stop at a hardware, pick up some tools. That's what mad will do. Make a person lose all their common sense. All I had was a large flathead screwdriver I found in the glove compartment, but that was all I needed.

I walked around to the front door, rang the doorbell and knocked and waited.

Nothing.

It took maybe all of ten minutes to go back around and attack the wooden door there, chew out the doorknob by chiseling around it like it was an ice sculpture. It always struck me as amazing how straights thought. They thought if you locked a door, that was all you needed. Or that a deadbolt somehow kept the bad guys out. Calvin didn't even have that, but it wouldn't have mattered if he did. Jobs in the past where the owner had installed a deadbolt just required a few more minutes to get in. If nothing else, I'd just chop a hole in the side of the house or building.

Once inside, I stood there a spell and just listened.

Nothing, except the sound of the rain hitting the roof and the occasional clap of thunder. Thank God for a rare December rainstorm.

Satisfied I was alone, I walked through the kitchen where I'd entered and into the living room. Off the living room were two other rooms, bedrooms. I went into one of them, looked around. Nothing there. No safe, no file cabinet. I came out and walked over to the other one and was about to step in, check it out, when a movement over at the kitchen door caught my eye. And my heart, which just about stopped. I still had the screwdriver clutched in my hand and I flipped it around into a stabbing position.

It was a man.

Fuck.

My first thought was that if he had a gun, I was dead. Even if he didn't shoot me, I'd be dead. I could already see that judge looking down over his bench, giving me The Bitch. Life without parole.

It was obvious the guy didn't see me. He looked around, then stepped into the living room. Too dark to make him out but just then, just as I was making up my mind that if he wasn't armed, I was going to have to take him out with the screwdriver if I could. Thinking, I don't want to kill this guy—Jesus!—but maybe I could threaten him with it, convince him I'd use it to stab him, and maybe lock him up somewhere and get the hell out of there—just then, when all that was going through my mind, a huge bolt of lightning struck close by and the whole room lit up, and I saw the man clearly at the same time he saw me.

"Walker!"

"Hey, Jake." He sauntered toward me, a huge grin splitting his face, acting like he'd just spotted me at his class reunion.

"What the fuck are you doing here? You just about got a Black and Decker up your ass, you stupid fuck!"

I looked down at the screwdriver in my hand and back up at Walker and both of us started laughing. I couldn't help it and Walker just didn't know any better.

"Changed your mind."

"Yeah," he said. "I see you got in okay."

I nodded. "Only there's nothing here. You parked out back, I hope."

For an answer, he put his hands on his hips and looked at me, shaking his head like I'd just asked the dumbest question in the world.

He turned back into the kitchen. I followed him. He stopped at the doorway, then walked over to a door by the sink.

"Basement," he said, opening the door. "That's where it'll be. That's where his workshop is."

He was right.

There it was, right out in plain sight, up against the wall

just beyond what must have been the man's work bench. You couldn't miss it. The safe. A black mother, roughly 6' x 4'. A large table with lamps clamped onto it in the middle of the floor, must've been Calvin's work bench. Shelves on the far wall stuffed full of all kinds of crap, must have been his tools. A refrigerator over in the far corner. Other bits of furniture. I didn't care about any of that. The safe was all I was interested in.

Only, all of a sudden, I wasn't.

I groaned.

"What's the matter?"

I answered by groaning again. "Let's go, Walker."

"What?" His eyes were wide as pie plates. "Whaddya mean, 'let's go'? There's the fucking safe. Open it and let's get the stuff."

I shook my head slowly. "You were right, Walker. The guy must have some serious shit in there."

"Yeah, yeah. Of course there's some serious shit in there. Why you think we're here? Quit fooling around and open it. We ain't got all day."

"I can't."

"Whaddya mean, you can't? You're the best. Jake Bishop can open anything."

"Except a Brown Super Fortress."

He stared at me, like he was trying to comprehend what I was saying.

"You can't open it? You *really* can't open it?"

I shook my head again. "I really can't open it, Walker. It's a top-of-the-line Brown. The TL-30. God couldn't break into that one."

I could see the gears whizzing around in his brain as he processed what I was saying.

"Okay," he said, finally. "You can't crack it. Then we'll carry it out."

I laughed but there was no merriment in my voice. "Yeah? That little puppy weighs over 5,000 pounds. I'm good for about 200 of that. Think you can pick up the rest?"

We were fucked. This was for sure our only chance at it.

Walker walked over to the safe, did the dumbest thing. He tried to lift it. Didn't budge. Then, he tried to pull it away from the wall. The only thing that budged this time was his pants. Bent over and straining, his trousers slipped down. Looked like the plumber on *Saturday Night Live* in that skit they used to do. I couldn't even grin at that, depressed as I was. Here we were, all alone with who knows how much in diamonds… and we couldn't touch it.

"Spencer didn't happen to give you the combination, did he?"

I knew he hadn't, but I had to ask. You never know.

Walker straightened up. "I wish." He looked back at the safe. "Hey, I'll run into town, get a welding outfit. We'll torch it open."

"Can't do it."

"Why not?" His voice turned whiny. "We got all the time in the world. Guy's in Chicago all weekend."

"That isn't it."

"Well, then, why not?"

"Because this fucker is the top of the line, Spitball." I was growing weary of our conversation and just wanted to get the hell out of there and figure out how far south of that Mendoza line my life was probably going to go. Somehow, I had to convince Spencer our task had been futile and get him to get Bobby out. Maybe there was another job I could do for him, but this one was definitely in the toilet. I tried to explain to Walker just how futile. "This is the best Brown makes, Walker. Which means it has a silent holdup alarm lock, a three-movement time clock and some other goodies. A lot of goodies. Even saying you could cut through two inches of the finest steel man can make, you just set off the alarm. It's useless."

His eyes narrowed. "Fuck you, Bishop. You don't know the alarm's even set. You're just a pussy."

I sighed. I wasn't even that mad at him anymore. All I was feeling was... defeated.

"Think what you want, Walker. You're just going to have to tell Spencer this job couldn't be done."

"I can't." The words came out in a little strangled cry. His eyes turned from anger to pleading. "Jake, I gotta do this job. I don't do this, Spencer's gonna have me killed. C'mon, buddy, *think.* There's just got to be some way to crack this mother."

There just wasn't. I didn't have to tell him again. He got it. His shoulders sagged and all the air seemed to go out of him.

I don't know what made him do it—desperation, I suppose—but he reached down and gave a pull on the door handle of the safe.

It swung open.

Walker's face turned toward mine and I'm sure the astonishment in his eyes was mirrored in mine.

Even from where I stood, I could see it was loaded. There must have been a hundred diamonds in there, lying on little tissue paper pallets, each tissue on top of a miniature kind of manila folder with a series of numbers on it. His accounting system, I guessed.

"Holy fuck!" It was all I could say.

Walker bent down, began scooping the gems out with both hands. I just stood and watched him, speechless.

He twisted, looked over at me. "I guess I'm the safecracker in this gang, what say?"

"Lazy fucker," was all I could come up with.

Walker's visage darkened. "What'd you say?"

"Not you. This Calvin dude. I shoulda known. Lots of guys don't want to go through the combination every time they open their safe. They just close it, don't twist the dial. Saves 'em a few minutes next time they want in."

He began stuffing diamonds into his pockets. "Say it, Jake."

"Say what?"

"Say, 'you're the smartest guy I ever met, Walker.' Say—"

Whatever he was going to smart off about next I'll never know. He was interrupted by a voice that came from upstairs at the door we'd come down.

"Calvin? You down there, Calvin?"

A woman's voice.

Chapter 19

Before I quite realized what he was doing, Walker had scurried over to under the stairs that led down from the kitchen.

"Call to her!" he stage-whispered hoarsely. "Tell her you're the phone man."

I saw his plan instantly. Once in a while, Walker used his brain. It always amazed me when that happened.

"Down here, ma'am," I said, in what I intended to be my phone repair dude's voice. "Phone company. Checking out the wiring problem you called about."

I saw her feet and then a pair of beefy legs appear. I didn't get to see her face—at least not immediately—because only her bottom half had appeared when Walker grabbed one of those tree trunk legs and yanked and she screamed and pitched forward, tumbling to the basement floor at the bottom with a thump on each step as she came down. She was face-down on the floor and not moving. Not after that last thump, which cut her last scream short.

I ran over and struggled to turn her over. One big woman!

Nice-looking though. A broad, pleasant face, with her eyes closed and the most incredible half-smile on her lips, she looked like she was dreaming of doing some housewifey thing, baking chocolate chip cookies or something. I could smell the fresh perm she must have just gotten for her chin-length brunette hair, and they'd done a good job, whoever did it. Nice bouncy curls, no frizz.

A tiny trickle of blood was coming out of her nose and there was a lump the size of a golf ball on her forehead, which must have been where she hit the stairs. I felt quickly for a pulse and at first couldn't find one, but only because I was feeling in the wrong place and then I felt her neck, located her carotid, and while her heartbeat was fast, it was relatively strong. She wasn't dead, but she was going to have a king-sized headache.

"Let's get the hell out of here," I said to Walker who had come out from behind the stairs and was standing there over me and the woman.

"Yeah," he agreed. "Just let me get the rest of the stuff."

He ran back to the safe and began stuffing his pockets with diamonds. I went over to help him. He was going to leave the little envelops, but something told me to take them. I gathered up handfuls and stuffed them in my own pockets. Walker gave me a funny look but didn't say anything.

"There's something in the back," I said. A canvas bag, one of those kinds artsy-fartsy women use for a tote bag. I'd seen 'em around at flea markets, such places.

Walker grabbed it, pulled it out. Opened it to reveal four stacks of money. Thick stacks. If the rest of the bills were like the ones on top, it was a lot of money. The bills were hundreds.

"Motherfuck!" We both said the same thing at the same time. There had to be a hundred bills in each rubber-banded stack. Maybe more.

"How much you think's here?"

I tilted my head sideways, looked at him. Walker's eyes were just these huge-ass glistening pie plates. "A lot."

He snickered and said, "No shit!" and began taking out the diamonds from his pockets and dumping them in the bag. I put the envelops I'd taken in there as well.

When we'd both emptied our pockets, the bag was nearly full. Walker picked it up by the handles, jiggled it, feeling the weight, grinning like a monkey with his own bunch of bananas. "You were planning to split this up later, right?" I said.

He stood up, reached his arm through the handles and stuck the bag up under his armpit. "Well, hell yes. We're pards, aren't we? C'mon. Let's boogie." He turned toward the stairs and I got up from my crouch and... the woman was pulling herself up. Moaning, shaking her head in little side-to-side motions like she was trying to clear it.

"Fuck."

I didn't say that; Walker did, but it was just about what I would have said if he hadn't first.

The woman struggled to get up. First, she pushed herself half-up with her arms, then tried to get her legs under her, splayed them out like she was a newborn foal getting up for the first time in his stall, and then she just kind of collapsed onto her butt, her legs out at right angles to the rest of her body and her arms pitched forward to prevent her from falling forward. The blood from her nose was still running, only thicker and faster now. It ran down her chin and began dripping onto the carpeted floor. It was probably that carpet saved her life, hard as she smacked it when Walker'd grabbed her and she fell.

She just sat there in a daze, hunched over, a low steady moan coming from deep inside her throat. Like she'd been poleaxed. Like I guess she had been.

Walker looked over his shoulder at me. "You know what this means."

I did, but I didn't want to say it. Or think about it. I wanted to have already left the place, only that wasn't possible.

"Maybe she hasn't seen us," I said, the first thing that popped into my mind. "Our faces, I mean. Maybe—"

"Come on, rappie. You want to take that chance?"

I really didn't want the answer to my next question. "What do you think we should do?"

His answer was a smirk.

"No," I said. I felt cold sweat in my armpits. "I'm not in for that."

"Oh, really?" I hated the way his eyebrows raised when he said that. "What *are* you in for, Jake? Going back to the joint?" He didn't wait for my response. "'Cause that's where you're going, we don't take care'a this bitch."

Whether the woman had or hadn't seen our faces suddenly became a moot point, as she raised her head and looked very clearly at both of us standing before her.

"Who… what…"

"We're your worst nightmare, lady," was Walker's response, echoing that old movie line. I could hear the glee in his voice when he said it, like he'd been waiting for years for a time and place to use it and now here it was, by golly. If it wasn't such a serious situation, I would've smiled. He took a step toward her.

And froze.

I froze right along with him. On the outside, that is. Inside, my organs curdled at the unexpected sound that shattered the silence.

The phone was ringing.

Chapter 20

It rang again. Somewhere in the basement. Loud. One of those clangy jobs. I swear it was the same kind of sound that the turnkey sets off just before he hits the lever that opens the cell doors. I flashed back to the tier in J Cellblock for the tiniest of seconds before I realized that wasn't what I was hearing, but just a phone in some guy's house out in the boonies.

Walker just stood there, us two looking at the lady, and the woman staring up at us.

It rang again and then two more times. I turned around, looking for the source of the sound and then found it. A white portable phone and answering machine unit, sitting just above the safe on a shelf.

"Whyn't you answer it?" Walker said, a stupid-ass smirk on his face. "Tell 'em we're closed. We're just taking out the garbage, pullin' the shades, counting the till. Come see us tomorrow, regular business hours."

Funny man.

A voice began speaking from a tinny loudspeaker, sounded like it had a rip in it or was maybe loose. "Sorry I'm not here to take your call…" All the usual phone answering stuff. "Leave your name and number at the…"

There was a beep and then a small, whiny male voice came on.

"Sally, if you're there, pick up." There was a brief pause and then the voice continued, starting with an audible sigh and then, "Mary and I had a fight. I bet you're not surprised, are you. Shit! Damn woman! Anyway, I'm on my way home… I'm leaving her off at her house. Be there in forty-five minutes. Stick around if you get this. It's…" Another pause, ostensibly while he was checking his Mickey Mouse. "…6:35. I want to go over the Bettenhausen account." There was a click and he was gone.

"That your boss? Calvin Brewer?" Walker was asking the woman, who nodded.

"I… I just came by to do the books. Are you going…" She looked back and forth between Walker and me. "…to kill me?"

Mother of God!

"Sally what?"

Walker tilted his head to the side looking at me. "You want her phone number, too? Ask her out?"

"Boxleiter," she said, her voice trembling. "Sally Boxleiter. I'm Calvin's bookkeeper. Are you…" Again, she looked back and forth between us, her eyes pleading. "…going to hurt me?"

"Walker, let's just go."

"Are you crazy? Why don't you just drive down to Pendleton, save the state a lot of time."

He was right. Those iron gates were already opening up for the both of us. Goodbye Paris, goodbye unborn son, goodbye Bobby, goodbye salon. But murder?

I couldn't do that. No matter what. I had no doubt I was already on my way back to the joint and for the rest of my natural life, barring some kind of miracle… and miracles didn't happen in my experience, but even if my body ended up in jail, I still had my soul. I participated in snuffing out this woman, my soul was gone, too. No.

"Walker," I said. "We've got forty-five minutes. Maybe less. Depends on how fast this guy drives. I've got an idea."

And I had. It had just come to me. Not much of an idea, but one that would buy us some time. And, at least temporarily, keep my old cellmate from carrying out his intention of killing the woman.

"Tie her up," I said. "We'll take her with us."

"Are you totally insane?" he said. "What, take her home to dinner? I say let's erase her, get the fuck out of Dodge."

"Yeah? And where do you figure to go? You know how long it's going to take them to figure out who did this? Look at your hands."

He didn't have a clue what I was talking about. I held up my own for illustration. I still had the rubber gloves on I'd donned before I broke in. He looked at his own bare digits and it dawned on him what I was saying.

"Fuck!"

"Yeah." I felt more in control now. "Don't even bother trying to wipe down. Take you an hour to do it, even if you could remember every place you touched, which I doubt. I give the boys in blue about two hours and they'll have your picture out to every police station in the U.S.A. And there ain't no way on God's green earth you're ever gonna be able to disguise that mug you got. You're cooked, buddy. And if you're cooked, I'm fricasseed. Once they got you, how long before you're gonna give me up?" I didn't wait for any of his protestations, which we both knew would be bullshit. "Day and a half, maybe. I know you, partner. The stoic type, you're not.

"Look," I went on, "here's what we do. We take this lady with us. My wife's parents have a place down on Chapman Lake. They're in Florida. I'll get the key and we'll take her there, figure out what to do."

"I already know what to do," he said. "Ex her."

"Naw, naw! That's stupid, Walker. They find her here dead, every law dog in the country is all of a sudden on the case. She's not here, it's a simple burglary. It'll take 'em time to figure out she's missing. It buys us time. Time to sell this stuff, get a stake, get out of the country. You want to kill her, kill her down at the lake. We'll hide her in a woods I know, take 'em years to find her. Maybe never."

The whole time Sally Boxleiter sat there, staring at the two of us. The best I could describe her expression was stunned. She never let out a peep, but I'd bet all I had in the bank she was praying up a storm.

I looked at my watch. At the outside, we had maybe forty minutes left. That is, if the guy figured his time to arrive there right.

"Whyn't we just wait and kill him, too?" Walker said.

Christ. There was no use arguing with the guy. I took matters into my own hands. I walked quickly over to the phone, unhooked the cord and then ripped the rest of it out of the wall. I took the cord back to the woman and grabbed one of her hands and pulled it behind her back and twisted the cord around it. I reached around her, got the other hand and brought it around and tied them together. Fifteen seconds maybe. I shoulda been in a rodeo.

"Now," I said, grabbing her blouse at the back and lifting her up, ignoring the short groan that burst from her lips as I hauled her up. "Let's get the fuck out of here."

I was expecting some grief from him, but surprisingly, he offered none. Just followed me and the woman up the stairs and out the back door. For all his talk, I guessed he wasn't much more anxious to actually murder someone as I was.

His car was parked next to mine.

I pushed the woman ahead of me. Tore my gloves off and stuck them in my back pocket. Got in my front pocket, got the car keys and unlocked the trunk.

"Gimme a hand," I ordered Walker.

"You puttin' her there?"

"Yeah, Einstein. I don't want some citizen looking over, I'm sitting at the light, and see I got this bloody, tied-up woman in the back seat."

He nodded and helped me lift her. She was heavy and not all that cooperative, but we got her in.

"Please," she pleaded.

"Keep it zipped," I said, trying to convince her with my eyes that keeping quiet was in her best interests. "I'm trying to help you here."

"What if she screams or something?" Walker said.

Damn. I hadn't thought of that.

"I saw some tape in the kitchen. On the counter."

He ran toward the house, came back in a few seconds with the roll of duct tape and her purse.

"Found this in the kitchen," he said, holding it up. Again, Walker was showing some brains. Twice, within the hour. "Excellent," I said. "They'd found that, they'd know she hadn't left willingly. No woman goes anywhere without her purse."

Walker beamed with the praise and tossed the woman's bag in the trunk with her. I held her face in my hands, and Walker ripped off a hunk of tape and pressed it over her mouth, the whites of her eyes bigger than I would have thought they could get. That done, I closed the lid on her.

"Her car," I said.

"What?"

"Her car. We've got to get rid of it." I walked around the side of the house and sure enough, there was the lady's car. Bookkeeping must pay pretty good. It was a two-year-old black Caddy. The keys were in it. Thoughtful of her.

"Get rid of it where?"

I thought.

"Back the way we came. There's a farmer's access road. Goes to a woods and a big field, looked like winter wheat. Maybe an eighth of a mile back. I saw a big ol' equipment shed at the edge of it. We'll put it in there. Chances are it'll be spring before anybody sees it."

"Okay, Einstein," he said. "Great idea, but who's gonna

drive it? You happen to notice there's three cars here and only two drivers? Unless you want to get the broad out, have her drive one of 'em."

"Look," I said. "You heard the guy. He just hit the toll road. I figure he's tooling through Gary about now. Got his windows rolled up for the smell. We've got some time. Enough to do this in. You drive her car there, we'll hide it in the shed, and I'll follow you in mine. Then we come back here, pick up yours."

For once he didn't give me any grief. He jumped in the Cadillac and switched it on. I ran back for my own wheels. Ten minutes later, we had the Cadillac stashed inside the shed in which fortunately the farmer didn't have any of his equipment stored. Some of the framing boards had worked loose to where you could see inside, but that wasn't a problem. We just tore some planks off the far side, propped them up against the spaces, and you couldn't see a thing. I hadn't figured on that and the chore ate up another fifteen minutes.

I got an idea. A great idea.

"Give me one of those diamonds," I told Walker.

"Say what?"

"A diamond. You'll see."

He shrugged and did as I asked. I put my gloves back on and opened the back door of the woman's Caddy and leaned inside. I could feel Walker behind me, straining to see what I was doing. I picked up the corner of the floor mat and put the diamond just under the edge of it and replaced the mat. You could just barely see a bit of the rock, but only if you were looking for it.

"Are you crazy? What the hell's that all about?"

"This might just save our ass, Walker. If the cops find this car... and eventually they will, they'll find this diamond. What do you think those Sherlocks are going to think when they do? When they put two and two together and get their usual five?"

A light went on behind his eyes. "That she robbed her boss!"

The guy had some brains after all.

"If they don't find her or her body, they'll just naturally figure she robbed the guy and flew off to Mexico or some place," he was going on. "Yeah!" He thought again. "Maybe we shouldn't hide the car so good."

"No," I said. "This is perfect. This makes it look like she hid it herself to buy herself time."

"You're right," he said, nodding in agreement. I opened the front door and went over the steering wheel with my gloved hand and did the same wherever else I thought Walker might have touched. Nothing I could do about any prints he might have left at the house. He looked away when I got out and closed the door. He just never learned.

"Let's book," I said. Our jawing had eaten up another five minutes. The guy had to be getting close. Maybe fifteen-twenty minutes away, if that. I wished to hell I knew how fast this Calvin guy drove. We ran to my car.

Less than three minutes later, I was rolling back down Calvin Brewer's driveway toward the road, Walker following in his own car. Pulling out onto the road, heading north, I saw a car coming toward us from the other way. I shot my arm out of the window, pointing as I hit the gas. In the rear-view mirror, I saw Walker wave and then burn out behind me. I didn't know if it was the jewelry designer or not, but if it was, that was about as close a call as I ever wanted to have during this particular day of my life.

A minute later, just barely visible behind us, I saw the car disappear, as it turned into the drive we'd just come from. The guy was becoming a fucking ghost in my life. This was the second time I'd just left his place and he pulls in right behind me. I tromped down harder on the gas pedal, slewed a bit on the ice, and then hit a patch of gravel and gained control. Goddamned country roads. That's all I needed, end up in a ditch with a kidnap victim in my trunk.

I had another problem.

The key to Paris's folks' cottage. I knew right where it was. Hanging on a hook just inside the pantry at the house.

There was no way around it. I'd have to go home and get it. And hope Paris wasn't there. And if she was, hope I could get it and go and avoid having to answer a bunch of questions.

Like if I'd just pulled a burglary. Or who that was curled up in the trunk of my car.

I pulled over to the side of the highway and watched as Walker slid in behind me. I walked back to his car.

"I have to stop at the house," I said. "Get the key. Just follow me. It's over on Twykenham."

The sun came out just as I was crossing over the state line just north of Notre Dame. Funny. It didn't feel sunny inside.

I went through a light as it was turning yellow on the outskirts of Roseland and glanced up to see Walker two-three cars behind. I started to pull over, wait for him, seeing as he didn't know where I lived, and then had an idea and hit the gas instead. I'd get ahead, hit a side street, jump out and unlock the trunk, let the woman go. No body, no murder.

No brains, Jake. Everything that was wrong with that little brainstorm swept through my skull like the still frames of a movie. Each vista that played on the big screen of my mind ended up with me sitting on a lower bunk and staring at a gray wall. For some reason, Walker was sitting on the top bunk, legs dangling over. Nowhere in any of these pictures was Paris or our baby.

No, letting the Boxleiter woman go now wasn't a good idea. Best keep with the original idea. Get down to the cottage, figure out something there. What, I didn't have a clue, but at least I could buy some time. For the woman in the trunk and me both. Maybe I'd get lucky, think up some genius plan that would save her ass and mine both. If not, if we had to kill her, at least I had that ace in the hole, that diamond I'd planted in her car.

"Damn," I said out loud, getting a headache over the whole mess, and sighed, cranking the car over in front of a florist's shop. In less than a minute, I saw Walker in the rear-view mirror, whizzing around cars like he was at the Indy 500. I eased back onto Highway 31, which was now Michigan Street and waved out the window as he came screaming up behind and slowed and five minutes later he followed me left onto Notre Dame Avenue, passing by the university golf course, the Golden Dome coming into view on the left a few seconds later.

Ten minutes later, I pulled up in front of my house and discovered what kind of lucky I was.

The kind that heads south.

Paris's red Escort was in the driveway.

Chapter 21

Of course, she was home. Story of my life.

After I motioned to Walker to stay put in his car, I walked up the sidewalk, trying to dream up a story Paris might buy.

Realizing my vow to never lie to her again was about to be broken once more…

She was on the couch watching TV. She didn't even look up when I came in the door. Just kept her eyes glued on the set. *L.A. Law*, I think was what she was watching. Perfect. Maybe she could get some legal tips that would help me out of my little disaster here.

"Hi, honey," I said, just about the lamest thing I could have possibly come up with.

She tore her eyes away from the TV and glanced over at me standing there in the doorway like she hadn't heard me come in and was totally surprised at my presence, even going so far as to do a little play-acting like I'd startled her in her deep reverie.

"Oh!" she said. "It's *you*. What're *you* doing home? I figured I'd see you tomorrow most likely. Maybe next week sometime. Maybe get a call from you. You know, to drop by and see you when I went to visit Bobby. In the cell next to his. What a nice surprise this is, to see you in civilian clothes and not one of those orange jump suits."

She looked beyond me through the door behind me, which I hadn't closed. I turned to see what she was looking at. Both my car and Walker's were clearly visible, Walker hanging his arm out the window, smoke curling up from the cigarette he was puffing on.

"That one of your clients from the Tangerine?" she asked. "Bring him home to do a kitchen haircut? You're not going to ask the gentleman in?"

She was really bringing it.

And I had to take it. I decided to play dumb. And figure out a reason to go to the pantry where the key to the cottage was.

And get out of there before Walker decided to come in.

And somehow get her over her mad.

"Nah," I said. "That's Walker. We're just going to go case the place. First, I just wanted to tell you where I was, so's you wouldn't worry."

She got up from the couch and walked over to me. She stood toe-to-toe with me, hands on her hips, and then did the oddest thing. She jutted her head forward until it was inches from mine and just mugged on my nose. Lasered it. Then, she stepped back and shook her head as if she was bewildered.

"What?" I said.

"I don't get it."

"Get what?"

"In that story, when the wooden puppet lies, his nose grows. Yours stays the same. I guess I'm just disappointed."

I started to say something, object, but she held up her hand like a traffic cop, then walked back to the couch, plopped down on it and picked up a magazine from the coffee table and began flipping pages.

Without looking up, she said, "Not disappointed at you, Jake. At that story. See, I always thought it was true. Now I know it was just a fairy tale. I guess this is the end of my innocence, eh? If a person can't believe in Pinocchio, who can they believe in?"

Well, fuck it. I couldn't think of any good reason for an excuse to go into the pantry, so I just went. Walked in, grabbed the key off the nail, stuck it in my pocket. Grabbed a box of Saltines and came out. I went to stand in front of her where she was still leafing through the magazine.

"I didn't know you liked *Sports Illustrated*," I said, nodding at the magazine. I could be a smart-ass, too. "You might want to check out that article on Barry Bonds. It's a goodun."

She didn't say anything, just kept flipping pages. The kind of flipping you do when you're mad.

"It's toward the back," I went on, pressing my luck. What luck? I was fresh out of that commodity. Maybe my temper was a little short as well. I turned and headed toward the door. "I'll be back in a little while. Don't wait up."

She said something and all I heard was "doctor." My mood changed.

"What?"

"I said when I got home from Niles I began to cramp some, so I called the doctor."

"And?"

"He said the swelling I've been having in my legs and the cramps might mean I might have preeclampsia. He wants to see me. I go in at four-thirty."

"What's pre—?—that thing you said."

"Preeclampsia. Lots of women have it. It's usually not serious, but it can be. Wants to see me just to be sure."

Jesus. What next?

"You going to be all right? You don't need me to take you in, right? I mean, I would, but..." I looked toward the door, torn what to do.

"Just go, Jake. Do whatever it is you think you need to do."

I didn't know what to do or say. This was the worst possible time in the world for all this. I wanted to say, "Look, honey, I'd love to stay and take you to the doctor, but the thing is,

I've got a kidnapped woman in the trunk, and, well...you know, I've got things to do."

I didn't though. I just stared at her a minute, then shrugged my shoulders, and said, "Well, then, sounds okay, right? I'd just be in the way, right? I've just got to do this...thing. I'll be right home after." This was shit and I knew it and she knew it, but what was I to do?

I'd just closed the door behind me when I heard a thump against it. I couldn't see, but I bet she'd thrown the magazine at the door. Pretending it was my head.

"Whazzup?" Walker said, sticking his head out of the window as I came up.

"A divorce," I said. "Never mind. Let's get going. Just follow me."

I jumped in behind the wheel of my own car and hit the ignition. I think he laid on the horn because I sprayed his windshield with berm gravel, pulling away.

Fuck you, I thought. And fuck you, too, Paris. I'm trying here. I'm really trying.

I felt like just getting out of the car, lying down on the road and letting a semi run over me, end all this happy horseshit. The situation was totally in the dumper. Here I was, driving down the road with a kidnapped woman in my trunk, a fucked-up burglary in my recent past that rubber-gloved cops were probably all over right this minute with Mr. Calvin Brewer.

Oh, man.

Probably already had Walker's prints, getting them analyzed and starting to type out the A.P.B. out on him. It wouldn't take them an hour to put two and two together, see who his cellmate in the joint was. Jack Bishop, ace burglar. The job had my mark all over it. I'd bet all the money I'd ever make in my life that both our kissers were plastered all over the cop wires.

I smacked the steering wheel with my fist in frustration.

I'd probably been an hour or two ahead of the cops when I was at my house. They'd be there before tonight, I bet, dredging up the worst scenario I was capable of. My glass-is-half-empty nature. What would Paris tell them? Would she give me up? One thing was in my favor. At least, I hadn't told her where I was going. If she was to give me up, she couldn't tell them where I'd gone.

My life was over. The free part, anyway. I was sailing right into the nasty part, and I had a feeling it was only going to get worse.

All I could hope for was to get down to the cottage, figure out a way to keep Walker from killing the broad, get him to get our money from Spencer and disappear off the face of the earth.

Except I couldn't. I couldn't just leave my brother until I knew Spencer had gotten him out, and then there was Paris. I still held onto the slim hope that we had a future if I could only dope out some kind of magical, happy-Hollywood-bullshit plan.

Problem was, I just didn't have an overabundance of faith that I could do that.

We'd just made the turn off of Highway 331 onto U.S. 30, heading east toward Warsaw and Chapman Lake. I must have slowed down without realizing it, deep in my misery. I heard Walker tooting behind me and glanced down at the speedometer. It was barely past forty.

That turned out to be a fortuitous thing.

Because just then, there was a loud report, like the sound of a .30-06 going off, just in front of me and to my left.

The front tire.

Flat.

It began flapping rubber immediately. I hobbled off the road, glad I hadn't been doing sixty-five as I had a couple of minutes before.

Walker pulled up behind me and jumped out of the car before I barely had my own open. I just got my legs swung out before he came running up.

"You got a spare?" he shouted, halfway to me.

Yeah. In the trunk.

Our friend Sally Boxleiter the bookkeeper lying on top of it.

That was bad, but I didn't have a chance to consider just how bad, because it all of a sudden got even worse.

Behind Walker's car a white sedan was pulling off the road.

A state trooper's white Ford sedan.

Chapter 22

Here it was. A curse on modern technology! They'd already gotten our mugs circulated. I could hear the angry clang of the steel doors shutting behind me in Pendleton. Or Michigan City. I'd forgotten I'd had some birthdays since my last stay in the joint. Pendleton was for felons under thirty; Michigan City for those over. It was Michigan City I was bound for.

I was so wrapped up in my misery that I failed to notice the trooper didn't have his gun out when he emerged from the prowler and that he had a smile on. When it penetrated my shock, at the same time I noticed that, I also saw Walker bending down to his boot. Where I knew he carried a piece, a little-bitty .25 caliber midnight special, a Raven.

"Hold it," I said, reaching out and putting my hand on his arm. Walker looked at me with a mixture of fear, puzzlement and just that plain meanness you get in your eyes when you're cornered, but he did as I said and straightened slowly back up.

The trooper walked up.

"Problem, boys?"

I nodded, trying to look pissed-off instead of the scared-silly Chicken Little I really was.

"Yeah. Looks like my horse threw a shoe."

He walked around me to get a better look at the tire.

"Yep. Looks like. You got a spare?"

I shook my head, hoping he didn't notice the lump in my throat I was having trouble getting swallowed. "Yes, but it's flat, too. I had another flat, about an hour ago. This must be my day for bad luck."

There was just no way in hell I was going to open that trunk with that uniform standing there. So far, this whole time we were jawing with the guy, the woman in the trunk hadn't made a sound. Either she didn't know it was a cop we were talking to or she'd passed out. Or had died. Oh, man... dead? Right then, I was pulling for the passed-out scenario. Either way, dead or alive, a tied-up and gagged woman in the trunk wasn't going to have a good result for us two ex-cons if that trooper saw her. That happened, we'd for sure lose the *ex* part of "ex-cons" in a nanosecond.

Walker gave me a look. I breathed a silent sigh of relief that he did the smart thing for once and said, "We're together, officer. I'll just take my friend down the road, find a gas station and get him a new tire. We'll have this out of here in half an hour."

The man considered that and then nodded. "Okay. Doesn't seem like much else you can do. You might want to pull a little further off the road, though. You're kind of close here. Lot of trucks go by. You wouldn't want your vehicle to get hit."

"No sir," Walker said. "We don't want that."

I got in and started the engine and steered the car over another four feet until I was at the very edge of the ditch that ran alongside. That done, I switched off the ignition, hit the door locks and exited the car, checking the door behind me to be sure it was locked, and then walked back to where Walker and the trooper were standing.

"Well, we're off," I said. "Let's go, Walker." As soon as I said his name, I wanted to pluck it back out of the air. Maybe the trooper hadn't gotten a picture of us, but I knew there was at least a chance he'd gotten our names. He wouldn't forget a name like "Walker."

If he'd received our names, he either didn't remember

them or connect it up. Walker and I started back toward Walker's car and the trooper trailed behind. Once inside the car, Walker fumbled for his keys and got them in the ignition.

And then the trooper tapped on his window. I saw Walker's hand start to move down toward his boot again and then he thought better of it and rolled down the window.

"Yessir?" he said, as nicely and pleasantly as a freshly-graduated Dale Carnegie graduate.

"An hour," the trooper said. "I can give you fellas an hour to get this changed and off the road. I'll swing back and if it isn't gone by then, I'm going to have to tag it for removal and put the boot on. Cost you pretty good to get it back."

I leaned over. "I understand, officer. Don't worry. We'll have it fixed long before that. Warsaw's just up ahead. Shouldn't take long at all to get a spare and get back."

"Okay, then," he said. "See that you do."

Walker started the car and put it into drive. The trooper walked on back to his car and got in. Pulling out, he went around us, waving. Walker waved back but didn't pull out.

"What're you waiting for?" I said. "Get your ass going. We got to get a tire and get back here."

He snickered. "Jake, you're something else. You believe your own story? You ain't got no flat spare. Let's just wait till he's out of sight and change the damn thing."

He was absolutely right. There was no need to go into Warsaw, buy a tire. There was a perfectly good one, keeping warm under the woman.

"But what if he swings back, sees us changing it? After we told him it was flat?"

"That's easy, buddy. We'll use mine. We'll just tell him I just remembered I had one that would fit it in my own trunk."

That made sense.

"Or," he went on, a new thought occurring to him. "We

could just leave the gal and the car and forget this cottage business. Just go get our money from Spencer. Although, I been thinking about that—"

"No!" I interrupted. "We'll change the damn flat and we'll go to the lake, just the way we planned. That guy comes back, finds my car still here and has it towed, that woman's going to make some noise. I can't understand why she didn't already. We can't take the chance she won't next time."

"Maybe she's croaked. From the stress and all that. Women have heart attacks too, you know."

"I thought of that. You think that'd be better? First thing this guy's gonna do is pop the trunk, he comes back and it's still here. Guys who wear uniforms and carry a gun are born suspicious. He comes back, finds the car still here, first thing he's gonna think is drug dealers. Count on it. Now, he's got probable cause to open that trunk. Cops don't count sheep at night to go to sleep—they keeping saying 'probable cause' over and over till they go nighty-night. He gets that trunk open, finds that woman—dead or alive—and we got maybe twenty minutes to get to some banana republic that doesn't extradite, if any such animal exists, which I doubt, least anywhere we'd understand the language. I don't think that can be done in twenty minutes or even a half hour. How long you think it's going to take him to look in the glove box, find my registration, get out an all-points, armed and dangerous out on us?"

He thought it over.

"Maybe you're right, Jake. I guess we better not leave it. We hide the body, they don't have a case, right?"

I breathed a sigh of relief. "Okay, then. Let's do it. Get your own trunk lid up in case he comes back. We'll use your spare, just like you said." I said that like I was just being logical, but the truth was, I wasn't ready to open my trunk just yet. If the woman was dead, I didn't know what I was going to do. At least if we got down to the lake and found she was dead, we had a place to hide her.

For once, my luck was holding.

Walker's spare fit just fine and we got the damned thing changed in less than ten minutes. If Mario Andretti had been watching, we would've gotten an offer to join his pit crew. And the trooper never came back.

And still the woman hadn't stirred. No thumping, no tape-muffled scream, no nothing. When we were done fixing the flat and had thrown the jack back in Walker's trunk and just before I hopped back in my car, I rapped on the trunk. "You in there?" I yelled.

No answer. No sound.

I felt sick down to my very bones.

Chapter 23

When we got to Chapman Lake, the first thing I did was go in and check the place out. The way the dice were falling for me, Paris's folks could have got a burr up their butt and come back from Florida so's the old man could do some ice-fishing and the old lady could hook up with her bridge club buddies. They'd been known to do such things.

They hadn't. The place smelled musty, the way lake cottages do when they're left unoccupied for a few months. We were also in luck. They'd left the heat on, no doubt to keep the pipes from freezing. It was turned down low, to fifty-five, but it only took a second to hit the thermostat, crank it up to seventy-two.

When I got back outside, Walker had my car backed up to the door and my trunk open and was trying to lift the woman out. She wasn't moving and her eyes were closed.

I felt even sicker.

"How'd you get it open," I asked.

"You left the keys in the ignition," he said, grunting as he wrestled her head and shoulders up. "You do that a lot? Surprised somebody ain't stole your ride."

I looked left and right, at the cottages on either side. Nobody was stirring. The house on the left was built closer to the lake, so even if someone had been looking out the window they couldn't have seen us where we were standing nearer the road. The cottage on the right was constructed on the same line with this one, but there were no cars in the drive and the only window that someone could catch a peek at us from was shuttered.

"I already checked," Walker said, seeing what I was doing. "C'mon. Let's get this bitch inside."

He didn't need to sell me on that idea.

Damn! She was one heavy lady. I grabbed her feet and Walker her shoulders and we lifted her out and I dropped her, surprised at the weight. Quickly, I reached down and got a firmer grip. Going in, Walker wasn't watching and her head hit the door jamb with a solid thunk.

She moaned. Sweet blessed sound!

"She's alive!"

"No shit," Walker said, his words whistling past his lips with exertion.

In a heartbeat, we had her inside and carried her through the kitchen to the living room and dumped her on the floor. I hurried back to the kitchen where I thought I remembered Paris's mom stored her clothesline. It was where I thought, all neatly coiled up and hanging on a nail just inside a little closet they used for a pantry.

Back in the living room, I had her feet tied in less than a minute. Together, we hoisted her up onto the couch.

"Maybe you ought to tie her to the couch," Walker suggested.

I thought about it a minute.

"Nah. When we go to sleep, I will. She ain't going anywhere."

"Let's kill her now," he said. "Be the kind thing to do. She's out cold, won't feel a thing."

"Jesus, Walker! With the killing thing again! Look, once you ice her, there's no turning back. It's murder, buddy. That's a place I don't want to go."

He laughed, a whinnying, horsey laugh. "You dumb shit, Jake. Kidnap gets you the same deal as murder."

That was true, but still. *Murder*. Kidnapping I could maybe live with—hell, I *had* to—we'd already done that—but murder? I was cursed with a religious upbringing. I could already feel the flames of hell and see my mom shaking an accusing finger in my face. I didn't know how I was going to keep Walker from killing the woman—at least, indefinitely—but I was going to try. And just hope I could come up with something, some idea, to convince him otherwise.

"You're right. But, I'm just not ready to do it just yet. Give me some time."

"Okay," he said. "But we're gonna have'ta do it eventually, pal. I'll do it. I don't mind."

For all his talk, I don't think he was all that eager to kill her either. He gave up the idea easily enough. For now.

"Let's count that money," I said, thinking of something that would distract him, get his mind on something else. "See how many diamonds we got."

That idea he liked.

We went out to the kitchen and pulled the kitchen table over to where we could keep an eye on the sofa in case she decided to come to. She seemed to be breathing all right, but she wasn't moving around any.

He dumped the bag out onto the table. The stacks of bills and the ice. There was a small mound of diamonds and other jewels.

"Must be a hundred diamonds there," I said. I had no idea what they were worth, but I knew it had to be a lot. "There's that canary!"

You couldn't miss it. It was easily the largest rock there and it was a bright lemony color. There was another, almost as large, and it was a clear brown. One of those mochas.

He picked up two of the four stacks of bills and pushed them over to me. "You count these and I'll count these," he said, pulling the other two stacks to him.

There was fifty thousand dollars in each stack.

Two hundred grand.

I couldn't make my heart slow down when I realized what kind of money was sitting in front of us.

"Hot damn," Walker said. He leaned back in the chair, clasped his fingers behind his head and got a dreamy look on his face. "We hit the lottery. You ever seen so much money before?" He unclasped his hands, leaned forward, picked up a handful of the diamonds from where he'd mounded them up and let them trickle through his fingers. "And that's nothin'. These got to be worth half a million. Maybe more."

"To a jeweler," I said. "What're they worth to a fence? That is, if we knew a fence. Half that? A third?"

The instant I said that, I regretted it. The last thing I wanted Walker to do was start scheming out a way to beat Spencer. Not with Bobby in jail and that fat pig the only key to his release.

"Not that we could do that," I went on, hastily. "Cross Spencer and you said it yourself. We're dead."

"Maybe not," he said, and the way he said it told me I hadn't given him any ideas he hadn't already had. "I know the guy in Chicago he uses—hell, I made ten trips to the guy's place already."

I could hear the excitement in his voice rise as he began to think out loud. "Hell, we're a day ahead of schedule," he went on. "Spencer's not even expecting us to do this until tomorrow. We could drive on up to Chitown, tell the guy these are rocks Spencer wants to sell him, wants us to bring the money back."

"You're forgetting my brother, Walker." I couldn't keep the dull ache I was feeling out of my voice. I could tell right then he'd just committed himself to this new plan. What the fuck was happening here?

"Shit, Jake, your brother's gonna be fine. It's just his word against Spencer's. What's the most he could get if he did get sent up? I mean, first offense and all. A year? A one to ten, that's it. Be out in ten months."

"First of all, armed robbery's ten and a quarter. Some get a one to ten, but that isn't Bishop luck. Bobby's already been popped once before this. He's on probation. They're not going to see this as a first offense they give those one to tens for. You can bet we screw Spencer, he's going to screw Bobby. Big time. He'll tell a story even you couldn't match. Time he gets done, he's going to make it look like that scene in that movie, *Dog Day Afternoon*. Besides, it doesn't matter we did this a day early. You don't think Spencer watches TV? This shit's gonna be all over the late news. Probably already is."

I was close to panic. I knew what Walker was thinking. We'd cash these diamonds in with the guy in Chicago, get that money, plus what we had, and disappear, go to Mexico or some other stupid shit. That was fine for him. He didn't have a wife he loved, a kid on the way, a business he was about to start. Or a brother in jail. I don't even think he minded being in the joint that much. He hadn't strung out a total of two years in a row outside time since he was fourteen. The joint was home. He was one of those guys his cell was his castle. For all his bitching, I knew he *loved* the joint.

"Walker, we aren't selling these diamonds and I don't want to hear any more shit like that. We're getting them to Spencer as quick as we can. We'll keep the money. Spencer doesn't know anything about that. All he wanted was that yellow diamond. He'll probably give you something for the other diamonds, especially that brown thing. Hell, you can keep all of it. The money, whatever he gives you for the rest. I don't want it. You can have all this, too." I waved my arm over the table and the four stacks of green lying there. "All I want is my brother out of jail and my life back."

I was desperate. And getting mad. Here I'd helped this asshole out, on the basis of what I owed him for what happened back in the joint, and he was about to fuck up what was left of the rest of my life. The anger took over.

I stood up. "Walker, here's what you're going to do. You're going to get your ass back up to South Bend, give Spencer his shit. You're not going to kill the woman. Then you're going to get lost. Go to South America, wherever. Fuck a bunch of Spanish broads, drink Mai Tais."

I was thinking ahead on my feet. My prints weren't at Calvin Brewer's house, Walker's were. Actually, with a little bit of luck, I could be clear. Cops'd figure it to be an inside job, the bookkeeper and Walker. If Walker and the gal both disappeared... I didn't want to think about what had to be done to make that come true. That the woman had to disappear, too. But... if she did and Walker did... All I had to do was convince Paris to give me an alibi.

That was the tricky part. Straights always get that wife testifying thing wrong. The law doesn't say a spouse *can't* testify against her husband—it only says *she doesn't have to.* She wants, she can. Knowing how Paris was probably feeling, I didn't want to hang my future on that, but it looked like I wasn't going to have a choice. Even if she started out wanting to save my ass, by the time she'd been in court five-six days running and the detectives messed with her head with all their threats and shit, I didn't have much optimism she'd end up lying for me. Still, it was the only hope I had.

I pretty much knew I was going to have to do the selling job of my life.

The other tricky part was being sure Walker did get lost, forever. They caught him, it was all over. I had no doubt he'd be singing an hour after he was in cuffs and the song he'd be singing would be titled, "Jake Bishop, My Dear Rap-Partner."

I didn't want to admit it, but Walker was right. There was too much at stake to let the woman live. She'd seen both our faces, plain and ugly. No getting around that. We let her live,

I was on my way back to the joint. For life. I wouldn't even have to worry about the Bitch if she I.D.'d me. They'd just throw that in for a bonus. That's even assuming I'd draw life and not the death penalty. Either way, it didn't matter. If I got sent up for life at this stage of my life, they might as well strap me into Old Sparky. Life behind bars would be even worse.

Even knowing that, I still wasn't mentally or emotionally ready to let Walker take her out. I sure as shit wasn't up to doing it myself. That old soul thing that kept fucking with my logic.

I had to get there. To that place where murder was think-able. Further than that. To that place where I didn't even think about it. Just let it happen, squirrel it away in the darkest corner of my mind to a place I would never go. Beyond the place where nightmares come from. I didn't know if that was possible.

Not yet anyway. My mind whirled with all the possible scenarios, none of them what I'd consider Disney material if this was a movie.

Deep in thought, I didn't realize Walker was saying something.

"…eat a horse. They got anything in this house?"

He got up, went over to the counter and began opening cupboards and slamming them shut, one by one.

"I've got some soda crackers out in the car," I said.

He turned, gave me a drop-dead look. "Crackers? You got to be kidding. We've got near a quarter million in bills and you want me to eat some stale-ass crackers? Buddy…" He laughed. "I'm for a T-bone steak. One 'bout three inches thick. Cooked in butter and slathered with onions."

I didn't think it was possible I could eat under this stress and worry, but when he said "T-bone steak" my mouth began to water.

"You know," I said. "I believe I could tackle one of those

my own self. Whyn't you run into town, get us a couple. I'll stay here, guard our houseguest."

He wasn't seeing none of that.

"I don't have no idea where the hell I am," he said. "You been here before. You know where the stores is and all. I'd get lost before I got six blocks from here."

I had to admit he had a point.

We argued a bit more and then I gave in and agreed to go. I picked up one of the hundreds from the table.

"Get some shovels," he said as I was leaving. "We got to bury this bitch, remember?"

I grabbed a second bill.

"All right," I said. "But you leave her be while I'm gone. I'm still thinking on a way to avoid a murder."

"You keep thinking, Jake, but I'm telling you right now. There ain't no way around it, gets down to the nitty-gritty. You know that's truth."

I did, but I wasn't ready to admit it.

"Maybe. Just hold off. We'll do it later. I'll help."

I was just going out the door, when Walker said, "Cigarettes."

I poked my head back in again. "Say what?"

"Cigarettes," he said. "Get me some butts. I'm low."

I got the steaks at the Owens' supermarket and, wouldn't you know it, they didn't have a single shovel in the entire store. The pimple-faced kid I asked said they were due in next week. He said most people didn't plant their gardens when there was still four inches of snow on the ground, and for a minute I thought about taking his little smart-ass tongue and tying it around his neck, but I didn't. Drawing attention to myself wasn't a goal I had right then. I did get two of the biggest T-bones they had and a bunch of other stuff to eat as well.

Back at the cottage, the door open, both arms full of groceries, I started to yell at Walker why he couldn't come out and help me.

He was too busy lugging Sally Boxleiter over to the kitchen.

A dead Sally Boxleiter. That was pretty evident even from the front door. If I hadn't seen her throat which looked like he had ripped it open with a rusty church key, I would have got a clue from the pool of blood by the couch and the trail of crimson gore that trailed along behind his load.

I felt my soul rip its way out of my body and tear loose.

Chapter 24

"Oh, shit," I said, dropping the groceries.

My knees threatened to give out under me. I could feel my stomach churning around in there and sweat popped out everywhere there were glands. I was in the middle of a Stephen King horror picture. "You done it, didn't you? Just couldn't wait."

Walker didn't even look around but just kept grunting and pulling on her legs.

"I could use some help here," he said. He dropped the woman's feet and turned around to glare at me. "This is a woman didn't believe in no diets," he said. "Bet she never saw a Hostess Cupcake she had trouble passin' up. Not to mention she probably played center for the Purdue Boilermakers in her day. C'mon, Jakey. Gimme a hand here."

I just stood there, looked at him. And the woman. The dead woman.

"Goddammit, Jake. You knew this had to be done. You knew you couldn't do it. Somebody had to. Once again, I save your useless ass."

I slowly woke up to what was happening. "You're right, Walker. Only this time, it was you who put me in this trick bag to begin with. You think of that while you're imagining you're some kind of hero on my behalf?"

He just shook his head, exasperated. "All right. Maybe I did. But we're in this thing, Jake, and this is what had to be done. Admit it. What were you going to do? Turn her loose, give her cab fare to the police station? You know what woulda happened we let her go."

He was right. Dead right. I supposed I owed him for doing what I couldn't and for doing what was the only smart thing to do. At least *I* hadn't killed her. Maybe that'd count for something with the Big Guy in the Sky.

For sure.

"Oh, hell," I said. "Okay, Walker."

I walked over and sat down at the kitchen table. "Leave her be a minute and let's figure out what we're going to do."

"Do? That's easy. We're gonna take her out to your car, load her up and find that woods you were talking about. Bury her ass. Then, get the hell out of Dodge."

"At midnight? Walker, we don't even have a flashlight. How're we going to see to dig a hole? To even find a place to dig a hole? You maybe didn't notice, but there's not even a moon out tonight. Woods are dark, brother. And what're we supposed to dig with? I couldn't find a shovel. You think we should use our fingers maybe? You want to mess up that nice manicure?"

"You didn't get shovels?" He came over and sat down beside me on one of the kitchen chairs. "Jesus, Jake. Why not?"

"Because it's nine o'clock at night, Walker. It's weird, but all the hardware stores seem to close before that around here."

"Yeah," he said, nodding slowly. "Okay. Then, let's just go dump her someplace. We can at least carry her back in some forest around here. Be days, maybe weeks before they find her. Meantime, we're long gone."

An immense feeling of emptiness swept over me. This whole thing was wearing me down. The whole situation was just… wrong. I realized I was at that point cops love to get the bad guys to. The place where they're so soul-sick and worn out and guilty that all they want to do is confess their sins and their crimes and lie down and sleep forever. A dangerous time, if I wanted to remain free.

There was a woman lying in her own blood not ten feet away. A woman who hadn't done anything to me and probably not to anyone in her life. Now she was dead and all because of two fucked-up worthless assholes. I wanted to blame Walker Joy for all of it, but I couldn't, not all of it.

All of a sudden, I saw my future—both here and in the afterlife—and I got dizzy. Physically. I leaned over and put my head between my legs.

"I already done that," I heard Walker saying, sounding like he was far away. "Ralphed. It gets you, don't it?"

I breathed as deeply as I could and little by little, got my stomach under control. I got the pack of butts out of my shirt pocket and lit one with shaking fingers.

"This is bad, Walker," I said, inhaling the smoke deep into my lungs.

"I know," he replied, his voice oddly out of character for him. Somber. I looked over and saw he was serious. Maybe he had demons himself. I'd never considered that.

"Look," I said, taking another deep drag. "We can't go off half-cocked here. First thing, we can't just dump her someplace. We've got to bury her. Deep. Some place where nobody goes. I know the place."

I told Walker about the place I had in mind. "Here's what we do," I said. The horror of what he'd done—*we'd* done—didn't disappear, but from somewhere within me a cold, logical sense took over and put the dead woman in the back of my mind. "We get some sleep. We're both tired right now. Too tired to make good decisions. In the morning, we'll go into town, get some shovels and a pickaxe t'get through the hard stuff on top, come back and load her up, go to this place I know."

My mind was racing ahead to the next day, covering all

the angles. "We'll get some black pepper. Don't forget to remind me."

"Black pepper?"

"Yes. We'll bury her and dump pepper all around. Keep animals from digging her up." I'd read that somewhere or seen it on TV.

"Yeah," he said, his eyes lighting up.

"You hungry?" I got up and went over to the spilled grocery bag. "I got the steaks." I bent over and began to stuff the steaks and potatoes and other things back into the bag.

"Yeah," he said. Then, "No, not really."

I straightened up, brought the bag over to the refrigerator, opened it and put it inside.

"Me, neither," I said. "Let's get some shuteye. There's beds upstairs. Me, I'm going to take a bath." I went over and locked the front door.

"What should we do with her?" he said, his gaze traveling to the woman's body on the floor.

"Let's move her back to the couch."

We got her body back up on the couch and threw a quilt I saw draped over my father-in-law Jerrol's easy chair over it. Made it look like someone had gone to sleep, gotten a chill and pulled the cover over her. That done, I headed for the stairs. "Take whichever bed you want. I'm going to take a bath."

A few minutes later, the tub was half-full of water as hot as I could stand it, and I slipped in and let the water keep running. I let it run to within an inch of the top and then turned it off and slipped down inside the heat until my entire body was covered except my face. Even my ears. I just lay there, trying not to think about the dead woman downstairs.

After a while, maybe ten minutes, I smelled something. Steak and butter. Looked like Walker had changed his mind, decided he was hungry after all. The smell made me nauseous. I reached over and shoved the door closed, but it didn't help much. I got out of the tub, pulled the plug and dried off. I put my dirty shorts back on. I could hear Walker messing around downstairs, pulling open drawers, probably to look for silverware, and then it got quiet. I went into Paris's parents' bedroom and lay down on the bed half-naked and half-damp, not even bothering to pull the coverlet down and get inside. I must have been really tired, because I don't remember even thinking about anything, but must have fallen asleep almost immediately.

Some time after that—I have no idea how long—the sound of voices downstairs brought me awake.

A man's—that was Walker's. And a woman's. A familiar voice. I fought the sleep cobwebs, sat up, listened, my heart racing and then I recognized the other voice.

Paris's.

Calling me.

Chapter 25

Screaming, actually.

"Jaa—aaaake!"

I took the stairs two at a time and cleared the last half dozen steps with a leap that landed me on the floor, twisting my ankle. I yelped, but scrambled up, ignoring the pain.

Jesus Christ.

It was Paris all right. She was backed up against the kitchen counter and Walker was two feet away, brandishing a gigantic knife in her direction.

Paris's mom's turkey carving knife. One of a set of cutlery we'd given her two Christmas's back. Probably the one he'd used on the Boxleiter woman.

"Walker!" I yelled. "What the fuck you doing? That's my wife!"

He took a step back, clear disappointment in his eyes. He was getting to enjoy this killing thing.

Paris's expression changed in a twinkling from terror to anger. She gave Walker's chest a forearm shiver, just like they teach in freshman football—although this was varsity-quality—causing him to stumble another step backward, and then she turned toward me with a full head of steam. I held my arms out to hug her. She stopped two feet from me, put her hands up, as if to say—whoa!—and then hauled off and rang my chimes with a slap alongside my head, making my ears ring and my senses temporarily leave, whether from surprise or from the force of the blow, I don't know.

I shook my head to clear the cobwebs and put my hand up to my ear. I could feel the heat with my fingers and knew it was fire-red.

"What the hell'd you do that for?" I asked, aware my voice was whining and wishing it wasn't.

"This must be your moron friend, Walker Joy," she said. "Hi Mr. Joy. I'm the wife." She didn't hold out her hand. "What kind of bullshit have you gotten my husband into?"

Walker didn't say a word. To her or me. He glanced down at the knife in his hand as if suddenly remembering it was there and walked over and tossed it clattering into the sink. He looked over at me, and I could read his mind. His expression said, "What the hell is she doing here?"

A question I was wondering about myself. What the hell *was* Paris doing here? Christ, could this get any more complicated? Or fucked up?

"How'd you—" I began.

"Know you were here?" She shook her head back in forth in disgust and then stalked past me into the living room. My heart jumped a beat, realizing there was a dead body two feet away from her, but she didn't even look at the couch, just kept walking through the living room to the sitting room her dad had built onto the back. A glassed-in addition to the living room where he'd put a couple of easy chairs and a couch in so you could sit there, have a drink or whatever and look out over the lake. She sat down heavily in the La-Z-Boy that was her father's favorite and put her head in her hands and leaned forward.

A memory flashed through my mind. This was the room I'd proposed to Paris in. The first time we went down to visit her parents. She'd sat in that same La-Z-Boy and I'd gotten down on one knee. Her parents had been out in the kitchen, doing the dishes, Gloria washing and Jerrol drying, in their every-night routine. I still remember Gloria shrieking when Paris went out a few minutes and told her the news. I forced the memory away.

I knew Paris was crying even though she didn't make a sound.

I went to join her, wondering what in the hell I was going to say to her. I sat down in the chair next to her, the one her mother usually sat in and knitted or watched TV on the little set on a bookcase along the far wall.

After a minute, she raised her head and looked at me, and I saw I was right. Her eyes were red-rimmed and moist.

"You're not too slick, Jake," she said. "It took me about ten minutes to figure out where you were going."

"How's that?" I said. "How—"

"Easy," she interrupted. "You left with that box of crackers. You hate soda crackers, Jake. You didn't even look in the fridge. If you were after food, that's where you would have looked. Since it was pretty easy to see food wasn't what you came home for, I wondered what was in the pantry you really wanted. That wasn't too hard to figure out. The only other thing in there besides food is our spare keys. I just went through them until I figured out which one was missing."

"Oh," I said. Well, hell…

"It's not important how I figured out where you were. What's important is…" She stopped, looked confused. "Jake, I don't know where to start. You broke into that man's place already, didn't you?"

I nodded. What else could I do?

"Makes sense. Something went wrong, didn't it? Otherwise, you wouldn't be here, I guess."

I didn't say anything. She was no dummy. One of the biggest reasons I'd fallen in love with her. The one word that could never be used to describe Paris was "bimbo."

"Yeah, we had a little problem," I said. "Nothing we can't work out."

"I imagine," she said, almost airily, as if whatever glitch we'd run into, couldn't be that much. That struck me odd. Why wasn't she going into histrionics? Crying and laying a bucket of blame and recriminations on me and demanding to be told what exactly the "little problem" was? This wasn't the reaction I was expecting. I decided to lay out the whole story, throw myself on the court's mercy, but I never got the chance to open my mouth.

"Are we—" I stopped. I wanted to ask her if the reason she'd come down was to tell me she'd decided to stay with me through this. Only, I couldn't. What if she said no?

"Jake, I wish there was an easy way to tell you this, but there isn't." She paused and I imagine there were two people holding their breath in that room. I was vaguely aware that Walker was out in the kitchen, opening cabinets and stuff. Probably looking for something else to eat. I guessed he was just trying to avoid Paris as much as he could, let us work out our situation.

What she was going to tell me would be one of two things, I figured. Either she was sticking by me, or... Or, the cops had come by like I feared. And she'd given me up. She must not have told them where she suspected I was, but that didn't matter. I'd be behind bars as soon as I ventured out from the cottage. They knew what car I was driving and most likely Walker's too, and even if we stole another car, it was only a matter of time before they found us. I wondered why she hadn't told them where we were, but decided she probably just wanted to see me one last time, tell me face-to-face what she'd done.

I was wrong.

"Jake," she said, about as bluntly as something like that could be laid on someone. "Bobby's dead."

I didn't hear her right the first time.

"What?" I said, an idiotic smile playing on my lips, like I thought she'd just played some sick joke on me.

"Bobby's dead," she repeated, her eyes suddenly hollow and gaunt and looking tired. "He... Jake, I'm sorry... Jake... he hung himself."

Chapter 26

It hit me all at once, what she was saying.

My brother.

Gone.

I couldn't believe it. Didn't want to believe it.

"Are you sure?" I said, the most inane thing I could have possibly uttered.

She nodded, tears suddenly flooding her eyes. She rose, came over to me and bent down and put her arms around me. Somehow, she ended up in my lap, and I was crying and trying not to and holding her to me like she was my mother or something.

"He was... attacked," she was saying. I had my head buried in her stomach and she was bent over, stroking the back of my neck. "He left a note for you."

I heard the rustle of paper and realized she was pulling a sheet of paper out from where she'd put it in her bra. She extricated herself and knelt on the floor beside me, gazing up. She handed up the paper and I took it. I was aware of a tremor in my fingers, but I couldn't help it. It was written in Bobby's small handwriting. Not the original; a photocopy. I'd always kidded him about his handwriting. Told him it looked like a girl's.

I thought of that, oddly, and experienced an overwhelming regret I'd ever said that to him, teasing or not.

"They kept the original," Paris was saying. "For the trial.

They said you could have it after that was over."

I didn't know what she was talking about, but it didn't matter. I focused on the words.

Dear Jake, it began.

This is a hard letter to write, bro. If you get this, I guess that means I've done what I set out to do. I've got some things to get off my chest and then I'm going to end all this bullshit. First of all, I got to say you're not to blame for my death. That's my choice. Nothing you could of done would of stopped me. You've been nothing but a good brother, Jake. Something happened here last night. A guy raped me. I don't know if that ever happened to you when you did time, but it sure as shit happened to me. Happened along about two a.m. this morning. Guy held a razorblade he had melted onto a toothbrush to my throat and "did his deed."

Jake, I wanted to fight him, but I couldn't. Little guy, too. I could of whipped him good in a fair fight. I just kept feeling that razorblade and knew if I did anything I was dead. After, I just kept wishing I'd said fuck it and at least tried to fight the motherfucker. But I didn't.

I can't live with that.

There's something else I can't live with. Been with me a long time. Before I tell you this, I want to ask you not to hate me, Jake. I can't ask you to promise, but I'm asking you.

I'm responsible for Mom and Dad's death.

There. I said it. I've wanted to tell you this for a year now.

You deserve to know what happened. What it was, was I was smoking weed. I'd been smoking all day. High as I've ever been. I came home about one in the morning and didn't want to wake the folks up. Everybody figured it was Mom put my clothes in the dryer, but it wasn't. You know Mom. She wouldn't put a load in and then go to bed. It was me, Jake. I was out of it, but I knew Mom'd smell the grass on my shirt in the morning and I'd be in big trouble. I washed out my pants and shirt by hand in the deep sink and then threw them in the dryer. I was feeling sick—bad gunge, bro!—and I went up to the sun room to clear my head. I figured I'd come back down, get my clothes out, and then go to bed.

Jake, I'm so sorry! I fell asleep and never went back. The dryer caught fire. You know the rest.

I wanted to say something when it happened, but I couldn't. Everyone would think I was the biggest creep in the world. Especially you.

This has torn me up forever.

That's why I got to do this. Check out. I just can't handle all this stuff anymore. I just hope I go to Hell so I don't have to face Mom and Dad.

It was signed: *Your loving brother, Robert*, and he had *(Bobby)* in parenthesis after it.

And a P.S.

It said: *And tell Paris I really appreciate her taking me in like she did. I'm sorry I was mean to her sometimes. I really do like her cooking. I guess I was just mad she wasn't Mom. Mad at me, not her.*

An incredible wave of sadness swept over me, so intense I couldn't cry. I felt as if I'd been hollowed out completely, there was nothing inside.

I dropped my hands into my lap, the letter falling to the floor somewhere, and just started off in the direction of the lake before me, but I wasn't seeing the water, the trees on the other side, nothing. If there were snowmobiles out I didn't see them. I was looking farther away than Chapman Lake, across the years. To a little boy I was giving boxing lessons to. Telling him to keep his right up, lead with his left. Calling him a punk and laughing at him as he flailed the air, missing my stomach by a foot at least. And then, quicker than I would have bet he could swing, my little brother Bobby coming in and catching me with his right, square on the jaw, with enough punch that I saw stars. Seeing me chasing him. Him laughing and then me, too, and both of us collapsing on the front lawn, out of breath and just two good friends on a warm Saturday morning in the summer.

Gradually, the image faded and I was aware Paris was talking.

"…can be proud of him, I guess. The guy who attacked him is in the hospital."

"Huh?" I said. She started again. I sat and looked out over the lake and Paris ran down everything she'd gotten from the police. An hour after he'd been raped, he got himself up, it seems, walked down to this guy's cell and attacked him.

"He took his eye out," Paris said. "My God!"

I nodded, dumbly. I remembered showing him that just before they took him back to the bullpen. How to make two fingers into a hook.

She went on, telling me how the turnkey had finally heard the noise and came and investigated. How they'd got Bobby up to another cell and the man on a stretcher and over to Memorial Hospital.

How Bobby'd tied bedsheets together and hung himself.

How—there was more she was telling me, but I don't remember what it was exactly.

My bones just all of a sudden and without any warning, kind of dissolved inside my body. Complete and numbing paralysis overcame every living cell. Not only physically, but emotionally. So many different kinds of feelings were crowding up to the surface that none could get out and instead of sorrow or rage or frustration or guilt—all of which I was aware were boiling around inside on some level—nothing came out. It wasn't that I didn't try. I kept opening and shutting my mouth and damned if I didn't begin to hiccup uncontrollably. Not those kind you normally get, about every ten seconds or so, but a steady run of chirps, like some kind of stupid bird or something.

"Jake?" She said it again. "Jake?"

I was aware Paris was looking at me with her big eyes even larger and brighter than normal and asking me if I wanted to lie down—I mean, I could hear her voice and understand what she was saying, but it was like she was sitting across from me on the edge of some great chasm that kept growing wider and wider between us and as the chasm opened up, a roar started up in my ears and the next thing I knew I was trying to sit up on the floor and Paris was wiping my forehead with an cold wet cloth and Walker was standing just behind her, looking down at me with an expression it seemed of slight bemusement. I was freezing cold and my teeth were chattering and I realized I was soaking wet, sweating ice from every possible pore in my body, salty perspiration running down into my eyes, making me blink at its burn.

"You okay, sweetie?" Paris asked, seeing me open my eyes. "You passed out. I thought you'd had a stroke!"

"Yeah," Walker said. "That's what she said, man. A stroke!" Seeing I was all right—or at least, alive—he threw back his head and laughed, which for some reason made me mad. "A friggin' stroke, she said! Like you was some kind of old fart, somethin'."

I pushed up on one elbow, waited a minute to see if I was still woozy, and when I saw I wasn't, I sat up and pushed myself back so that the wall could support my back and wiped my sleeve across my eyes. Gradually, I got my breathing back under control.

"He's really dead, isn't he?" I said, the question more directed at myself than at Paris.

"Yes, he is, Jake. Jake, I'm—"

"It's okay," I interrupted, holding my hand up. "I just need a minute to get used to this."

I'd need more than a minute.

An entire lifetime wasn't going to be enough for this.

My poor baby brother.

I should have seen this coming. Bobby wasn't equipped for jail. What he was equipped for was skateboarding and hanging with his buds and checking out the babes and working on his curve ball. Worrying about next Friday's algebra test. Not this. Not dying in a jail cell with a bunch of perverts and the other sad cases in a place like that. For something he had nothing to do with. In a place only because some motherfucker wanted me to do a job for him and maybe to exact a little revenge for something I'd done to the motherfucker's retarded uncle years ago. The guilt I was feeling was so palpable and overwhelming I could taste it, like a mouthful of rancid meat I'd just put in my mouth and swallowed.

And what was that bullshit about him being the cause of our parents' death? If he'd only told me what he was thinking. I would have set him straight, made him see it wasn't his fault. That it was just one of those fucking accidents we get in life.

Now, that chance was gone.

Bobby was gone.

And me, the cause of his being where he was and creating the situation for him that led him to take his own life... me, the older brother who should have been out in the back yard playing catch with him and taking him to get pizza... me, I... was sitting in a lake cottage with a dead woman's body on the couch—a woman that had never done me an ounce of harm and was only doing some overtime on her job when our paths crossed. Sitting on the floor of a cottage with a partner hustling about in the kitchen looking for something to stuff into his ugly face, a partner who was a moron and could only get me in deeper trouble than I already was in—if that was even possible. Sitting in a cottage with a wife looking at me with anxious eyes, a woman I adored and was about to lose. Not to mention a business that was fast disappearing and no longer even mattered in the face of everything else. What was appearing in its place was the onrushing specter of gray prison bars and concrete walls, mouth-breathing mesomorphs all around me, scheming unholy ways to get my pink eye for the rest of my natural days, years and years until I died alone, without my soul mate and without a single other human being who might be considered normal, in one of those institutions filled with the mentally-ravaged and doomed, called a prison.

I think I was close to feeling some of the same emotions that Bobby must have felt when he took his own life.

I just didn't have the guts he did. I wanted to, though, for the most intense few seconds of my life. I wanted to pick up a gun—that one Walker kept strapped to his ankle—point it at my worthless skull and pull the trigger, let the anonymous bullet speed toward my fevered brain and end all the agony and pain that was just flat-crushing my useless ass.

But I didn't.

In the middle of all this self-misery and feeling sorry for my pitiful, worthless self, I looked over and realized that was my wife sitting there looking at me, and she was smack in the middle of all this, and that too was my doing. And realized, if I took the way out Bobby had, I was leaving her to Walker Joy's mercy, and I had no doubt what he'd do.

I knew then what had to be done.

Chapter 27

Make all this right, somehow.

For Paris.

No matter what it cost me.

First, I had to know if she was with me. I didn't know any other way to find out other than to just ask.

"Yes," she said.

"You're sure?"

She hesitated before answering. "When I came down here, I wasn't sure. I just knew I had to tell you about Bobby. But..." she paused, lifted her chin to look into my eyes, almost defiantly, "...when you went out, for a second, I thought you'd died. That's what made up my mind. I knew then that I didn't want to live if you weren't with me."

She cleared her throat and looked out at the lake and then back at me. A new look of raw determination was in her eyes. "But, you have to be straight with me, Jake. I mean, completely straight. As much as I love you..." she stopped, as if to gather herself, "...you lie even once to me and I'm gone."

That's when I knew what was required of me. The whole truth, nothing left out, nothing glossed over, nothing sugar-coated.

It was hard.

It got harder, watching her eyes as I revealed to her the events of yesterday, unfolding each detail and each step that had plunged me deeper and deeper into the toilet. Watching her hand fly to her mouth in horror and her eyes dart to the couch when I told her about the woman lying there under the blanket and how she came to be there.

After that, I could no longer look straight at her, but continued my sorry account by staring fixedly at the wall behind her the whole time.

All I could say when I finished was that I was sorry.

Sorry! Like I'd knocked over her favorite plant or something.

When I was done, there was nothing. Silence.

I didn't know what to expect and I couldn't bring myself to look at her.

A scream? An attack? Her flailing at me with both fists, bloodying my face? That would have been almost preferable to this silence.

And then...

She surprised me.

Floored me, actually.

No recriminations, no shrieking, no accusations. None of that. Just Paris joining the team. Not just joining it. Taking over.

"You've got two choices, the way I see it."

I was aware that Walker had come back into the room, was standing leaning up against the doorsill, listening, arms folded, his eyes on Paris.

"One," she continued, "you can turn yourselves in."

Walker gave a derisive grunt at that one.

She turned to look at him. "No? I kind of figured that was how you'd feel, Mr. Joy. How about you, Jake? That an option you don't like?"

Not at all. Only...

Maybe that's what I should have done. If I'd stopped this runaway train earlier, just gone to the cops, told them what Sydney Spencer was up to, then maybe Bobby'd still be alive.

It was for sure Paris wouldn't be knee-deep in this with me. When do you jump off a speeding train headed for destruction? I said nothing.

"Okay," she said. "That's what I figured. I'm just throwing it out. All right, then. What we've got to do is figure out how to get out of this mess."

She hadn't mentioned Option Three. That she go to the cops, turn us in. I hoped Walker had noticed that.

I should have felt good, maybe even great about Paris's decision. The truth was, it added even more misery added to the mix. Now, my "straight" wife was saying she was in this with us. My wife, who heretofore had only dreamed of a nice house, a successful business, a child or two with her husband. My wife who was crossing that line into criminality while I watched helplessly. Who only crossed the line because of me. The love of my life who I'd pulled down into the cesspool with me.

It couldn't get much worse than this…

I cleared my head, shoved down the emotions I was feeling, forced myself to listen to what Paris was saying.

Which was amazing.

"The way I see it, unless your intrepid partner here, Mr. Joy…" she paused and gave him a funny look. "…unless Mr. Joy left his fingerprints back at this man's house, you're probably in the clear."

A wife and career girl one minute, a master criminal planner the next. I'd expected anything but this. Paris was totally into the situation and thinking more logically than either Walker or me. I listened, growing more fascinated by the second by this sea change in her.

"The thing to do is just wait. If they've found his prints, it won't be long before they put it all together and figure maybe Jake was in on this too. You guys' past backgrounds, you know?"

I nodded and saw Walker's head bob up and down along with mine.

"I'll go home and if the cops pay me a visit, then we'll know they're onto you. If they don't, then you're probably in the clear."

"You're right," Walker said. "Let's say they find prints and come looking for Jake. You gonna warn us, right?"

That was my question as well.

"Of course," she said. "You guys just stay here in the cottage. We'll go into town in a while, find a pay phone someplace, get the number, and every day at say, five, I'll give you a call. Let you know what's going on, if anything."

"How long you think we need to do that?" he asked.

"Two days?" I offered.

"Two days sounds right," Paris agreed. "Yes. Two days. If nothing happens during that time, you're probably both okay."

Walker grinned. "This is some old lady you got, Jake! Brains *and* looks! Whooey!"

"I'm not done," Paris said. "Don't go celebrating just yet. You boys still have a problem out there that needs an answer." She gestured toward the living room and the body on the couch. "I want her out of here."

"I've got that figured out," I said. "We're going to bury her tonight. Over in that woods by the county highway department. You know, on the road we take to town?"

She thought a minute and nodded thoughtfully. "Yes. That'd be the best place. If she disappears, chances are the police will think she pulled the job and got out of the country somehow. Especially when they find her car. They'll figure she had an accomplice."

"Exactly," I said. "What I was thinking when I put that diamond on the floor in back."

Then, something occurred to me. I couldn't believe I hadn't thought of it sooner.

"Bobby," I said.

Paris immediately caught my thought.

"His funeral."

"Exactly."

She thought for a minute. "Okay. Here's what we'll do. I'll go home, make the arrangements. You'll come back for the funeral. Anyone asks in the meantime, I'll tell them you're on a trip, looking for salon furnishings. I'll say you're over in... Pennsylvania. Looking at antiques. I've left messages, but you must have changed motels."

I hated to have her do that. He was my brother. That should have been my duty. But she was right. If they were onto us and I came back, that was it. Another thought logically came from that one. If we had to make a run for it, how was I even going to be there when they buried Bobby?

This was all shit.

Fuck it. I made up my mind to go back with Paris, make the arrangements myself.

But then...

...Walker Joy.

I couldn't leave him here by himself. I just didn't trust the guy. Knowing him, he'd just take off. It wasn't the money and diamonds—I could care less about that. It was simply that I didn't trust him not to get caught if he was on his own. And if he got nabbed, I knew he wouldn't take the fall alone. Sooner or later—probably sooner than later—after a headslap or two—my name would surely come up and I'd be downstate getting that visit from someone like Toles again. The joint was full of guys like Toles. Fuck, the *world* was full of 'em... I saw the future and it was clear. Me, ending up with a reserved seat on a blue bus headed for Michigan City and a lifetime diet of beans.

Which brought me full cycle to my original thought a few minutes earlier when that brief thought of suicide had entered my brain, and I'd realized what leaving Paris with Walker would mean. Her certain death.

Walker had to go.

But could I do that?

Could I kill someone?

Could I waste the guy who'd once saved my life?

I had to.

Only…

I'd never killed anyone before. Well, except for Toles, but that didn't count. That was more like self-defense.

This would be… murder. Of someone who passed for a friend.

Jesus.

Paris had one more thought.

"You know what's in two days, don't you?"

I looked at Walker and he shrugged his shoulders.

"What's in two days?" I asked.

She looked at the two of us. Her visage was grim.

"Christmas."

Chapter 28

The way it was finally decided—well, actually, Paris decided; she'd just sort of taken over—was that she and I wouldn't go into town and find a payphone and get a number, but that Walker would. On his way to doing a couple of other errands. He was to buy some shovels and a pickaxe and pick up some chow for the three of us.

That was all right with me. In fact, it was better he went and left my wife and me at the cottage. I needed to talk to her.

I drew a little map for him so he could find the way into town and get back to the cottage okay.

As soon as Walker pulled away, I said to Paris, "You know he's going to call his contact in Chicago, don't you?" She looked puzzled, so I explained. "Walker's kind of a criminal, Paris." Before she could make a smart remark, one I'm sure would involve my own self, I went on. "His brain has been working overtime trying to figure out how to keep the diamonds and the money for himself. My bet is he's got the number of the fence in Chicago his boss uses and he's going to make a beeline for a phone and set up an appointment with him."

"What?" she said, that look I always called her "smart-ass" look on her face appearing. "You think your bosom buddy is capable of double-crossing you? Why, I never!" That last was delivered with her best Scarlett O'Hara impersonation.

"Afraid so," I said. "Anyway, I don't care about that. Fuck the money. He can have it all. I just want our lives to go back to normal. The problem is, Walker will get caught. You can make book on it. He always does. He gets all that cash, in a week he'll have half of it spent and that'll be his downfall. Ours, too. It won't take ten minutes by an ugly cop with an attitude to get everything out of him."

"Then, it's simple," she said. "We'll have to kill him."

Stunned couldn't begin to describe the effect her words had on me.

"Paris," I said. "Paris."

"Get it together, Jake," she said. She walked out to the kitchen, leaving me standing there with my mouth open.

A moment later, trance-like, I wandered into the kitchen where Paris was slamming cabinets, her back to me, her shoulders hunched forward like some feral animal.

"Now where in the hell would Mom hide the coffee?" she said, more to herself than to me. She found the canister, slammed it onto the countertop and began opening cabinets and drawers, pulling out cups and saucers and spoons. She crossed over to the refrigerator, giving me a little shove to move me from her path, her eyes blazing and her lips pressed tightly together. She retrieved the bowl of sugar cubes from where her mother kept it in the fridge and took it back over to the counter and proceeded to prepare the coffee pot. They were the brown raw sugar cubes her mother always bought. They were in the blue and white bowl we'd given her for their last wedding anniversary, part of a set of china Paris had found on one of our excursions to Chicago. I had a weird thought, wondering what Gloria would say about Walker being in her kitchen. Or me, considering.

"Paris—" I began, not having a clue what I was going to say to her, but knowing I had to say something, get a dialogue started, try to figure out who this person was that I'd thought I knew. I guess I should have been happy that she'd come out with the very same thing that I'd decided I'd have to do to Walker, but I wasn't. Never in a million years would I have thought my sweetheart capable of such a thought. Our relationship had shifted and gone to a new place. A dark place.

"Don't 'Paris' me," she said. She turned to face me and I saw she was fighting tears. For some reason, that made me feel okay.

She went on. "Don't look at me like I'm some alien. Or..." She struggled to find the word she wanted. "...some kind of monster. I just said what you were planning to say. I'm right, aren't I?" Only she didn't say it as a question, more like a statement.

The tears she'd been fighting had vanished, replaced by a look of aggressive belligerence, her jaw jutting out, her eyes narrowed and harsh. She moved forward until she was right up in my face.

"Well..."

"Yes. Well, yes." She turned and went back to her coffee pot, picked it up and poured the steaming liquid into the two cups she'd prepared.

"One cube, right?" she said, her back once more to me.

She handed me a cup and I sipped it without thinking, scalding my mouth. I could feel an instant blister on my bottom lip. She stalked past me with her own cup and I followed her like a dumb animal trailing after its master back out to the front porch. She walked up to the window to stare out at the lake. A snowmobile was just passing by, a man and woman on board, both flashing toothy smiles as the man leaned far out, hiking the machine like it was a sailboat, the woman shrieking in pleasure, which we heard faintly. He navigated the turn successfully and they headed to the opposite side of Chapman, the snowmobile going flat out, flying across the ice.

I moved up beside Paris. She didn't turn her head, but

spoke in a quiet tone. "Remember the Hobie Cat we used to have?" she said.

"Tequila Sunrise," I said.

"Yep," she said, turning to stare at me. Her eyes had softened, which confused me. From stone killer to the old Paris. Just like that. "I wanted the blue one and you wanted the red sail. You won."

"We had a lot of fun with that boat," I said.

"We did," she said, nodding. "Wonder how many Hobies we can buy with all that money?"

"One apiece, for sure," I said, wondering where this was going. "You can get your blue one and I'll get another Tequila Sunrise."

"Do you suppose that will make us happy?" she said. She turned back away from me, staring out at the disappearing catamaran. I didn't know how to answer that. And, for some reason, the question made me almost feel like crying.

Out of the funk I was in, I heard her say, "You're wondering about me, aren't you Jake? You're wondering about this person you thought you knew. Well, there's a reason."

Chapter 29

It was that preeclampsia thing.

"It made me realize there was a human being inside me."

Well...*duh*...I started to say, then thought better of it.

"I knew that," she said, touching her forehead with her finger, "...up *here*...But I didn't know it here." She pointed the same finger at her chest. "Now I know he's a real person. And I'm responsible for him."

"You mean," I said, "*we're* responsible for him."

She hesitated, averting her eyes for a second, then brought her eyes back up to mine. Somehow, something happened in that instant that felt wrong. I sensed a circle that excluded me in an important way. I shrugged, shook my head to clear the feeling. It was just the pregnancy, I told myself. She put her arm around me and squeezed.

"So. What are we going to do?" she asked. She disengaged and sat back.

"You mean..." I hesitated. "...the baby?"

"No," she said, a slight smile on her lips. "I know what to do about the baby. I'll handle that shortly. No, I was talking about the immediate problem. *Problems*. That body out there. Your friend Walker Joy. How are we going to take care of him?"

"Walker..."

"You have to admit that would solve a lot of this," she was saying. She lowered her head and stared at the floor for a long moment and then raised her eyes to mine. "It would solve most of it."

Exactly what I'd been considering myself, but that was *me,* the ex-con considering that, not my wife, the woman who worked in an insurance office and believed in aliens and something called "positive life forces."

"Maybe we could just run away," she was saying.

"What would that do?" I asked, our debate roles somehow becoming switched. "Besides, no one's looking for me yet and chances are they won't be. It's a stretch, but Walker may not get caught his own self and if he isn't, then we're in the clear."

"How big a stretch is that, truthfully?" she said.

I didn't know how big a lie I could get away with here and in the end figured it wasn't worth it.

"Almost nil. If I was betting on him to not get caught… well, I wouldn't bet."

She sighed out loud. "That's what I thought. I haven't known him but less than an hour and I see nothing but a loser."

"He's got his good points." Then, "Yeah." I sighed the same as she had.

We sat there in silence for a few minutes.

"How're you going to do it?" she repeated her earlier question. The quiet had gone on so long, I jumped slightly at her voice.

It appeared that Paris had joined the avalanche…

Something came over me. From where, I don't know. All I know is that somehow the whole miserable mess just crawled away and vanished, way back in the blackest part of the cave that was my mind, and even though I didn't say the words or pray the prayer, I knew I'd just made an unholy pact for my soul. It was a deal that didn't require words, only an understanding that transcended mere language.

For my family. My wife and son. Why I kept thinking it

was a boy, I don't know, but I knew what was inside her was a male. Paris herself had said "he." Women knew.

"Here's what we're going to do," I said.

My mind was clear for perhaps the first time since Walker Joy had come back into my life.

"Go home, call the funeral home and get things done for Bobby. When you finish that, I want you to call a guy named Jimmy Barnes. He's in the phone book. Lives on Colfax. Call him up, tell him you're my wife and that I want a .45. Only don't say that. Say I want one of his *products*. He'll know what you mean. He may want to call you back from a different phone. He probably will."

She looked puzzled, so I explained.

"Jimmy's an old friend. Deals in guns. His phone may be tapped."

She nodded again, her face pale.

"A .45. With a clip. You with me so far?"

"Do you think you can actually do it, Jake?" she said. "Kill him?"

"I have to. It's him or us."

"Okay, then," she said, after peering into my eyes intently for a long second. Then, again, nodding thoughtfully, as if satisfied with what she saw there, "Okay."

"Get going," I said. "You've got a lot to do and not much time. Try to be back here by seven. It gets dark by six, six-thirty."

"I'll try," she said.

The only clue that she was shaken was the slight tremble I felt in her lip when she kissed me on the cheek before left.

Just before she went outside, she paused at the door and looked back.

"What do you really think will happen, Jake?"

I stared at her.

"I'll kill him or something else will happen."

"What?"

I didn't answer her and after a few seconds, she shook her head, tossing her hair. She got up and walked to the door and stood there, her hand on the knob, watching me.

"Bye," she said finally, going out and quietly closing the door behind her.

Chapter 30

I went upstairs, took a quick shower. In the kitchen, I poured out the coffee Paris had made and started a new pot brewing. I plugged in Gloria's little portable TV on the counter and turned it to one of the South Bend channels, 22, hoping to catch the news when it came on. The picture was fuzzy and kept rolling, but that didn't matter. All I needed was the sound, in case something came on about a break-in up in Niles. Or a missing person, one who just happened to work at that same place.

The noon news segment came on, but no mention of either of those two events. That didn't mean a lot, I guessed. Maybe the cops weren't reporting it. The break-in, by itself, wouldn't rate a mention. Something like that would be lucky to get a couple of paragraphs in the paper, much less anything on TV, but tie in the woman's disappearance and that's a story. Either no connection between the two had been made, or if it had, the cops weren't letting anyone in on it.

I switched off the set, turned on the radio to some oldies station instead.

Half an hour later, Walker Joy came walking in the door, a cheesy grin splitting his face. A guilty grin, by my estimation. I'd bet the farm he'd set up something with the Chicago fence. Probably for tomorrow.

"I got everything, buddy," he said. "Hey, where's your wife's car? She go someplace?"

"You had a few drinks too, didn't you?" The smell of cheap whiskey permeated the room. "How drunk are you?"

"Not near enough. Hey. Lighten up, pard. I don't need a dad, fucker." He laughed, craned his neck, looking into the living room. "Your wife's gone, huh? Where to?" I could see he was trying to act casual about the question, but that underneath, he was tense.

"She'll be back," I said. "She went home to take care of Bobby's funeral. She'll be back tonight, help us bury the body."

"Yeah," he said. "That body."

He was silent for a moment and then he said, "So. What you gonna do about her?"

What was he talking about? The dead woman?

"Her?"

"Your wife. What's-her-name? Patsy? Paris. Yeah, Paris. Funny name."

"Whaddya mean, what am I going to do with her?"

"Just that, ol' buddy. She's a civilian, Jake. You know what that means."

"No, what does it mean? You tell me."

"Christ." He plopped down in one of the kitchen chairs and took out his cigarettes and lit one up. He squinted up at me through curling smoke, and said, "You've been on the bricks too long, Jake. Maybe you've become too straight your own self."

"You think she'll talk. That it? Turn us in?"

He smirked. "Something like that. Uh, duh, homeboy. Get your head right."

I'd figured the guy right. I wasn't going to let him do this easy, though. Make him squirm a bit, trying to tell me. That the smart thing to do was get rid of my wife.

He didn't squirm all that much. He seemed almost happy about the idea.

"Hey, Jake, she's kinda cute and all that, but man! You're

talking about your freedom here, dude. Ain't no pussy ever lived worth doing time for. Is there?"

Not in his world there wasn't.

"Don't tell me you think she'll keep her mouth shut," he continued. "Hell, for all we know, she's talking to the cops right this minute. Maybe not, but how long you think she's going to go along with this?"

"How do I explain her disappearance?" I said.

He snorted. "You don't. You and me, we'll be sitting on some beach in Rio. You'll be knee-deep in broads then. Won't barely remember this one."

"Then why kill her? That's what you're talking about, right? Killing her?"

"Well, yeah."

"Why not just go, leave her? If I don't tell her where we're going, then she can't very well tell the cops anything, can she?"

"Well, maybe," he said, trying to sort out his argument. "But it takes time to do all this. Sell the stones, get fake passports, all of that crap."

I was halfway enjoying this.

"Tell me, Sundance, you know how to go about getting a fake passport? You been on the lam to Bolivia before? Which reminds me—you keep talking about Rio, places like that. How do you know which countries don't have extradition treaties with us? I've got a sneaking suspicion you don't have a clue. How're you going to find out? Call up the State Department, ask 'em? Say, 'Hi there, Mr. Government Man. Can you tell me what countries a guy can get his sorry butt to that won't send him back for a murder charge? Hypothetically speaking, of course.'"

His face turned sullen. "I ain't never got no damn passport, if that's what you mean. But, there's ways. There's guys you can call. I know a guy can get 'em for us, I think. He'll know the best places to go, too."

I laughed. "Walker, I bet you a dollar the farthest you get is Las Vegas or some beach in Florida." I had another bet I didn't share with him. That his plan wasn't just to kill Paris but me as well. Too bad I didn't know a bookie would take that kind of wager. That'd be easy money.

Three bodies in the same grave. That was Walker Joy's vision, sure as birds fly south in the winter and junkies rob their mothers.

Outside, just then, it began sleeting. Ice began pelting the kitchen windows with a fury.

I changed the subject.

"Getting colder," I said, gesturing toward the window. "Did you get a pickaxe? That ground's going to be like a brick."

"Yeah," he mumbled, still pissed at what I'd said. "I'm not a complete moron, you know."

"Well," I said, "I did give you a list, didn't I?"

"So? I knew what to get anyway. You didn't put no flash-lights on your list though, did you? How you figure we was gonna see? Lemme ask you that, smart guy."

"Bet you bought one, didn't you?"

"Two."

We sat there in silence after that, Walker smoking and glowering, and me just staring out the window. That sleet was really coming now. Which made me think about Paris. She wasn't the best driver in the world and the way this stuff was coming down, the roads must be pure ice. Maybe South Bend wasn't getting what we were.

"Okay," I said, finally, breaking the silence. "What're we fighting for? You're right. There ain't no pussy in the world worth going to the joint for. How you think we should do it?"

That was all it took for him to brighten up, bring a smile to his ugly kisser.

"That's my boy!" he said, slapping his thigh as he said it. "We'll do it tonight. When we bury the broad. Roll 'em both in together. Hell, *I'll* do it, Jakey. I wouldn't expect you to. I know you love the broad. I understand that shit. We'll dig a hole and you say you got to take a piss. Walk off behind a tree, sumpin', and I'll take care of it. She won't feel a thing. I can make it painless."

He laid it out so quickly and easily it was evident he'd spent a lot of time working it out.

He was happy now. He figured he was home free. I could almost visualize the picture that was on his mind's Sony at that moment. Him, sitting on some beach in Rio, three-four Latin beauties in thongs rubbing suntan lotion onto his back with their tits. Him, superimposed on some scene he'd seen on the *E!* Entertainment Channel.

I was certain I wouldn't be anywhere in that scene.

"Hey," he said, standing up. "I got a bottle in the car. How 'bout it? Feel like gettin' shit-faced?"

The moron must have thought I needed to get drunk to go through with this.

"Sure," I said. "Go fetch it." Great idea, Walker. *Beautiful* idea. A man with his reflexes dulled by alcohol would be infinitely easier to handle, come time to do the deed. Plus, a Walker drunk was an even more obnoxious Walker than the sober version, which would make what I had to do somewhat easier to carry out.

He came back in with a fifth of Bushmills.

"Bushmills?" I said. "I thought you were a Wild Turkey man, Walker."

He giggled. "Before, I was. Fuck, Jake. We're *rich*, man. Get used to it."

He was halfway there to that beach in Rio, the poor, sad fuck.

Chapter 31

In less than two hours, Walker was rip-roaring drunk. A "put the lampshade on and act silly" quality of drunk. Funny, even though he was drinking top-drawer Bushmills, his voice still retained that Wild Turkey mush to it.

As for me, I'd pretended to toss 'em back with him, but had actually consumed less than the equivalent of a single stiff drink. He hadn't noticed I'd been barely putting any whiskey in with the ginger ale I was using as mix. I was proud of myself for my control. Maybe I wasn't the alcoholic I thought I was.

At the moment, he was rambling about something pretty much incoherent, some sort of word association thing going on in his booze-scrambled mind.

"...bitches that shave their pussies," he was saying. Something about the women we was going to be able to get as rich men. He'd already landed on Fantasy Island and was walking up toward the hotel with the midget.

And me...me, I was pretending to listen to him ramble on about all the great things we were do with our money, but inside I was dying. I was acutely aware of the time and of the fact that only hours remained before I was going to have to end the life of this man who sat across from me at my mother-in-law's kitchen table—a man who had once saved my life and without whose intervention at that time would have meant I wouldn't even be here or any place else at this moment. For all his stupidity and for all his own evil intentions, this was a man who had saved my life when I was helpless, and I was going to take his.

That was more than bothering me. It was caustic lye working on my gut.

At last, I couldn't stand the images in my imagination—seeing the scene that was to happen later on that night—so I had a drink. A serious drink.

Before I'd even drunk half the glass I'd filled with amber Bushmills, I knew I was making a mistake. The clear head I knew I'd have to maintain to carry this thing off wasn't going to be. At that point—glass raised to my lips, burning liquid trickling down my throat—I knew I was going to end up more soused than Walker could ever hope to get. I realized what I was doing and couldn't stop. I knew then what I'd always said I'd known but really hadn't. I was an alcoholic.

A really fucked-up alcoholic.

Like there were other kinds…

Before I knew it, it was going on six o'clock and we'd finished the bottle.

"We need a new soldier," Walker said, looking back and forth between me and the empty bottle sitting on the table as if he expected me to fetch us one.

"I'd go," I said. "But Paris should be getting back soon."

"Hell, then," he said. "I'll go. Although…"

He stopped and looked at me.

"Although what?"

"If you went and she happened to come while you were gone, I'd be happy to go ahead and take care of our problem."

"What problem?" I said, like a dunce, and then it hit me what he was saying.

I had to think fast.

"Nah," I said, trying to give my face and voice a nonchalance I certainly wasn't feeling. "If it has to be done, it's my job. It's my wife."

He nodded, seemingly satisfied by my logic.

"Yeah. Makes shense." He said it like that. *Shense.* "Do th' right thing, huh, bro?"

"Something like that," I mumbled back.

"You all right, homeboy," he said. He got up, walked around the table, stumbling a bit, and slapped me on the back. "My man."

He was totally fucked up. *I* was fucked up, but he was a total waste. Watching him had the effect of sobering me up a little. Now, a new worry arose. Was he physically capable of driving all the way into town and returning without wrecking the damn car?

I considered talking him into drinking some coffee, waiting a while before he went after another bottle, but rejected that, knowing it would be futile. Also, the thought occurred that maybe I'd get lucky. Maybe he would get in a wreck and kill himself. That'd solve a whole lot of problems.

Or create new ones.

Was life ever going to become simple again? I ached for the days when the biggest headache I faced was how I was going to fill the two-hour space my no-show perm client had left me with.

In the end, I did nothing. That was my big decision.

Walker lurched out the door and climbed in his car. I watched out the kitchen window and grimaced as he revved up the engine, over and over. I saw him struggle with the gearshift and then shoot out in reverse, slamming on the brakes in the middle of the road. There was a grinding of the gears, and then the car leaped forward and he was gone.

Going at least sixty down the narrow lake road.

Too late, I ran for the door. The money. He had the money and the diamonds with him. I hadn't realized he'd grabbed them off the table until he was moving away like Mario Andretti, and then it dawned on me what I'd seen him toss on the seat beside him when he climbed in the car. If he did get in a wreck, they'd find them. What would otherwise be a routine traffic accident would turn into something entirely different. FBI different, without a doubt.

He was already out of sight when I reached the road.

The oddest image crept up in my mind. My dying mother. My promise to her to "find God."

I almost wished I'd done what I'd promised her. Maybe then my prayers would've had a chance of being answered.

Fat chance.

Chapter 32

An hour went by.

Then another.

Half a dozen times, I started for the door, car keys in hand, thinking I'd go look for Walker. Each time, I changed my mind.

It was agony.

It was eight-thirty and still no Walker. No Paris, either. She wasn't due back for at least another couple of hours, maybe three, but I'd hoped she'd take care of our business early and return. It didn't look like that was going to happen.

Maybe I should have gone for the bottle instead of Walker. I just hadn't wanted to take the chance Paris would return early with me not there.

It looked like I couldn't make a single blessed move without it turning into a mistake.

I wanted a drink in the worst way.

I also had to take a bowel movement.

Diarrhea.

Always got diarrhea back in the old days, the hours before I knew I was going to pull a job. I'd forgotten that.

I barely made it to the downstairs bathroom which was just off the living room and sat down before it all let loose. I must have been really stressed. Doggie! I was just finishing flushing for the third and final time, when I heard the front door open and then close.

Walker.

Or was it Paris?

I called out, but no one answered.

I yanked up my shorts and pants and hurriedly zipped and buckled them and pushed open the door.

It wasn't Walker.

It wasn't Paris, either.

It was a woman, her back to me, standing in front of the couch where we'd put the body. Holding the blanket we'd thrown over the corpse in her hand. Even though her back was to me, she looked strangely familiar. I just couldn't make my mind tell me who it was. She slowly turned around.

It was Gloria Meecham.

Paris's mom.

Chapter 33

Gloria's eyes were as wide as they could get, and she kept reaching up with her free hand to grab a handful of her hair and pluck at it, let go, reach up again and do the same, over and over. Her usually well-coiffed hairdo was a mess already.

I guess I'd be agitated, too, I was in her shoes, walking into my house and finding a dead woman lying on my couch.

I was pretty much in first-degree shock myself.

She quit tearing at her hair and pulled the blanket she was holding close around herself, almost as if she was nude and was shielding her nakedness from me.

"I saw your car," she began. "I thought… you and Paris…"

Jesus.

I took a step toward her.

"Don't!" she said, her voice high-pitched, almost a shriek. She held up one hand, like a traffic cop. She still clutched the blanket with the other. "Stay!" she ordered, like I was a dog. "Where's Paris? Where's my daughter? What's going on here? Who's this?" With each question, her voice rose higher and higher and her eyes got even wider.

"Paris?"

At first, I didn't know why she was asking about Paris and then I realized she must have assumed we were here together.

"Paris is home," I said. "She's all right. Where's Jerrol?"

"He's in Canada. Fishing. He'll be here Wednesday."

This was bad. This was worse than bad.

"Who's this woman?" Her voice had lowered, but she hadn't lost her wide-eyed expression.

"Just somebody… who had an accident," I said. I was furiously trying to think of some kind of story to concoct to buy me time. Although… for what? No matter what I came up with, the truth would come out. What would happen when Paris returned?

I knew what would happen.

I knew what I had to do.

There was just no choice in the matter. All those thoughts about killing someone—could I do it, couldn't I?—just flew out the window. If I let her go, she'd call the police.

If I wasn't already decided, Gloria helped me out.

"This was no accident," she said. "This woman's throat has been cut." She stopped. "My God…" she began, as if realizing what she'd just said.

"I'm sorry," I said. I walked toward her.

"Jacob," she said. Just my name. And then, she began screaming. Only she didn't run or even try to. She just stood there screaming and screaming while I walked toward her. When I reached her, she stopped abruptly in the middle of a scream, slid down to her knees and shut her eyes tightly and began reciting a children's prayer. And hiccupping.

"Now I (hic) lay me down—"

Near the end, she made a feeble attempt to fight me, reaching up and slashing her nails across my face. She must have been nearly unconscious then though, as that was it, the extent of her struggle. It was easier than I would have thought.

Long after she was dead, I remained in the same position, my hands around her throat, pressing as hard as I could. Only when my arms began to cramp did I let go. She crumpled softly to the floor and I realized I'd been holding her up.

Mother of God, I thought. What have I done?

What I had to, I told myself. Only what I had to.

I folded my arms across my chest and bowed my head, twisting my torso from side to side. I wanted to cry but I couldn't. For some strange reason, I thought if I could only cry, it would be all right.

I stood like that for a few minutes more, swaying back and forth, my mind swimming. I took deep breaths and started to get dizzy and realized I was hyperventilating. I ran into the kitchen to the closet where I knew trash bags were kept, grabbed one up and began breathing into it, quick, hard breaths at first and then consciously, I made an effort to go slower. My breathing slowed down but my heart still pumped furiously. I could feel it in my ears. I felt a burning sensation and knew they were bright red. Somehow, I got myself under control and forced my brain to begin thinking about what I needed to do.

I walked back into the living room, over to where Gloria lay crumpled up in a tiny heap. I stood over her, staring at her, incongruously worrying that maybe she wasn't dead after all. I didn't think I could do it all again if she wasn't.

After long seconds of watching her face, not daring to blink in case I missed any movement or sign that she was still breathing, I was sure she was dead. I suppose I could have just reached down and felt for a pulse, but I didn't want to touch her skin.

My mind raced.

I couldn't let Paris find her mother.

I had to hide Gloria's body.

If I could just make her disappear, I'd be able to figure everything out. I just needed time.

I kept thinking about my own mother. I could see her, pointing an accusing finger at me, shaking it. Telling me I was going to Hell for sure, now. I'd committed the one unpardonable sin. The Bitch had slipped to second place on the list of bad things that could happen to me. Third. Maybe not even on the list now. For this, I could get the needle.

I heard someone groaning and started, thinking at first it was Gloria, and then realized the moan was coming from myself.

I pushed my mother-in-law and her accusing face away from me, and just like that, a half-formed plan came into my head.

I'd put Gloria in my trunk. Then, when we went to bury the Boxleiter woman later that night, I'd carry her body out and put it on top of her body. I didn't know how I was going to do that—keep Paris from seeing there was another body already in the trunk—but I'd cross that bridge when I came to it.

I went upstairs, grabbed the quilt off her parents' bed and took it downstairs and wrapped it around Gloria. That done, I ran to the kitchen and went outside to take a look around. There wasn't a soul in sight. It was just lucky it was the winter. All the nearest neighbors were "lakers" I remembered—folks who only came up in the summer. Even more luck—it had begun snowing again, thick, big, sloppy flakes—and I could see only a few feet in any direction. The closest house to Gloria's was almost completely shrouded by whiteness and none of the others were even visible. If any of the other neighbors across the road were home, I couldn't tell. Not even the few streetlights were able to penetrate the dense snowfall. If this kept up, we'd be buried out here.

It occurred to me that instead of cursing the weather, it might be more appropriate to give thanks. Nobody would be out driving around in this stuff, not even the cops. If Paris and Walker got back soon, we could get these bodies buried and out of here and no one would be the wiser. Any tracks we made would be covered up in five minutes, if this kept up.

I jumped in the car and quickly backed it up to the kitchen door, the tires spinning a bit. It was already hard to gain traction. After popping the trunk open, I ran back inside and hoisted Gloria's body up on my shoulder. She was a small woman, no more than 5'2" and didn't weigh much more than a hundred pounds, if that. I took another quick look outside, then opened the door and carried her the five feet or so to the car and bent over to lay her in, only she slipped from my arms and dropped into the trunk cavity. When she landed, the car bounced a tiny bit and the edge of the quilt came loose, exposing her face. In that instant, in the gloom of the falling snow, she looked exactly like Paris.

My heart stopped.

I reached down, pulled the quilt back over her face and slammed shut the trunk lid. Crying.

Fighting for control of my emotions, I forced myself to think about what I had to do next.

Her car!

I'd almost forgotten it.

That was stupid. There it was, the T-Bird they'd bought two years ago, canary yellow and sitting less than twenty feet away in the drive. I was so used to seeing it there when Paris and I had come down on weekends, I hadn't even thought about it.

Christ, what else was I overlooking?

I'd have to get rid of it.

Maybe I should put Gloria's body in her own car…

There was a house a block away I knew. The owner was an artist and worked in Chicago, designing jewelry. He only came down in the summer. Paris's folks were friends with the man, I knew, and had a key to his house. As a favor, they kept an eye on the place for him. Gloria would even go down and dust occasionally for the guy when they came up for a weekend when they were back in Indiana. I knew just where the key was. And, it was one of the few houses on the lake that had an attached garage. Most houses and cabins just had carports or breezeways. In fact…

In an instant, I knew what I'd do.

Half an hour later, it was done.

I'd found the guy's house key—it was right where it always was, even had his name, Bill Tyler on a round white disk—then driven down to his house in the Meecham's car and let myself in. The T-Bird handled better on the snow than my Lumina had. I'd unlocked the garage and drove the 'Bird inside, locked everything up and left.

I knew the artist wouldn't be visiting his place any time soon. Most likely, at least not until spring and maybe not even until early summer.

Way before that, I figured Jerrol would be calling our house up in South Bend, wondering where on earth his wife was, then come there, see what was going on, try to figure out where Gloria had disappeared to. Or why. My plan was, once that happened, I'd wait a few weeks, then place an anonymous call to the Warsaw police, tell them I had a tip for them. Look in this guy's garage, I'd tell them. They'd find the car there, but no body, and this guy would become the chief suspect. If I could get Gloria's body buried without Paris seeing me remove it from the car, I was home free. I thought that possible. I could see me taking the Boxleiter woman out to the trunk while Paris was in the house and then, once we got to the woods, I'd think of something to get her out of the way for a while so I could dump Gloria in the hole we planned to dig. I'd have her be the lookout while we dug the hole.

I'd have to let Walker in on that—at least some of it—and just play it all very carefully, so that I killed him before he spilled the beans. In fact, that would help convince him I was going to kill my wife. If he saw that I'd killed her mother, that would be easy.

And I needed a cover story for the scratches Gloria had made on my face. Walker could supply that—say he'd been drinking, we had a fight. I began making up something plausible for him to tell. I'd gotten him down, and he just reached up and scratched me and then he sobered up and we quit.

This was all going to work out.

It had to.

Back inside the cottage, I checked everywhere I thought Gloria might have been before I'd come down for any signs she'd been there. It was lucky I did.

I don't know how I missed it, but right there on the kitchen counter was her purse.

Jesus.

I'd almost overlooked it. Probably because I'd seen it there so many times in the past, it didn't even register.

I kept forcing the horror of what I'd done to the back of my mind.

I ran outside and opened the trunk and threw it in on top of Gloria's body.

Chapter 34

Five minutes after I'd returned to the house, I heard a car pull up.

Then another one.

Muffled voices outside.

I ran to the window, rubbed a circle in the frost and looked out. It was Walker and Paris. They must have pulled in together.

Fuck.

I walked over, yanked open the door just as they were reaching it. Even though they were maybe only ten feet away, the swirling snow so obscured them that if I hadn't recognized the colors of each of their coats—Paris's a bright red parka I'd gotten her last Christmas and Walker's blue jean jacket—I wouldn't have known who they were. The wind whipped the snow first one way and then another, as if it couldn't make up its mind the best way to go.

"Did you see that cat?" I yelled, sticking my head out and craning it all around, looking. Shouting, to make myself heard above the shrieking, vacillating gale. My voice seemed to bounce back at me.

"Cat?" Paris said.

"What the heck happened to your face, Jake?" Walker asked, walking behind her, both coming up to a couple of feet from me. They glanced around.

"A cat," I said. "Is he still out here?"

Paris came up close and reached up to touch my cheek and the scratches. "A cat did this? What cat?"

"Come on, get in here. We don't want to all be standing around out here, get the neighbor's attention." I held the door while they entered and began stamping their feet to rid themselves of the snow that clung to both like an extra outer garment. They removed their coats and put them on the coat rack beside the door. Paris crossed her arms and hugged herself, shivering.

I sat down at the table and the other two did likewise, Paris slipping into the chair next to me, her arms still wrapped snugly around herself, and Walker across the table, facing us.

"It was this big-ass, huge cat," I began. I tried to keep my face from betraying the lie I was making up on the fly. "I heard something upstairs—scared the shit out of me!—and I went up to investigate. Found this big ol' tomcat up in the bedroom, scratching to get out of the closet. Must have either been up there the whole time we were or else snuck in down the chimney or something."

"We get squirrels in here that way sometimes," Paris said.

"Yeah," I said, quick-like, elated she seemed to be buying into my little tale, even helping it along. "That's it. Must've crawled down the chimney, something. Anyway," I went on, surprised I could lie this effortlessly to her—I'd come a long way in a week!—"I got hold of him, picked him up and was just going to take him downstairs and dump him outside."

"That's when he nailed you?" Walker asked. He asked it in a bored tone, glancing around the kitchen, as if he was satisfied; let's get to what we got to do now.

"No," I said, feeling that even if he bought it, Paris still needed a bit more. "The dang cat was fine. I carried him downstairs and all the way to the door. It's when I opened the door to throw him out he attacked me."

"He didn't want to go out in the cold," Walker said.

"Yeah. You're right, I bet," I said. "Fucker didn't want to leave the warm house."

I looked at first Paris, then over at Walker, then back to Paris.

"You guys didn't see him outside then?"

Paris leaned over, placed her hand on my cheek and ran her fingers lightly down the length of the scratches. "That must have been some cat," she said. "His paw's as wide as my hand."

"Well," I said, stammering. "It was a big 'un… And… he scratched me a couple of times."

"That must be it," she said. "Otherwise, that was no house-cat. Mountain lion would be more like it. You sure it wasn't maybe a bear cub?"

"Fuck, Paris." I stood up, indignant. "You don't believe me, I'll go find the cat, show you."

"No," she said, sighing. "You say it was a cat, it was a cat. Just doesn't look like cat scratches is all. Maybe one of these days you'll tell me exactly what it was that scratched you. You didn't go into town while I was gone, by chance, did you?"

I didn't get what she was saying for a minute and then it hit me that she thought some woman had scratched me.

Which she had…

"Goddamn it, Paris! I said. "I've been right here the whole time! You think I could go off whoring at a time like this? Jesus! Get off that shit, willya!"

I walked over to the sink, turned the cold water on, leaned over and cupped my hand and drank, my back to the other two. Standing up, I twisted the water off and said, "You gonna keep this other woman shit up, Paris?" I made my voice as cold as I could.

"No," I heard her voice and thought I detected resignation in it. "It's not important. You say it was a cat, I believe you. Besides, we've got more important stuff to talk about."

I didn't push it. If she was going to let it lay, at least for the time being, then I was up for that. You make the sale, shut up. That's what they taught us in Dale Carnegie, that course I took in Pendleton. Even a half-ass sale like this.

"You're right," I said, coming back to the table, wiping my hand dry on my jeans.

"It's..." she held up her wrist, glanced at her watch. "... nine o'clock. Let's get this over with."

She meant bury the woman.

"Don'tcha wanna wait till midnight or something?" Walker said.

She turned his way.

"I don't think so, Mr. Joy. Midnight might look a little suspicious to any county mountie who comes by, sees the car. This early, we could be coon hunters, something legitimate. This is the season. Lots of the men around here are hunters. And, being as most of them are family men with jobs and all that and have to get up early for work, they don't hunt late. I suppose if they were criminals and got to sleep in till noon they would. Maybe that was your reasoning. If you're capable of reasoning, that is," she finished, brightly.

"Good thinking, honey," I said, hastily, to avoid the argument between the two I saw coming. "Besides, I just want to get this over with."

"Jake," Paris said, twisting around in her seat to face me. "You're becoming quite the diplomat, aren't you? Jake, the Peace-Keeper."

"Well, yeah," I said, defensively. "This isn't the time or place to be putting each other down."

"You're right," she said, her eyes softening. I wasn't expecting that.

She went on. "You're right, but not for the reason you think. You're right because I was about to let Mr. Joy here rent space in my head."

"That's perfect, honey," I said. "Good advice for all of us."

During our exchange, Walker just sat there, switching his gaze back and forth between us, a smirk on his kisser. I could read his mind. *Glad I'm not married...*

"Yeah, whatever," she said. "Anyway, it's agreed we need to do this now, right?"

I nodded and Walker said, "Yup. Good a time as any." He got up. "I'm gonna take a whiz. You guys get ready and let's go. Get this done. I got all the stuff in the car."

As soon as he left the room, I leaned over whispered to Paris, "You get it?"

She answered by opening her purse, which she'd kept on her lap, and reaching in and coming out with a standard Navy-issue .45. She handed it to me, gingerly, holding it by her thumb and forefinger. I took it from her, quick-jacked a shell into the chamber, checked the safety, and stuck it in the waistband of my trousers, pulling my shirt out and over it to hide it. She dug around in her purse and came out with two extra clips, which I took from her and slipped one in each of my front pockets. Three clips, including the one in the gun. I was ready for a war.

"Bobby?" I said.

"Thursday at one o'clock," she said. "Day after Christmas. Jacobson's Funeral Home in Mishawaka. You have to give them a list of pallbearers. Any speakers you want."

Pallbearers. Who the hell would I get? And when would I have time? I supposed I could make a call to Adams High School, talk to the counselor, find out who Bobby's best friends were. It struck me that I didn't have a clue who his buddies were, except maybe for the kid he'd got caught with stealing the car. With me, that'd make two criminals carrying his body to his final resting place.

I was glad Mom wasn't around to witness that.

I wished I wasn't.

The Bishop that should be lying in that casket wasn't. Christmas! Jesus! I hadn't even thought of that.

Chapter 35

"Paris," I whispered, urgently. An idea had come to me.

"What?" she said, leaning toward me, sharing my urgency. She glanced over her shoulder toward the direction of the bathroom where Walker Joy was.

"You're going to stay here while Walker and I go bury the body."

"Like hell!" she exclaimed, her voice a harsh whisper.

"Yes, you are," I said. "Something happens, we get caught, you go straight to jail." I looked pointedly at her stomach. "You and the baby. I don't want my child born in the joint, do you? Have it grow up in foster homes and institutions." I could see by the expression that came over her face that she was visualizing that and I knew I had her. I applied the clincher. "Besides, I don't want you to see what I need to do." I patted my own stomach where I'd put the gun, for emphasis.

"Oh," she said. She started to say something, then paused.

Before she could come up with a counter-argument, I said, "The problem is convincing Walker to leave you here. He thinks I'm going to kill you in the woods."

Her eyes got round. "He does?"

I told her the gist of the earlier conversation I'd had with Walker. "He wanted to kill you right away. Thinks you'll snitch. It's the only way I could keep him from it."

"I see," she said. "Tell me, Jake… did you consider it? Killing me? For just a second, maybe?"

I couldn't believe she'd think that. Which was exactly what I said to her.

"Well," she said, apparently satisfied. "That would solve a lot of problems, wouldn't it? You and Walker could sell the diamonds, split up the money and be on your merry way to some island in the Caribbean. No millstone of a wife around your neck. Think of all the babes you could have."

"Paris," I said. "Talk like that makes me think I should do what Walker thinks I'm going to do." I grinned to show her I was kidding. "Not the babes part, but the millstone part."

I heard the bathroom door open.

"Let me talk to Walker in private," I whispered. "Tell him I'm going to ex you when we get back."

"Think he'll buy that?" she said, and I didn't have time to answer her as he walked into the room.

I was positive he'd buy it. I had an ace card, Paris didn't know about. Her dead mother. That'd give me the excuse I needed for Walker.

He came over and sat down and Paris got up and excused herself.

"I'm going to take a bath," she said.

Walker looked at me, puzzled. "A bath?" he said. "Aren't you going with us?"

"Seems this is a guy thing," she said. "Jake'll explain." She left the room.

"I told her to stay here," I said, as soon as I heard her clump upstairs. "What I told her was I didn't want to take the chance we'd get stopped or something and she'd be nailed with us, go to prison for accessory to murder."

"Are you nuts, Jake? I thought we agreed you'd kill her. How you going to take her out now?"

I smiled, tried to look assured and like a man with a plan. "No problem. I'll do it when we get back. Later, tonight, while she's sleeping. I just don't think I could do it with her looking at me."

"Christ!" Walker said. "Fucking pussy. *I'll* do it." He stood up.

"Siddown," I said. "There's something else."

He did as I said, sat back down.

"There's already a body in the trunk," I said. His jaw dropped and he started to say something, but I held up my hand for him to keep quiet. I ran down what had happened earlier with Gloria. "I don't know if I can keep Paris from seeing her when we take out. She sees her mother out there, dead, what do you think's gonna happen?"

Before he could answer, I went on. "She's going to start screaming, is what's going to happen. You want that to happen? She sees her mom, starts screaming like a banshee, then what? I kill her, sure, but by now half the neighborhood is up, looking out their windows. Maybe somebody calls the cops. Maybe somebody comes out to see what's going on. See?"

I neglected to tell him that there probably weren't any neighbors, that the folks who lived around the cottage were all lakers who only came down in the summer. I was pretty sure he hadn't made that observation.

"Yeah," he said, slowly, thinking it over. "I see what you mean. Only why don't we just tell her we need her to go with us, be the lookout? Like you said before."

"Because. Because I just talked her into staying here. Because I don't think I can kill her with her looking at me. Jesus, Walker, this is the woman I married, you know! I love her, fucker. This is going to be hard enough, but I know right now the only way I can do it is when she's asleep."

I don't think he was totally convinced, but he gave up. Shrugged his shoulders, said, "Whatever," and we both stood up. "Let's do it, then," he said.

I got my jacket on and we went into the front room.

"You killed her goddamned mother?" he said, as if he'd just realized what I'd told him, trying to get his mind around it.

I nodded.

"Motherfucker!"

"Yeah," I said. "Exactly."

It took us less than five minutes to pick up Boxleiter's body and take it outside to the car. We laid it down on the ground while I fished for my keys. When I opened the trunk, Walker reached inside and threw back the quilt covering Gloria's body, exposing her face.

"Yo!" he said. "She looks just like your wife!"

I reached around him, flipped the quilt back over her face.

"Let's throw this one in," I said. "I don't want someone to look out their window, see us standing around gabbing with a dead body lying there in plain sight."

Walker grinned. "You got a point, homeboy. Let's load the truck, make our run."

About a mile from the woods I was headed to, Walker began to talk. Joint talk. We'd both been silent during the first leg of our trip, listening to the Warsaw oldies station. They'd just played Bobby Bare's "The Green, Green Grass of Home" a Pendleton favorite, and I knew from the way he got quiet he'd been thinking about the joint, same as I had while it played.

Not only had the song triggered memories of Pendleton, it had sent a shiver down my back. They'd played that song over and over on the prison radio station and more than one inmate had hung himself after listening to it on his earphones late at night. All that was needed to put me right back there in that cell again was the sound of the freight train going by at midnight like it did every night, blowing its whistle as it went by.

Jesus!

The good thing about hearing the song was it reminded me why I was going through all this. To escape the Bitch. To not end up back behind those walls for the rest of my life. Or…get the needle.

To not have to hear that goddamned song ever again.

I switched the radio off.

"Yeah," Walker murmured. "Some shit, huh?"

I didn't answer him.

Which didn't stop him from going on. "You know why I helped you out that time back in J-Block?" Walker began.

He was talking about Toles.

"Cause you're a good guy?"

He turned his face sideways to glance at me and he wasn't smiling.

"Maybe," he said. "You don't think much of me, do you, Jake?"

How the fuck could I reply to that?

"Don't answer that," he said, saving me from lying. "I know you don't."

I started to protest, but he waved his hand.

"Save it, Jake. You and I both know you don't. I think maybe you did before I dragged you into this thing, but it's pretty obvious you don't now."

Again, I started to say something, but he didn't let me.

"That's okay, homeboy. I understand. I understand a lot more than you know. I want to tell you why I saved your ass."

He didn't mention the secret we carried between us. I guess he didn't think of it.

We were at the woods. I pulled down the narrow dirt lane that led partway into it about the equivalent of a city block before it ended in a clearing where I killed the engine and turned off the lights.

"Here," I said. "Over by those little mounds is where I figured we'd bury 'em." Just in front of us, beyond a line of poplars, were the hills I referred to, covered with freshly-fallen snow and looking like a woman's breasts.

Walker grabbed the pickaxe he'd thrown on the back seat and I picked up one of the two shovels there, and we walked over to the spot I had in mind. "How 'bout there?" I said. I gestured where I figured we should dig, and Walker grunted in agreement. He began tearing up chunks of the frozen earth, laying out the outline of a rough rectangle about six feet long and maybe three feet wide, and I followed behind digging, throwing shovelfuls of dirt over to one side. The ground was surprisingly soft for the season. The rain the day before must have defrosted it, as there were only a couple of inches of hard earth before the digging got easy.

As we worked, Walker continued to talk.

"Loyalty, bud."

"What?" I said, forgetting what he was talking about.

"Why I saved your butt, braced Toles that time."

"That never made sense," I said. I was getting somewhat tired of his bringing that stuff up all the time. "You barely knew me then. I appreciate it, but—"

"We were both from South Bend," he said. "Homeboys."

I didn't like the way this conversation was going. The last thing I wanted was to be reminded about how he'd saved my life. Not when in a few minutes I had in mind to shoot him and dump his body in with the other two.

"That's stupid," I said. He stopped chopping at the sod at that. He laid his pickaxe down to the side and dug around under his jacket in his shirt pocket and pulled out a pack of Camels and got one out and fired it up. I shrugged and went on digging. He'd just about finished the outline of the grave anyway.

He squatted on his haunches, smoking, his cigarette dangling from his lips, hands in his jacket pockets. I could see the derision in his eyes as he squinted at me through the smoke. Fuck it, I thought. I concentrated on digging.

"Stupid, huh?" He sucked down a lungful and began hacking. I just kept digging. A second after he was done with his coughing spell, I saw the flare of a lighter out of the corner of my eye and knew he was firing up another one.

"You didn't think it was stupid then, didja?"

So what? Of course, I didn't. The guy, Toles, had just told me during chow—he walked over, with his tray in hand, leaned over where I was sitting, eating, said he was making me his "boy", that I better get ready for a visit during the rec period.

What I'd done, what I was regretting now, was I went up to Walker when we got back in the cell house that night. I scarcely knew him—had seen him around, back in South Bend, but we weren't buddies or anything—but I knew he could get me what I wanted. A weapon.

"I need a shank," I'd said, remembering.

"Sure," he'd replied. "Who sold you a wolf ticket, bro?"

No harm in telling him, I figured, so I did. I guess if I was honest about it, I might have had a hope or two that he'd do just what he ended up doing. I knew he had a rep, guys respected him. Or feared him. Same thing. I told him what the guy had said and he just laughed, said "point him out" and I did. When we got let out for recreation, I saw Toles making a beeline toward me on the tier walk, and I nodded my head toward him and said to Walker, who'd come out of his own cell, three doors down, "That's the guy."

What happened next was amazing. Walker intercepted the guy just as he was coming up, and so fast I missed it he had the guy hanging over the railing, holding onto one of his legs. Dangling over the edge, third tier up, the guy started crying. Pissed his pants. Had piss running off the end of his nose. A hack started around the corner, saw what was going on, and made a one-eighty, turned and disappeared back around the corner. Toles was begging Walker to let him up, crying like a baby.

"I oughta drop your ass," Walker said, grinning like he was having the best time.

He didn't though. It might have turned out better if he had. I probably wouldn't be in the mess I was in now if he'd just let go. What happened, though, was he let him up after a bit, made him look at me and swear to leave me alone.

That should have been the end of it, but it wasn't. Time went by, as it does, and about six months later, Toles came up to me again and said one word. "Tonight."

I knew what he meant by that.

I also knew I couldn't depend on Walker to bail me out this time. Once, yeah, but not again. He saved my ass again, I'd have to become his kid. Law of the joint. I was on my own.

"Fuck you, Toles. Not tonight. Tomorrow. Meet me during noon chow up on the laundry roof."

That's when I stabbed him. He'd brought his own shank, but I was faster. Luckier, too. I got him first in the throat and he went down, just like that. I stabbed him with a straightened-out laundry pin so many times I couldn't lift my arm any more. I switched hands and nailed him four or five times more and then rolled off the guy, thinking he was dead for sure and left.

They found him a few hours later after he didn't show up for a check at his work station, the machine shop, and they shut us all down while they searched for him, made us all go in our cells in a general lockdown.

He wasn't dead.

I couldn't believe it. Turned out, he had thirty-some holes in him and he was still alive! A regular fucking vampire.

They took him to a hospital in Indianapolis and three months later I got the word that he was back.

Working at the library.

That's when I took care of him, once and for all. That was the secret Walker and I shared. No matter how you cut it, it wasn't self-defense that last time. That was pure murder, all the way.

My reverie ended when I became aware of Walker shouting at me.

"What?" I said, looking up. I was at least three feet lower than where he stood on the edge of the pit I'd been digging. I looked around me, amazed. I hadn't realized I'd dug that much. I shook my head to clear the memory cobwebs, spoke to Walker. "Keep it down, fucker. You want somebody to hear us?"

"Ain't nobody gonna hear us, Jake."

He was right. It had started to snow again—something else I hadn't noticed—and it was snowing as hard if not harder than it had earlier. You could probably yell your lungs out and couldn't be heard more than ten-twenty feet away. It was like the whole world was snow, coming down so thickly there was barely any space between the flakes. And the flakes! Huge, looked like clumps of snow falling instead of flakes. This kept up, it'd be a worse storm than the one in '78.

"What is it?" I said, realizing we could talk in a normal voice or even shout as Walker had done and no one could possibly hear.

"That's deep enough, ain't it?" he shouted.

For two bodies maybe. Not three.

"No," I said. "Lots of dogs run in these woods. We need to bury 'em deep so they can't smell them."

"Yeah," he said. "You're probably right."

He sat down on the edge, feet dangling over the side and gave a little hop and was down in the hole with me.

"Take a break, Jake," he said, thrusting his shovel into the ground and turning a spadeful that he tossed up on the bank.

I hoisted myself up and sat in the spot he'd just sat in

and lit a cigarette. I could feel the damp seeping up from the ground into my trousers and discovered if I kept still it wasn't that cold.

"You know what, Jake?" Walker said, grunting as he shoveled.

"What?"

"I don't like people in them 12-step programs. I like 'em *before* they go."

I laughed.

"That a poke at me?"

He stopped his digging, leaned on his shovel and tilted his head sideways up at me.

"I got to admit you were more fun when you were drinking."

That was nuts.

"Walker, I was in the joint. How do you know what I was like when I was drinking?"

"You was a dry drunk," he said. "You might not have had any booze, but you had the mindset of a drinker. Now, you just changed. Big-time, partner. I think it's because you quit drinking."

"That doesn't make any sense. If you recall, I've been drinking lately."

"Yeah, but your heart ain't in it."

He was right there.

"Walker," I said. "You're an idiot." I laughed, to show I was kidding. "Your brain is about six over par. What's bad, is you're only on the second hole."

That got a smile from him. He shook his head and resumed his digging.

The hole was getting deep. He'd gotten it close to the standard six feet graves are supposed to be.

It was time.

I'd had my hands in my pockets and I brought them out and they were shaking. I stuck my left hand back in my pocket but kept my right hand—my shooting hand—out, placing it over my trousers where the gun was, feeling its shape.

"That's good," I said.

Walker nodded, bent his head and looked around him at his handiwork.

Now's when I should do it, I thought. Before he looks up. I didn't know if I could shoot him while he was looking at me.

He didn't look up, though. Just kept looking around at the dirt he was standing on. And began talking, his voice so low I had to strain to hear him. Almost like he was talking to himself, but what he said was directed to me.

"Why'd you marry that gal, Jake?" he said. "She's not your type attall. She's gonna be the death of you, you know. She's bad news, brother. I seen that right away."

That made me mad.

"What the hell do you know about what my type is?" I said. "What the hell business is it of yours who I marry?" I suddenly felt better about what I had to do. Who the hell'd this cocksucker think he was, talking about Paris that way?

"Oh, she's a looker, all right," he said. He looked up at me for the first time since he'd begun talking. There was something different in his eyes, something I'd never seen there before. Sadness? That's what his eyes looked like. Sad. Mournful, like.

He was going on, flapping his yap. Let him go, I thought. More he talks, the easier this is going to be.

"Yeah, she's a looker. Kind of gal a guy'd give up a kidney to get in her pants. But you know what? I think you hooked up with her cause you were feeling all guilty and all about being in the joint. Started to think you wasn't a criminal but belonged in nice society, somethin'. You know what I think? I think you're like the hillbilly finds a tampon in the first girl he dates. Guy's like a Democrat gets a government benefit. He don't know yet there's a string attached to the thing."

I almost laughed.

"You're fulla shit, Joy," I said. "Paris isn't the first girl I dated, stupid. Fuck you and your nickel psyche."

"You missing the point, Jake. The point is, your old lady is the first of her kind you been up against."

"What kind is that?"

I hadn't been paying attention like I should have. I'd looked away and when I looked back, he had that little .25 out in his hand and pointed right at me.

"The kind that makes you do dumb things," he said. "Like that gun you got stuck in your pants there. You think I didn't see that?"

A wave of nausea passed over me. I fought it, tried to regain control.

"So what?" I said, trying to act defiant and not quite succeeding. "How you think I was gonna kill Paris?"

He snorted. "Last I heard, you was gonna smother her or something while she was asleep. Hey, Jake? Remember what we used't say back in the joint? Don't shuck a con?"

I suddenly noticed it wasn't snowing any more. I didn't know when it had stopped. While we'd been talking, I guessed. Kind of ironic, I thought. Kind of like the curtain going up on the last act.

My last act…

"Hop on down here with me," he said. I did what he ordered. We were face to face.

Chapter 36

"When were you gonna do it, Jakey?"

"About now," I replied, dully. "I should've speeded up the program, I guess." I'd lost. All that was left now was to go out like a man. Don't explain, don't complain. Take your medicine. In a way, this was all a relief. I'd be out of the whole sorry mess I'd created.

Except…

Paris. And our baby.

I realized what would happen once he killed me. He'd bury me and the others— getting us about half-covered before saying fuck it, thinking he'd be long-gone at some beach in Rio when they found us—and then he'd go back to the cottage and take care of my wife.

I knew then I'd have to make a play. I'd known that before, in an instinctive sense, but now I knew I had to succeed. Even though it was hopeless.

Keep him talking. Maybe something would come to me. Maybe he'd let his guard down long enough for me to draw my own weapon and fire.

Maybe pigs could really fly…

"You gonna kill your partner?" I said.

"Spencer's my partner," he said. He took one and then another step toward me, and his gun was twelve inches from my head, pointed directly at my nose. "Spencer's always been my partner, Jake. He's loyal. You're not. You figured every time Spencer sat down, I got a nosebleed, but that's not the way it is. He's been like a father to me. More'n my own father ever was. When I was a kid, I had a photo for a father. And it didn't even look like him. The only clear thing on Pappy's picture was his number. Something you need to know. I didn't make a mistake, telling Spencer about you. I did it on purpose. Why? 'Cause I like you, is why, you dumb fuck. I wanted you in on this job. *Me*, not Spencer. You were my best friend, Jake. It woulda worked out fine, too. 'Cept for that gal of yours."

It *was* sadness I'd seen in his eyes. I saw it clearly now, heard it in his voice.

"Goodbye, Jakey," he said. I couldn't help it. I didn't reach for my own gun, try to make a play, desperate or otherwise. I closed my eyes. It was over. I almost felt at peace.

Click.

That's what I heard. A sharp click. I opened my eyes, saw Walker's eyes widen, squeeze the trigger again, another click.

Misfire.

What went down next went down fast, but everything seemed in slow motion. He pulled the trigger a third time, same result, a *click*, and I reached in under my jacket, found the handle of the .45, started to pull it out from my belt, lost it in slippery fingers, found it again, pulled it out, thrust it forward, leaning with my body, jamming the barrel hard into Walker's stomach, tearing a gasp from him, and pulled the trigger, falling into the pit.

And heard a loud retort ringing in my own ear. From his gun. At almost the exact instant I fired my gun, Walker's had finally fired also as he fell back.

Everything after that was more or less a blur.

I'd been hit.

It didn't hurt at first.

I just slumped down on my haunches beside Walker's prone body, gulping down lungfuls of air. I thought I would start shaking—*wanted* to, as if somehow that would prove my remorse, but even though I trembled once or twice, that was it.

I concentrated on my body. I knew I'd been hit, but wasn't sure where at first. I knew I was in shock and just had to wait it out. And then, it began to ache and I knew where. My chest. Not my chest, exactly. My left pectoral. Walker would say, "my boob." I reached up under my jacket and shirt and felt with my fingers, starting a few inches away from where the pain was emanating—it was really starting to hurt now—and working my way slowly to the place the throbbing was coming from. All I could feel was roughness, and I realized my fingers were too dulled by the cold to feel accurately. As best I could tell, there was a general roughness, about the size of a quarter and a raised bump. It dawned on me that the lump I was feeling was the bullet. My shirt and jacket must have taken a lot of the force. I pressed harder on the spot and that seemed to relieve a bit of the pain for a second and then it returned, twice as bad, and I felt nauseous. I pulled my hand out and looked at it. In the brightness of the half-moon and the white snow, I could see clearly and feel the warm stickiness on my fingers.

Blood.

I sat there a minute, trying to clear my head, figure out what to do next. I struggled to stand, pushing up with my legs, using the bank to support my back. Once standing, I remained there a few moments, listening to the wind, which had decided to begin blowing. Little swirls of snow danced here and there, and it had turned decidedly colder in the last few minutes.

The wound didn't seem to be all that bad. It hurt like crazy, but I was getting used to it.

I sat back down. Looked at Walker lying there. Then he moved. Just a twitch.

"Walker?" I said.

He twitched again, moaned.

I bent to him. His eyes fluttered, opened.

"Guess you win, Jakey," he said, his voice barely audible. "Fucking cheap-ass gun."

In spite of everything, I smiled. I couldn't help it. It was just like Walker to make a joke at the worst time.

His eyes were clear, wide-open. He grinned back, albeit weakly.

"At least I'm gonna go out a free man," he said.

I knew what he meant. Back in Pendleton the one thing he'd always said he feared was dying in the joint, being buried in the pauper's field outside the walls.

"Yeah," I said. "That's good, right?"

He gulped down air, making a raspy sound. I reached down, lifted up his shirt. The blood had stopped except for a little bubbling from the hole in his stomach. It shone on his skin where it had splattered, and I realized it was blood mixed with perspiration.

"You bet your ass, it's good," he said, trying to raise his head and laugh at the same time. His head fell back and his eyes left mine to stare at the night sky. The snow had begun again, scattered flakes falling on his face and melting as soon as they touched his skin.

"Your secret…" he began, and then stopped to gather his energy. He looked at me again. "I never told Spencer. I never told anybody about that."

"I know. You told me already. And I believed you."

My secret…

That I'd killed Toles. Twice, in a way. The first time up on the laundry roof with the laundry pin and then, for good, in the library with the shank Spitball got me.

"I'd never do that, Jake. You're…my…partner."

"I…" What could I say? "I…appreciate that, Walker."

"Yeah," he wheezed. Then: "Jakey. I can't feel my legs. Or my arms."

My bullet must have hit his spine.

"Walker," I began. "I never told you my real secret. Nobody knows this."

I told Walker about the rape.

It's kind of funny, what goes on in a guy's mind when a razor blade is held to the tender skin of his throat and he is being fucked in the ass…against his express wishes. That an erect penis forcibly entering the anus is not unlike that of a proctologist's fingers. Or, in my more immediate experience, that of a prison guard conducting a body cavity search. Those were some of the thoughts that swept through my mind while I was being raped, early one morning in the South Bend city jail.

A kind of detachment separated my mind from my physical body as my butthole was being violated. Your mind remains oddly calm at moments like this, even though witnesses say later that you struggled frantically. Go figure. If only your body could travel to where your thoughts flew.

I didn't struggle frantically or otherwise while I was being raped. I held about as still as I could, what with a Gillette Blue Blade, melted with a match into a toothbrush, held just below my Adam's apple with enough pressure that it slightly pierced the skin. It wasn't a time for movement, not if I wanted to stay alive. Or so I thought. Later, I wondered if a razor blade could have really cut deep enough to kill me. Just one of the things you think about in hindsight that lends to your guilt at not resisting.

What I remember mostly after Toles left is climbing back up onto the top bunk and lying there, his jism oozing down between the inside of my legs, turning cold in the air. I didn't want to wipe it off. I didn't want my fingers touching it. It was bad enough that my legs had to. There was a sink out in the bullpen but I couldn't make myself go use it. I was convinced everyone in the cells lining the bullpen had heard what happened, were laughing at me, even though only the usual snoring and sleep-twitching sounds came from my fellow criminals in the other cells.

I lay there on the bunk, on my side, my face to the wall, not even pulling my blanket over me. The only way I could deal with what had happened was to reduce it in my mind to solely a physical level. The emotional part, I shoved aside, pushed way back in my mind, kept it there until the present moment, some four decades later. That night, I compared what happened to a proctologist probing me with a gloved finger. Doctor Happy Hand. This is all it was, I thought, amazed. It wasn't that bad. I wasn't bleeding, at least I didn't think I was. The pain wasn't that great. It hurts worse to get hit in the mouth, sometimes. Of course, a poke in the chops doesn't carry nearly the same stigma.

While he was raping me, I remember being surprised. He wasn't that big. Much smaller than I was. Weren't black guys supposed to be hung? Somehow, that knowledge gave me a bit of perverse pride, helped me endure what was going on. Ego had been at the center of everything in my life; no reason to expect it to disappear in a little crisis like this.

Weird stuff went through my head during the rape. I worried I would like it and if that would make me a homosexual. I worried I would end up so traumatized I could never go to bed with a woman again. Either one was bad.

The way it started, I told Walker, was earlier that previous afternoon two black men approached me as I sat at one of the two picnic tables set up in the bullpen. Around the bullpen, which was just a big, square open space, were cells on two sides, the concrete wall of the building at the back, and open bars and the one entrance at the front. The cells contained two beds, one above the other, and they swung down on steel bands from the wall. There were doors on the cells but they were never locked. One or two men were in each cell, depending on the current population. This particular area of the jail was for those already convicted of their crimes and awaiting transportation to either Pendleton or the Michigan City Prison.

"Hey, man, 'sup?" asked the smaller of the two, the one I later learned was named Toles. The other, a huge, blue-black hued man named Cleaves, didn't say much. It never crossed my mind that I was being set up. I hadn't had that much experience at that time with what went on in the joint, and the rumors I'd heard were sketchy. Rape just never entered my mind.

We started playing cards and I started smoking the squares Toles offered. Now I know you don't accept gifts in jail, but this was before I got to Pendleton.

I had a lot to learn. Mr. Toles was about to "educate" me…

Lights went out at ten and I rolled over on my side, face to the wall. I was just about to go to sleep, when all of a sudden somebody grabbed my hair and I felt something sharp at my throat. It was Toles.

"Get on down, white boy," he whispered, and I didn't know what else to do but "get on down." He walked me over to the side of the cell, against the wall, and when we got there, he reached around and undid my belt, unzipped my pants and pulled them and my underwear down to my ankles. Naturally, he kept the razor at my throat during all of this.

What I remember most was thinking what my father would do if this had happened to him. My father was the most powerful man in the world to me. Is today, too, I guess, even though he's been dead twenty years. He never took shit from anyone in his life, except his mother-in-law, my grandma. I knew exactly what he would do if he ever found himself in the same situation I was in. "Cut my throat, punk," is what he would have said. "You better kill me, though, or I'll kill you." More probably, he wouldn't have said a word, would've just turned and broke the guy's neck. Even more probably, he would never have been selected for rape. He carried himself in such a way that I can't imagine something like this ever happening to him. This is exactly what I thought about the whole time Toles was raping me. What my dad would have done. Thinking I would never be the man my father was. I just didn't have it in me. I was too afraid of dying. I was weaker than my dad and that was the worst part of the whole deal, knowing that.

Other things go through your mind. Weird things. I was looking at the wall before me while Toles was penetrating me and wondering when the coat of gray paint had been applied and by whom. Inmates? Outside contractor? I thought of people driving by on the street outside, totally unaware of what was going on just a few feet from them. A million things go on at once, a hurricane of ideas, but at the center I was calm. All during the act, I concentrated on the razor blade at my neck, thinking that when he came, he would be so focused that his hand would waver and I could turn and hit him. It never happened.

Instead, he was gone and I was standing there. I stood there a moment, just listening, hearing nothing but the sound of my own breath.

I didn't cry and I kept thinking I should, but I just couldn't. My mind was just numb. After a couple of minutes, I walked over to my bunk, the top one, and climbed up and lay down, facing the wall.

I lay like that for hours. I heard the first stirrings of prisoners, first the coughing, then the squeaks as men in the other cells swung their feet over the edges of their bunks, and then the plop of feet hitting the floor. Laughter, talking, the sounds of the one stool being flushed over and over, guys joking about different stuff, cursing. The guard coming around with the day-old rolls and the coffee in tin cups, and the men bitching about how stale the rolls were as they formed a line at the front bars where they shoved the food through the opening designed for that purpose. A little later, the sounds of cards being shuffled, guys walking by my cell in pairs, talking. All the while, I just lay there, not moving, and then I began to think about what had happened. I had kept my mind away from what had gone down, but I let it back in.

For some odd reason, I didn't get mad. I remember thinking that I didn't deserve to get mad. After all, I had let Toles rape me and hadn't resisted in the least. By my nonaction, I had surrendered the right to anger. What rose up, in the place of vengeance, was a weird kind of resolve. Feeling that I had relinquished my manhood completely, and that surrender had rendered me dead in spirit, and I decided, without dwelling on it, that I was going to kill Toles. Somehow, I knew that was the only chance I had of recovering myself, although I also felt even if I succeeded in killing him, I would still be less of a man forever. But I had to do it. The emotional climate I found myself in was that of floating around something big and that I didn't dare think about it directly. It was like plunging into a quarry—you know the water will be freezing and since you've never dived into that particular body of water, you could easily break your neck on something submerged and out of sight, a rock, perhaps, so you don't think about it, you just do it and you have to do it head-first, never feet-first.

And that's what I did. I walked out, saw a mop standing in the corner in the back, and walked over and picked it up. Toles and Cleaves were sitting at the table at the front and I walked toward them with the mop. Just before I came up to them, I stopped, put the mop on the floor and put my foot on it, breaking off the mop head. I walked on up to the two and instead of going after Toles, I went after Cleaves, the bigger of the two. I cracked him across the face with the handle, coming from left to right and then came back the other way. I nailed him good. Blood flew from his nose the first time and then the side of his head on the second blow and he dropped on the floor, a surprised look on his dull, churlish face. Toles just sat there, no doubt stunned by the suddenness and ferocity of my attack. I hit him next, a glancing blow alongside his ear and he stood up, rage in his face, and I took the handle and thrust it as hard as I could into his Adam's apple, like a spear. Cleaves was trying to get up, reaching for the edge of the table, when I hit him again. I went back and forth, just swinging methodically at both men like it was a job of work, and then there were three guards who came in the bullpen and grabbed me. Toles and Cleaves both lay on the floor, Toles silent but not knocked out, looking up with hatred in his eyes, and Cleaves sat there, legs splayed out in front of him, blood streaming from where I'd caught him across the front hairline and from his nose, just looking up at me like some cow that had been pole axed.

The thing was, I felt nothing. Completely dead, devoid of all emotion. It was like it was some job, a piece of work I had to do was all.

The guards didn't even ask me what had happened. They hustled me upstairs to a cell they used for solitary and pushed me in. I lay there all day. Nobody came by, not even to deliver a meal. Finally, about six o'clock, a guard came up and told me to come with him. He took me downstairs to another bullpen and told me to take a shower. I did and he tossed me a pair of orange coveralls and another guard came in with a tray of scrambled eggs and toast, which I sat and ate at one of the tables. The first guard sat across from me and didn't say anything. When I was done, he told me to grab one of the cells on the other side, and I went over and lay down and went to sleep almost immediately.

Three days later, I was transported to the Pendleton Reformatory. During those three days before I was led to the police bus to be driven to the joint, shackled by handcuffs and ankle chains, no one talked to me nor I to them. I ate my meals when they came and otherwise stayed in my cell except to go to the bathroom.

I concentrated very hard on not thinking about what had happened.

"That's why Toles fronted me the time I came to you for a weapon. That's the part you didn't know about," I said to Walker. "That I was raped. It's why I can't go back to the joint. Toles's brother is there. I saw him the day I got released. I go back…He's doing life. He told me what would happen if I ever ended up there again. He wouldn't kill me, he said. He told me what he'd do—what he and his partners would do—and he made it clear I'd wish he would kill me. You knew I killed Toles that day at the library. You just never knew the other. The rape part. Until now."

I waited for his response to everything I'd told him. He just lay there like he had the whole time I'd been talking. Then, I noticed his eyes. They were open…but they weren't seeing anything.

That's how my secret died. With Walker.

I sat there a little while longer, and I kept seeing Walker in the cell we shared back in Pendleton.

Kept remembering what it was like. Being scared every single minute of every single day. It didn't matter how big or how bad you were. Some guy wanted your booty it didn't matter. Even if it wasn't your brown eye they were after, a guy could just go off for no reason at all. I'd seen half a dozen guys shanked like that, for no good reason. An inmate just sat there in the corner, say, during recreation, all kinds of thoughts and memories building up inside him and then, wham! just like that, he'd be up and stick the first person he saw.

The fear didn't go away when they locked you down for the night, either. I remembered the first night out of quarantine, out in population, when a guy walked by my cell to the cell on my right and threw acid in that guy's face. A black guy. All night long he screamed and screamed like an animal, the screams turning to little whimpers toward dawn. The whole time, I could see the hack downstairs, just below our cells, sitting at his desk, his feet up, reading his *True Crimes* magazine. Hadn't looked up, not once all night. In the morning, when we came back from chow, the guy was gone. They'd hauled him over to a hospital in Indy. When he came back, his face was splotched the color of bubblegum and he'd lost one eye completely and was half-blind in the other.

No, it didn't matter where you were—if somebody wanted your ass they could get to it.

That was the biggest thing I remembered. The fear that never went away. That, and the noise. It never got quiet, not even in the middle of the night. Always—*always*—someone was sobbing for his mother, or someone was yelling at someone else, or someone was crying and pleading while some other inmate or *inmates* pounded his pink eye.

That's what Walker had done for me. He was the only one I'd ever been able to trust. Once we'd celled up, I was able to sleep most of the night. I knew he'd never go nuts on me. I could trust him.

And now I'd killed the only true friend I'd ever had.

If I got sent back I would be going to something worse than death. And no Walker to watch my back.

• • •

It took the better part of half an hour to lug the two bodies of the women up to the grave and shove them over the top. They landed, one on either side of Walker's form. The second one, the Boxleiter woman, was stinking to high heaven, but the odor kept my mind off my own pain for a few seconds. As cold as it was, I was sweating. Once they were in, I stood there a minute, thinking I ought to say a prayer or something and then decided any invocation I'd offer up God was only going to laugh at, or worse, get more pissed off at me than He probably was already.

I'd thrown four-five shovels of dirt on the bodies before I remembered something. I dropped the shovel and climbed down into the grave, wincing at the pain that generated in my chest. It felt like the flesh was being torn, but I realized that was unlikely. I brushed the dirt that had fallen on Walker away and rummaged through his jacket.

Bingo.

Both the packet of diamonds and some of the money were in his pockets. I knew where the rest of the money was. Back at the cottage, in his own car.

That was stupid, almost forgetting the diamonds like that. I knew I'd better get it together or I was going to keep making mistakes like that. Wouldn't that have been something! Go all through this and then end up without anything to show for it. True, I'd done everything out of loyalty—to protect others—first Walker, then Bobby, and now Paris—but to end up at this point with nothing besides a dead brother and a dead partner and a relationship forever altered with my wife and no money either?

Paris deserved more.

Hell, maybe *I* deserved more.

I found something else. Something good. A paper, folded in squares, with writing in Walker's hand. The name Bill Bradley, a phone number, and a Chicago address. I'd bet the farm it was the guy in Chicago that Walker delivered diamonds to for Spencer. The fence.

I wiped both guns down and threw them in with the bodies. Once the grave was filled in and tamped in, there was still a mound. I thought about leveling it off, but decided the spring melt-off would take care of that. Just before I heaped snow on the grave, I went back to the car and got the box of black pepper Walker'd bought and came back and sprinkled the whole can all over the dirt. That done, I heaped snow up over everything and took a last look around before plowing through the deep snow back to the car.

There was an anxious moment when I put the car into gear and the wheels spun without going anywhere, but I only had to rock it back and forth a time or two and I was free, back on the road and headed back to the cottage and Paris.

And the rest of our life together.

How was that going to be?

I tried not to think about it, just concentrate on what remained to be done.

Get rid of the diamonds.

Take care of Spencer. That part, at least, was going to be enjoyable. I had some ideas about how to do that.

I thought of something else. What was I going to do with Walker's car?

Chapter 37

The second I pulled into the driveway at the cottage, Paris shot out the door. She must've been watching from the window. She ran up to the car before I could get out.

"Is it done?" She peered past me at the passenger side. "You were gone forever!"

"Yes," I said. "It's done." I opened the door and she stood back to let me out.

"My God!" she said, her hand flying to her mouth. "You're hurt!"

She'd seen the blood or maybe the hole in my jacket.

"It's not bad," I said. Adding, "I don't think."

Once inside the house, I peeled off my jacket and shirt and Paris inspected the damage.

"You're right," she said. "It doesn't seem to be that bad. The bullet's still there though. I can just see a bit of it."

"It'll have to come out. I think that's how you get lead poisoning," I said and laughed, not knowing if that was true or not.

She nodded and went over to the silverware drawer and got out a small steak knife and brought it back over to the table where I was. She asked me for my lighter and clicked it on and held the tip of the knife over it. Blowing on it to cool it, she said, "Hang on. This may hurt."

It did.

I jumped the first time she slid the knifepoint in and

applied pressure but told her to go ahead, and this time I grit my teeth together and focused on a spot on the wall and she flicked it out, the hunk of lead shooting across the room and bouncing off the far wall. I yelled, roared, rather. The pain was so intense I thought I might pass out, but I shook my head violently back and forth and it began to subside.

"I'll never believe the movies again," I said. "Those ones where the guy takes a bullet and it's a foot inside him and they dig it out while he bites on a rag and takes a hit of rye and cracks jokes. This was only in an inch, inch and a half, and it about killed my ass."

"Hold still," she said. She picked up the bottle of vinegar she'd brought over and put on the table. Dumb me, I hadn't asked what it was for. I did now.

"You're going to make a salad?"

"No, silly. I'm going to sterilize your wound. Maybe you ought to believe the movies—you're doing the joke thing just fine."

"With *that*?"

"Well, alcohol would be better, but I think vinegar'll work."

"No, no," I said. "Use that." I reached over and grabbed the bottle of Bushmills sitting across from me on the table. "My body's used to this."

She grinned before she could help herself and instantly replaced it with a frown. "I think your body's a bit too used to whiskey, if you want my opinion."

I let the remark go. My renewed drinking wasn't the biggest problem I had just then. Besides, I'd only leaned off the wagon, I figured, not fallen completely off.

While she worked cleaning the wound and applying a bandage to it, I told her the details of what had gone down. Not *all* of the details, just the essentials.

"Now what?" she said, when I was done.

"Now we—*I*—go to Chicago, fence these diamonds. In the

morning." I told her about the name and address I'd found in Walker's pocket. "Then… Spencer."

She was silent for a while.

Finally, she stood up, began gathering up the scissors and bandages she'd brought out from the bathroom first aid kit. "I'm going with you to Chicago," she said.

I started to argue, then decided against it. I was just too tired. And hungry.

"What's to eat?" I said.

"Nothing," Paris said. "I'll run into town, get some stuff."

While she was gone on her errand, I decided to take a bath. I felt grimy all over, felt my skin tighten when I moved because of the dried perspiration my efforts back in the woods had brought. I got up and walked toward the stairway and was just about there when something caught my eye.

On the far end of the countertop by the sink, over in the corner. On top of the stack of cookbooks her mother kept there.

Something orange.

Something I'd missed, earlier.

Gloria's winter hat, a little cloth French beret she always wore.

Chapter 38

I grabbed the cap, stuck it into my pocket, cramming it down deep, and frantically rushed through the house, searching every inch of the downstairs for anything else Gloria might have taken off or laid down.

Nothing.

I sat down heavily on the bottom stair step and concentrated on all the possible scenarios. Paris couldn't have seen the beret. If she had, we'd be discussing that right this moment, although "discussing" probably wouldn't be an accurate way to describe that kind of scene. Although… maybe she had seen it and just thought it had been there all along, something her mom had left behind months ago. If that was the case, then if it came up missing…

For a second, I considered putting the beret back.

But what if she hadn't seen it?

Put it back or get rid of it?

The wrong decision and it was all over.

I decided to get rid of it. If she had seen it, I was cooked. Maybe not right that minute. After all, Gloria wasn't even "missing" yet. But, that fact would come out and fairly soon. I had no doubt Jerrol would be calling in the next day or so—maybe he'd already left a message on the phone at home—and might even show up. Once that happened, once Paris knew her mother was supposed to be there and hadn't shown up, it wouldn't take her six seconds to put two and two together and figure out she'd been at the cottage. And that I would have had to have been there since I hadn't said anything about going out.

On the other hand, if she hadn't seen it, that whole scenario was moot. Besides, even if she had seen it and it turned up missing, arousing her suspicions and confirming them once she learned her mother was to have come here, if I got rid of the cap then there was no proof linking me to her, except through Paris's story. If the cap was nowhere to be found, it'd be that much harder to connect me to her disappearance, even if Paris testified as to what she knew about it.

I felt my neck muscles tighten up and the beginning of what I could tell already was going to be the granddaddy of all headaches over all this. A week ago, I'd been stewing about the first lie I'd ever deliberately told my wife. Our relationship had undergone a sea change since that day. Sea change! It was a fucking tidal wave!

I had to protect my wife from learning the truth. That I'd murdered her mother. Not only Paris, but our son or daughter. That was the worst thing I could imagine. That our baby would someday be told I'd killed his or her grandmother.

I had to get rid of the cap. Without the cap, even if the worst came to pass, without the physical evidence of the beret, there would still be a reasonable doubt in Paris's mind. With it, there would be none.

But where?

I racked my mind for possibilities. I couldn't just throw it in the trash. In fact, I couldn't hide it anywhere on the premises. If Paris went to the police—and I was positive she would if she thought I'd done something to her mother—they'd turn this place inside-out. I thought about burning it, but Paris would be back in minutes and she'd smell the smoke and I'd have to concoct some wild story about that and right now I didn't feel capable of dreaming up a plausible lie.

No, I'd just have to keep it hidden from Paris until we were away from the house and then, at some opportune moment, dispose of it.

I knew.

When we left for home in the morning, I'd pull over at some rest stop and get rid of it there. Go to the restroom and just throw it in the trash.

The only thing I had to do between now and then was keep her from finding it.

I got up from the stair step to look for a hiding place and headed upstairs.

Halfway up, I heard the front door open.

The instant I heard the noise, I remembered I hadn't locked it.

Chapter 39

I knew it couldn't be Paris. She'd just left, maybe ten or fifteen minutes ago. Not nearly enough time to go into town and back.

But who? Cops? Were they onto me already? By now, they'd know Calvin had been robbed and that the Boxleiter woman was missing. They would have dusted for prints and knew that Walker Joy had been involved. By this time, they'd know everything about him. Including who his cellmate had been.

The notorious burglar, Jacob Bishop…

I was such a dumb ass! I'd thrown both my .45 and Walker's gun into the grave with the bodies.

Although…

If it was the cops, they would have just barged in. It wouldn't be a lone policeman, but the SWAT team, half the county mounties.

This was just one guy. I could tell from the way he was moving around in the kitchen.

Walking toward where I was on the stairs.

Heels clicking on the linoleum.

Clicking? Heels?

"Honey?"

It was Paris.

I stepped down just as she got to the stairway. Self-consciously, I pressed my hand against the outside of my pocket, flattening as much as I could the cap I'd put there.

"I almost nailed you," I said. "I didn't know who it was. Cops, maybe."

She frowned, a look of distress coming over her face. "I'm sorry, babe. But… if it was the police, would they walk in just like that?"

I didn't want to admit I'd come to the same rationale, but not as quickly as she had.

"Maybe," I said. "Anyway, what're you doing here? You haven't been to town already?"

"No," she replied, taking off her mittens and stuffing them into her coat pockets. "I was almost there when I thought of something. Two things."

"What?"

"Well, one, I realized I only had a five on me. I need gas, too. I could have used a credit card, but then I thought of something else."

"Which was?"

"Which was, why on earth are we staying here tonight? There's nothing more to do here, is there?"

She was right.

"So, I thought I'd come back and see if maybe you didn't want to just go home tonight. Now. We can stop and eat on the way. Sleep in our own bed tonight. Unless you're too tired…"

"Makes sense," I said. "I'm whipped, but you're right. There's no percentage in staying here. The longer we stay here, the more chance we have of attracting notice. It'll be nice to be in our house."

She brightened. "Good. That's what I thought, too. Besides, I forgot to tell you. My mom and dad are coming up."

"They are?"

I didn't have to feign surprise. I wasn't surprised that her folks were coming—not hardly!—but I was startled to hear that she knew they were.

"How'd you—"

"Dad called. Right before I left to come down here. He was still in Florida, but he said Mom was driving up."

She must have seen the look of consternation on my face.

"Oh, don't worry," she said, quickly. "She won't be here till day after tomorrow. Dad said she's going to visit a friend in Indianapolis on the way."

"Oh." It was all I could think of to say.

"But," she went on, "I think it might be best if we left early. You know Mom. She doesn't always follow her schedules."

Gloria Meecham hadn't this time, it was certain. If only she had...

Before we left, there was the little matter of Walker's car. We talked it over and Paris came up with the best idea. I'd drive it to the rest area just on the other side of Warsaw on Highway 30, leave it there. Her idea was that when the cops found it, and if they ever put him on the robbery scene with Sally Boxleiter, they'd just assume that had been their meet-up spot. The only thing about that that worried me was if the state trooper who'd stopped us would remember his car and remember I'd been with him. I didn't know if they recorded license numbers in a situation like that or not. I was sure he'd run a check before he'd even gotten out of his car. There was no way around it, though. I was just going to have to take the chance.

We parked it down toward the end, behind a semitrailer.

Back at the cottage, we packed up quickly, checked the place twice for anything we might have left behind that could tie us to anything that had happened in the past two days, and hit the road. I put the bag with the money and the diamonds in my trunk, under the spare tire in the wheel well. Not that they wouldn't look there first, but if I got stopped for something innocent, like a taillight out or something, at least it wouldn't be in plain view on the back seat or something.

We stopped along the highway outside of Warsaw at the McDonald's and grabbed a takeout, both of us going through the drive-thru, Paris first and then me.

It had begun snowing again, and the wind picked up, creating drifts across the road. Grimly, I kept a steady pace of fifty miles per hour—about the max I could do under the conditions—and kept my eye on Paris's lights in my rear-view mirror. I didn't curse out the elements as I usually would, however. Let it snow and blow. The more, the better. Cover everything up so deep it wouldn't melt till spring. The more it snowed, the harder the wind blew, the better I felt.

Except for thinking about my mother-in-law.

My *murdered* mother-in-law.

Unbidden, and fought against, memories surfaced. Our wedding, when Gloria'd walked up, happy tears running down her cheeks, and put her arms around me and said, "Welcome to the family, Jake. We're so happy to have a son like you."

I'd killed this woman, this woman who'd never been anything but a second mother to me. If there *was* a heaven and Gloria and my own mother had hooked up…

I didn't want to think about that.

Gloria, I articulated silently, *I killed you to save your daughter. Because of what I did to you, she won't go to prison. You see that, don't you?*

I shook my head violently and turned the windshield wiper to go faster. Jesus. I was becoming one of those loons who think God is speaking to them through drainpipes. I made Gloria's face disappear and focused everything on the road ahead, straining to see beyond the hundred-foot visibility that ended in a black void filled with swirling and gusting snow devils.

I thought of Walker, too.

I wanted a drink in the worst way.

Chapter 40

I woke, my throat dry and sore, and my nose stuffed with phlegm. A damned cold. Just what I needed. I turned over and saw Paris wasn't there. Faintly, I could hear signs of her doing something in the kitchen downstairs. Probably cooking us up some breakfast, a guess confirmed a second later when I thought I caught a whiff of bacon. I couldn't be sure, what with a stuffed nose and all, but I thought I could smell bacon being fried.

The night before, we'd finally made it home a little after one and went right up to bed. Well, almost immediately. Before I collapsed, I suddenly (and fortunately!) remembered that damned cap in my pocket. I should have thrown it out! I waited until Paris was in the john, then hustled downstairs to look for a place to hide it. My mind drew a blank. Everywhere I considered, I thought of a reason why that wouldn't be a good place. Just as I was debating whether to run down to the basement, I heard the bathroom door open and Paris called out, "Jake?" The next sound I heard was her footsteps on the stairs and quick-like I stepped over and jammed the cap under the couch cushions, not a second too soon, as she appeared in the living room.

"What're you doing down here?" she said and I mumbled something about wanting a drink of water and forgetting why I'd come downstairs.

"Senior moment, eh?" she said, and I went into the kitchen and got a drink, cupping my hand under the faucet.

A minute later, I was back upstairs and hitting the sheets. I figured the cap was all right where it was for now and in the morning I'd retrieve it and get rid of it. I was almost asleep, seconds after pulling the covers over me, but just before I went under, I thought I remembered Paris reaching over and putting her hand on my thigh. I also thought I remembered mumbling something like, "Not tonight, honey. I'm just beat," and turning over, my back to her, and her saying, "I guess I don't have Willie Mays's electricity any more, do I?" It might have been a dream.

I hoped it was.

Although… Putting the moves on me would mean she hadn't seen the beret at the cottage.

"Morning," she said, when I walked into the kitchen. I was right. It was bacon she'd been frying. A dozen slices were on a paper plate on the kitchen counter, draining on a piece of absorbent paper. Two pieces of browned bread jumped up in the toaster and I saw a plate with one of her Spanish omelets at my place at the table. Even with my stuffed-up nose I could smell the food, but I just wasn't hungry. Even for her omelets, which ordinarily I loved. I walked over and picked up one of the bacon pieces from the plate and bit off a bit of the end, thinking that maybe the taste would make me hungry.

No way. I put the rest of it back and swallowed what I had in my mouth.

"I'm sorry, babe," I said. "I don't think I can eat." I pointed to my nose. "Cold."

"Great," she said. "I wish I'd known that an hour ago. Those were the last eggs. And I hate omelets."

She stepped over, grabbed my plate and took it over to the trash can in the pantry and dumped it all out.

I felt like I was walking on eggshells here. And I knew why.

That terrible secret that I carried with me lay between us, even if she didn't know about it. *I* did. And I'd always know it. Somehow, some way, some day, I was going to have to resolve it or it would only fester and grow worse, like some inoperable cancer.

I wasn't going to resolve it today, though. I had to just go on. *We* had to just go on. Else there was no value to what I'd done. I knew there was value there. There had to be.

"Okay," I said. To her back. She'd walked over and stood leaning over the sink, staring out into the back yard. "You're not mad about the eggs."

"You're right." She turned, faced me. She came over to the table and took the chair across from me, turning it around so that she straddled it, her arms across its back. "I'm mad because I'm scared."

I could deal with that. That was easy. All I had to do was be the coach in the locker room at halftime. Give the ol' pep talk to get the troops fired up again.

"What's done is done," I said, choosing my words carefully. "I can't undo what's happened, sweetheart. Neither can you."

I could tell by the way she leaned forward she wanted to hear something positive, wanted me to put a spin on the events of the past few days that would convince her that…what? Fuck, I didn't know. Convince her that everything would be all right in our brave new Martha Stewart, Republican, Ozzie and Harriet Nelson world. That the child she was carrying would be little Ricky Nelson and would have his wonderful life, sans the unfortunate plane crash at the end.

I tried.

"Everything's going to turn out all right," I went on. "You'll see. We're past most of the bad stuff now. Couple more little odds and ends to clean up and we're home free."

Christ! I sounded like an insurance salesman explaining the merits of whole life versus term and how easy it was going to be to pay for this here little ol' policy. Snoopy, giving his Met Life schtick.

I forged onward.

I talked to her about life's vagaries, kismet, karma, bad and good luck. I threw in everything but the kitchen sink and I even eyed that for a minute, considering. I think I even quoted Thoreau, some shit I remembered from that first lit class I'd taken at IUSB.

The more I talked, the more glazed-over her eyes got, the less and less time she held my gaze before staring at other objects in the kitchen, and frankly, all this shit was just wearing me out.

Finally, just a second or two before I think she would have picked up the frying pan she'd cooked the bacon in and belted me over the head with it, I came out with a thought I'd had earlier.

"I guess what it boils down to is that we probably aren't going to be asked to play Ozzie and Harriet in the silver jubilee commemorative movie," I said, out of the blue. "But," I added, "we've probably got the inside track on the Bonnie and Clyde flick if they ever redo that."

She laughed.

Out loud.

And long. She began with a short, sharp burst of unexpected laughter, stopped for a second, then started up again with giggling. The longer she went on, the less able I was to keep a straight face, and I ended up joining her like we were two teeny-boppers at a sleepover.

At last, we both stopped. Together. It was almost like we'd got our nut at the same time.

"Now I'm hungry," I said. I walked over to the trash can and reached in and picked up her omelet with my fingers. "Umm, good," I said, stuffing it into my mouth with one hand, brushing off the coffee grounds stuck to part of it with the other. Paris looked at me in disbelief for a moment, then began laughing again, this time softly, chuckling.

"You're nuts," she said, getting up and coming over to me and putting her arms around my neck and kissing me on the mouth. I looked down at her, brushed off an egg crumb from her cheek. "I know," I said. "But I'm *your* nut."

I don't think I ever loved her as much as I did that moment. Best of all, I saw a glimmer of hope for us. I think she did, too.

We made love right there, on the floor in front of the pantry. Neither of us got all our clothes off. When I finally collapsed to her side, out of breath, she still had her jeans on one leg and only one button of her flannel shirt came undone and that wasn't because of me, but somehow because of our twisting around. My own jeans were bunched up around my knees, my shoes weren't even untied, and all my shirt buttons were fastened.

Best sex I ever had. I think, for her, too.

Chapter 41

I had me a plan.

Weirdest thing. I came up with this plan while I we were making love.

It wouldn't solve all of my problems, but it'd take care of a big chunk of them.

The part it wouldn't solve was the Gloria situation, but first things first. Take care of the other stuff and I'd come up with something. At least that's what I was counting on. That a miracle idea would come to me. I refused to consider the odds of that happening.

We took turns taking a shower—Paris first, and then me. I think she wanted me to take one with her, but I didn't want to make love again so soon after what we'd just done. I wanted to kind of bask in the glow of that one for a while, not dilute the memory.

Besides, my mind was already busy with how I was going to implement the scheme that had come to me. I'd gotten the basic overall shape of it, but the details needed fine-tuning.

I brushed my teeth while she showered, talking to her in that mushy way you do when you've got a toothbrush and toothpaste in your mouth.

"I'm going to Chicago, see Walker's guy," I announced. "Fence the diamonds." I heard her say something over the roar of the shower, only her words were muffled. I could tell by the tone of what she was saying, she planned to go along.

"No," I said, half-yelling. "It's better I go by myself in case something goes wrong. For one thing, you don't want this guy to see you, be able to identify you. We don't know a thing about him. For all we know, he could be a snitch."

The shower stopped and she slid the glass door open. Surprisingly, she acquiesced. "All right," she said, stepping out and reaching for the towel she'd put on the stool we kept beside the shower. "I need to go to work, anyway. No sense in losing my job."

"That's right," I said. I leaned over the sink and spit a mouthful, then leaned over more and cupped my hand for water to rinse with. I held the toothbrush under the tap, shook it, and put it in the ceramic holder alongside Paris's orange one. I wiped my mouth dry with a hand towel, put it back on its hook and said, "Not that I will, but if I somehow get caught, get sent up, you'll have that."

"What I was thinking," she said and for some reason that bothered me.

"Yeah, well… Don't worry. I won't get caught."

"I'm past worrying," was her reply.

Irrationally, that bothered me too.

Before I left to Chitown, I read the newspapers from the last two days. The first day, Saturday, the break-in at Calvin Brewer's merited only half an inch of type, back in the felony reports section. A simple burglary was all it said. It was probably lucky it even made the *South Bend Tribune*, being as it had happened across the Michigan state line, in Niles.

It got a lot more space in the Sunday paper. A fairly long article by some reporter named Alan Wiskeroff. Important stuff, to rate a byline. Page two, the rest of the piece continued on page 15. The gist of the article was that an employee of Mr. Brewer was missing and the police had located her car a short distance away, hidden behind an equipment shed on a neighboring farm. The police had refused to speculate on what that meant, but the reporter didn't seem to have any trouble including his own spin. He hinted broadly—without actually coming out and saying so—that it was an inside job.

There was no mention of a diamond being found in the car, but I knew the cops always withheld information from the press. In the event some moron confessed to see if he (or she) would know that kind of inside information to prove if they were real or not, and for other reasons. Probably mostly because that's what it said to do in the police manual, I always thought.

The police also refused to divulge how much and what had been stolen, except for "several diamonds and other gems of indeterminate value."

The article made my palms sweat. I knew the police would have been on the case five minutes after we'd fled the premises, seeing as that was most likely Calvin Brewer who was pulling in while we were beating it, but seeing it in the paper made it a fact. And I guess I was a bit surprised they'd found Boxleiter's car so quickly.

The good news was this reporter had come to the same conclusion I figured the cops had. The way the article was written gave me reason to believe it was based on some "off-the-record" info they'd given the guy.

If so, then the scheme I'd just dreamed up was going to work like nobody's business.

I left as Paris was reading the same articles.

"Looks like we figured right," I said, my hand on the doorknob.

She didn't look up, just held her hand in the air while she continued to read.

"Back by supper," I said, going out.

Ozzie telling Harriet bye-bye as he leaves for the office…

•   •   •

I made one other stop before hitting the Indiana toll road.

Had a meet with Jimmy Barnes at a McDonald's in Roseland.

"You're becoming a regular," he said. "I thought you were out of the life."

"I am," I said. "I just need something for protection. I'm opening my own business."

"Yeah," he said, passing over what I'd asked for, an Army issue .45 with an extra clip and a box of shells. "That's what your wife said when she bought hers. Must be a dangerous business, hairstyling. Lots of customers packing, are they?"

He sold me a pair of handcuffs, too.

"What kind of shop you opening?" he said. "I might want an appointment. Looks like an interesting clientele."

The guy was easy to find.

There was his name on the front window, just the way Walker'd written it down. "Bill Bradley Designs, Wm. Bradley, Prop."

Bill Bradley, just like the basketball player.

I knew my way around Chicago fairly well. Years ago, during my "roaming" period, I'd lived out in Ford City, on Cicero, worked downtown on Ontario as a waiter at a little Italian restaurant that had gone out of business while I worked there. I'd been without a car then, so I caught a bus to work and on Saturdays used to just get on the bus and use my pass, ride all over hell. I got to know the city, at least the main drags, the tourist spots. Spent a lot of time around Wrigley Field in Yuppieville.

Which was where the guy lived. A few blocks away from the Cubs' park on Lakeview Avenue. Lots of old mansions, one of which his office was in.

"Mr. Bradley?"

"Yes. You're the gentleman who phoned?"

He wasn't what I expected. I didn't realize that until he

introduced himself. He almost looked like the NBA star, except he had a thick mane of gray-flecked dark-brown hair, tied back in a ponytail. He was the same height as the other Bradley, looked like. Close, anyway, six four, six five, I'd say. Just not what I'd expected. I think I'd been anticipating someone who looked like Sydney Spencer.

He caught me staring.

Chuckled.

"It's the name, right?"

"Sir?"

He'd let me in and flipped the "Open" sign to "Closed" and turned the lock on the glass door. I was following behind him as he walked through a large room with three long display glassed-in cabinets. He headed for a curtained doorway behind the back cabinet.

"Bradley. Bill Bradley."

We were in his office. Standard office equipment—desk, executive chair, computer, monitor and keyboard on a computer table in the corner. A tall filing cabinet and a workbench with what I assumed was jewelry equipment over in the corner. Another door that led somewhere over in the corner behind the workbench. He sat down behind the desk and I stayed on the other side of it, standing.

"Please," he said, indicating with a sweep of his hand that I was to take the chair at my side.

"Thanks," I said. "Sorry to stare. You've got to know you're a dead ringer for—"

"Bill Bradley, the ex-Princeton basketball player. I know. Fact is…" he paused and I could see he took pleasure in this, "Bill and I went to Princeton at the same time. I was in several classes with him. In fact, we were sometimes confused for each other. After a while, I quit explaining and just gave out my autograph. I already knew how to spell it." He laughed and I smiled.

He turned off the smile.

"You're an associate of Mr. Joy's, is that right? Mr. Bishop?" I said I was.

"Let's see what you have."

I reached inside my jacket pocket and pulled out the small manila envelop I'd put the diamonds in and handed it across to him. All the diamonds we'd gotten at Calvin's minus two. The one I'd planted in Sally Boxleiter's car wasn't there, of course, and neither was the canary yellow Spencer'd wanted, the original object of the burglary. I had plans for that one.

He reached into the middle drawer of his desk and pulled out a deep blue velvet cloth and spread it out before him on the desk. From the front pocket of his jacket, which looked like one of those things they used to wear in old-time movies, a whadyacallit, a smoking jacket, he extracted a jeweler's glass and a large pair of tweezers and placed them on the desktop. Then, he undid the clasp on the envelope and dumped the contents on the cloth. He picked up the loupe, fixed it to his eye and moved the diamonds around on the cloth, finally selecting the largest, the one I recognized with the naked eye as the mocha.

Putting it down after a look at it, he said, "I don't see the canary."

I was stunned.

"How'd you—"

"Know there was a canary yellow?" He laughed. I didn't. This was getting irritating, this guy finishing my sentences. Like he could read my mind or something. "Very easy, my friend. Even before I went to Princeton I knew how to read. It was in the newspapers, you know. Also, in our online newsletter. Not to mention that Calvin Brewer is an acquaintance. A fine craftsman. One of the very best."

"Newsletter?" I felt like an idiot.

"What you might call a 'hot sheet.' Whenever there's a

robbery like this, they send out a list of the stolen merchandise. And descriptions. I knew what you'd be bringing me. The only thing that surprised me was that I'm meeting you. I'd expected Walker Joy. I assume he's tending to other business?"

Christ. Everybody and their brother knew about this.

"You'd assume right."

Fuck all this. I just wanted to get rid of the rocks, get the hell out of there.

"How much?"

"You mean how much am I prepared to give you for this merchandise?"

"You really did go to Princeton, I guess," I answered. "Yeah, college boy. How much?" I was tired of all this polite society shit. The guy might be degreed up the ass, might be sitting behind a mahogany desk, might own half of Chicago or at least this block, but you got right down to it, he was a fucking fence. A crook, just like I was. Just better dressed. He reminded me of those rich assholes in high school with their customized hot rods. Fastest cars Daddy's money could buy, and they acted like they had something to do with the drag races they won, other than by accident of birth and access to a checkbook.

"Forty thousand."

I sat there, and felt my jaw drop.

"Forty thousand? Apiece?" Although, I knew that wasn't what he meant.

He snorted. "In your dreams, cowboy. For the lot."

I rose out of my seat—to do what, I don't have the foggiest—just a reaction to what I was hearing out of his mouth, a movement born of just plain shock—and he reached, quick-like, into the side pocket of his jacket, extracting a snub-nosed, nickel-plated .38 Police Special and laid it down on the table.

"You gonna rob me?" I asked, amazed. "Don't you think

an offer of forty G's is robbery enough? There's got to be half a million bucks of ice sitting there."

He gave that goddamned sniggering look again. "You're actually very close. My estimate would be a bit higher. Some good stuff here. I'd say retail on this would fetch close to seven hundred thousand."

"And you think I'm going to give it to you for forty lousy thousand? Is Princeton where you first started using LSD? And what the fuck's the gun for? You like the taste of gun metal? 'Cause if you don't, I was you, I'd put that away."

He just stared at me, a more-or-less blank look on his face. No narrowed eyes or anything like that, just a blank look. More threatening than any version of a Terminator scowl. The pro version of a wolf ticket look. I had no doubt the guy was for real, soon as I saw that look. "I don't think so, Mr. Bishop. Sit down. If you think someone else will give you more, you're free to do so. I think you'll find I'm being extremely generous."

If that was his idea of largesse, I was glad I wasn't in the Christmas exchange with him.

"Tell you what," he was saying. "I know these diamonds are all top quality. I shouldn't have any trouble selling them. I'd be willing to give you fifty. I can tell you right now, that's going to be the best offer you'll get."

"I don't understand. When I bought my wife's engagement ring, the guy said we were making a 'wise investment.' He said diamonds had never once depreciated in value in the course of history." I don't know why I was repeating this. I was just plain stunned, flummoxed.

"Your jeweler was right," Bradley said. "Diamonds always go up in value."

"Then—"

"But only to the retailer. That's the part we always neglect to add. Look…" he sighed, picked up the gun and slid it back down into his pocket. "You seem like a fairly nice man. Not the usual sort I do business with. Let me explain how the diamond business works. First of all, normal markup is about fifty percent. I buy a diamond for five thousand from the nice DeBeers folks, sell it for ten. Plus whatever for the setting, design work, et cetera."

"Then, why won't you pay me half the retail?" I said. "I'd be happy with that." I tried to keep the whine out of my voice.

"Because," he said, with that slick little smile. "I don't have to. Nobody pays full price except to a legitimate diamond wholesaler. You want proof of that? Take one of these to a diamond dealer. Not a wholesaler, a dealer. Wholesalers won't deal with you. Dealers are in most malls. Those folks who buy gold and silver. See what they offer. I'll tell you right now what they'll give you. Ten percent. Maybe even up to 15 percent. And that's for legitimate diamonds. You know, the ring your Aunt Victoria left you, the one you can prove is yours. Take one to a pawnshop. Same deal. Maybe worse. More than likely, worse. Say seven percent of its value."

"Then diamonds are a lousy investment."

"You got it, slick," he said, switching from his Princeton diction into a pretty good imitation of one of those guys selling knockoff Rolexes over on Maxwell Street a five-dollar cab ride away. "My congratulations. You just graduated from Diamond Investing 101. You want to feel rich, just keep the merchandise. You'll be worth three-quarters of a million dollars. At least until you sell it."

In the end, the guy took pity on me. Or else he just knew he was going to make a killing on the rocks anyway and wanted me out of the store before teatime. I walked out with fifty-five thousand dollars in the same manila envelope I'd brought the diamonds in.

Before I left, he said, "You want to make some serious

money, Mr. Bishop, bring me cocaine. I pay top dollar if it's pure."

"You're a coke dealer?"

"I'm a dealer in anything that pays well, sir. I've got a son in Princeton. A son who didn't get the best grades in high school. Missed getting a scholarship by… let's see… ten or fifteen miles. Princeton's expensive. Thank God for legacies. He's going to be a minister, so I don't think he'll be able to pay me back, either. Not unless he ends up on TV, but we're Episcopalian, not Baptist. Plus, he doesn't really believe in God and that will make it difficult for him to convince folks to send in their rent money. John just basically doesn't like to work very hard. Ergo, his father deals drugs and hot ice. Stolen John Deere tractors if the money's right. Someone in the family has to take responsibility seriously."

I left almost liking the guy.

On the drive home, I assessed the situation. Paris was going to be disappointed, maybe more than I was. Seeing fifty-five thousand instead of the three or four hundred G's we'd expected to get was bound to depress her. On the plus side, with what we already had—the cash from Brewer's safe—we now had a quarter of a million, which wasn't exactly chopped liver.

And I still had Spencer to see.

I expected to come away from that meeting with a lot more.

Chapter 42

I phoned Paris at her job as soon as I got off the toll road, from a little coffee shop by Memorial Hospital. I decided it would be better to let her know the bad news over the phone, let her digest it before I got home after seeing Spencer. That way, she'd have time to get over the disappointment before I saw her. I didn't see any need to tell her about the visit I planned to see Sydney Spencer, although I think she had an inkling of what I was going to do.

She had news of her own.

News that gave me a jolt.

"Daddy called," she began and that spot in my stomach where my old ulcer lurked flared up with a major twinge.

"And?" I said, not knowing what else to say.

"He said Mom would be calling us. He said she was headed up for the lake. He's coming later."

Her voice didn't sound suspicious. I took a deep breath.

"Good thing we got out of there when we did," I offered.

"No kidding," she said. "That would have been awful."

"Well, we did and we cleaned up the place. There's nothing there to say we'd been there."

"Yes there is," she said, and when she said that my heart gave an extra beat.

"What?"

"We forgot to turn the heat off."

"Oh," I said, furiously thinking. "Well, if she notices or says anything, we can just tell her we went up for the weekend. They know we do that, sometimes. Isn't that why we have the key?"

"Yeah. I guess."

We talked a couple minutes more, then I told her I had some errands to do, I wanted to look at some equipment I'd heard about a lady was selling over in Gilmer Park from the shop she was closing.

"I'll see you later this afternoon," I said. "Probably be home before you."

Unless I was dead or in jail.

I kept that possibility to myself.

Paris's comment about our oversight in not turning the heat back down reminded me of a lapse of my own.

That damned cap of her mother's.

It was still stuffed up under a cushion on the couch. I'd forgotten to retrieve it. I remembered my oversight about a mile from my destination.

Spencer's jewelry store.

I was in luck. Spencer was behind his counter when I walked in and no one was in the store. I'd parked three blocks away in a supermarket lot and came up to his store through the alley. Before I came around to the front and into the store, I'd put on the pair of rubber gloves I'd picked up down the block at a drugstore and stuck my hands in my pockets so no passerby would notice I had rubber gloves on.

He tried to come across as cool and collected, but a glance at his face when I walked in told me otherwise. His eyes widened for a split second, and the color rose from his collar to his jowly cheeks.

Make that his fat cheeks.

"I've been waiting for you," he said, recovering his composure quickly, at least appearing to do so. "What took you so long and where's Walker Joy?"

I didn't say anything. I turned my back to him and locked the door and swung the Open/Closed sign around and pulled the shade down over the glass door. That done, I turned back around.

"Walker Joy won't be joining us, Spencer. He's indisposed."

I didn't fuck around. Just reached into the canvas bag I'd brought in with me and took out the .45, leveling it at him in the classic Western shitkicker movie draw.

"Where is it?" I said.

"Where's what?" he said. Then, "Jake, I just heard about your brother. I'm sorry, man. I'm really sorry. Who would've known? You can't blame me for—"

"Fuck you!" I screamed the words. "Don't even talk about my brother. I don't want his name on your filthy lips."

"Jake," he said, a begging note in his voice. He put his hands palm-up in front of him and backed up a step. "Don't be rash. I've got a letter—"

"I figured that," I said. "That's what I just asked for, asshole." I waved my gun. "Back room."

I had a pretty good idea what the letter was and I'd thought about where it would probably be. I walked Spencer over to his desk, had him sit down and cuffed him to the arm. I opened each drawer to see if there was a weapon in any of them.

"The letter's not there," he said. "You don't think I'd be that stupid, do you? It's in a place where if something happens to me the police'll find it. Lays out everything. You'd better let me go, you know what's good for you."

"I'm not looking for a letter, greaseball," I said.

Actually, I was… sort of. I didn't really think he'd do the obvious, create an actual letter in an envelope, addressed to the police. But… one never knows.

If he had written such a thing, it wasn't in his desk. I even checked underneath it, in case he'd taped it up under a drawer. Nothing there, either.

I pushed Spencer in his rollabout chair to the front of the desk and planted him in the middle of the room, facing it. I wanted to be able to see his face for what I planned to do next. All the while, he kept silent. Just as good, for him, anyway. I was itching for the opportunity to pistol-whip him. I think he sensed that.

I went back behind the desk and began turning his computer and its components on, watching his face as I did so. It remained stoic, to my disappointment. I don't know what I expected, a look of chagrin, I suppose. For a second, I thought maybe I'd guessed wrong.

I hadn't.

There it was. In a Word file. Under the filename "Intheeventofmydeath.doc."

"Jeez, Sydney, couldn't you be any more original than this?"

He couldn't see what I was looking at, but I knew he knew what it was. This time I got the look I'd hoped to get when I'd switched his computer on. His forehead turned into a corrugated tin roof and there was outright pain in his eyes. He even delighted me with a small groan.

I read the document. It had everything. Names, dates, even his own part in the robbery at Brewer's, setting it up. I guess he figured if it got read he'd be dead and he didn't much care about his own reputation at that point. I deleted it and then decided to go a step further, make sure it was gone forever.

I pulled up his Excel program and there was his inventory, under that name. I deleted that as well.

"I'm just going to reformat your hard drive," I said. "You got a lot of garbage in here. This'll make it run faster." I rubbed my hands together with glee, just as Simon LeGree would have. A couple of clicks and a "Yes" to the "Are you sure" box that popped up—"You bet!" I said out loud—and every single record the man had was gone. Disappeared into computer purgatory.

"I've got a hard copy," Spencer said, his voice smaller than I know he intended it to be. "In a safe place. With a friend. If I die or disappear, he has instructions to mail it to the police."

"That so?" I said. "Know what, Spencer? I don't think so. If you do, you do, but I'm just going to take the chance you were too lazy to do that. I'm at a place where I take chances like that now." I could tell from his expression I'd guessed right. It was the look a man gets when his ass is in a wringer and he can't reach the "off" button.

"Besides," I continued. "I doubt very much if you have a friend. That's what makes your little story unbelievable."

The safe was even easier than finding Spencer's letter file. Another one of those Brown TL-30's. The Super Fortress. An identical mate to the one Calvin Brewer had. I'd bet anything they'd gone together to purchase their safes to save a few bucks.

Even better, the two jewelers must have gone to the same Locking-Your-Safe-Up School. Like Brewer's, the door on Spencer's 5,000 pound behemoth swung easily open. Fucker was just too lazy to keep it locked.

His bad. My luck.

Although, in a way, I was disappointed. I'd kind of hoped it'd be locked and I'd have to pull out his fingernails or something to get the combination.

I heard his voice from behind me. "You're going to rob me?"

I turned around. "It's what I do, remember? Wasn't that the reason you hired me, Sydney?"

"You won't get away with it," he said, his voice whiny, desperate, the tone of his voice in contrast to what he was saying. "You're not a killer, Jake. We both know that. You think I won't go to the cops? You think they'll believe you over me? I'm an established businessman. You... you're an ex-con. If I was you, I'd let me go, pray I'm a nice guy. Tell you what—you don't even have to give me the diamonds you got at Calvin Brewer's. Just consider us even, what with your brother and all."

Nice try, Spencer.

"You know," I said. "At one time you're right, I wasn't a killer. Things've changed. You're not curious why Walker's not here?"

It was enormously satisfying to watch his jaw go slack.

"But…" he hesitated, "…Walker's your *friend*. He saved your life back there. You owed him. He told me the story—"

I interrupted him. "What I really wanted to do wasn't kill you, Spencer. What I really wanted to do was set you up, get you sent to the joint. Guy like you, know what would happen? Fat, white ass like yours is prime meat, Spencer. They'd be lining up, t'get your brown-eye. See that creamy white ass, the ol' love bug's gonna bite a certain kind of guy. First night you're in population, some big, black mother would pay you a visit. You'd scream for the hack, but the hack wouldn't hear you. He'd be busy reading his Zane Grey at his desk, counting the green this big buck just slipped him. Your cell door would be open. Only one on the tier open. Besides your visitor's, that is."

I was really enjoying this, watching his face go through the permutations.

"This guy—you want to call him 'Daddy'—this guy will have a ballpeen hammer with him. Know what that's for?" I paused for effect. "The hammer's for a little dental work. He needs it to smash out your front teeth. You know… for better blow jobs. Don't ask him for any Novacaine. It's not in his dental budget. He takes care of that, then he's gonna fuck you where you don't want to be fucked. Maybe he's got a few buddies waiting outside, arguing over who gets to be next. Whatever. Later on, the hack is going to make his rounds, 'discover' you, get your sorry ass hauled on over to the hospital. A week later, you'll be back in population. Have you a new cellmate. The guy I hoped you'd learned to call 'Daddy'. He's your new best friend.

"That's what I *wanted* to do, Spencer. That would have been perfect. Poetic justice, I think they call it. Even out things for what you did to Bobby. To me. But…" I sighed. "…to make all that happen means I'd have to get sent up too, and I decided I didn't want that. I've got a wife to take care of. So…" I shrugged my shoulders. "And yeah, Walker saved my life. You're right. But then he took it back. When he got me mixed up in this shit. With you."

"What…" he said, the word escaping his throat in a raspy, strangled whisper. "…what are you going to do?"

I said, "You'll see," and turned back to the safe.

I scooped up the diamonds and other gems and dumped them in a heap on the floor. For my plan to work, I didn't mean to keep them. I knew now they weren't worth diddly-squat to a guy like me. A guy who didn't have the convenience of his own jewelry store to unload them to unsuspecting starry-eyed lames walking in with their little gold digger girlfriends. I planned to leave them in his car, in the trunk, make it look like he hid them there. Along with the canary yellow we'd taken from Calvin's safe. What I planned to keep was his cash, if any.

There was. A large velvet bag, way in the back. Stuffed with packets of bills, fifties and hundreds. Ten packets in all. I counted one of them and it came to twenty-five thousand. The way they were bundled, I figured they all had the same.

A quarter of a million dollars.

Motherfuck.

"Looks like I struck the mother lode," I said, grinning. "This your pin money, fat boy?"

I stuffed the bundles into my coat pockets. Their weight felt nice against my hips.

I reached in the canvas bag and felt around until my fingers found the item I was looking for. I picked it up, walked over to Spencer.

"Recognize this?" I said, opening my hand to reveal what lay in my palm. It was the canary yellow. He nodded. Looked to me like he was somewhat speechless.

I tossed the rock to the mound of diamonds and other gems I'd taken from his safe. Perfect shot. Landed right on top.

"There," I said. "You got your diamond. What all this fuss was about."

"I don't understand," he said.

I said, "Too bad. The police will. That's all that counts."

All that remained of the contents of my bag were a bunch of miniature yellow manila envelopes. The ones I'd taken from Brewer's safe. I didn't want to make this too obvious. There were probably a hundred of them, made quite a stack. I picked up one and took it over to Spencer's desk, looking for the best spot to plant it. I wanted it to look like it had fallen there and Spencer hadn't seen it. Finally, I decided to crush it into a ball and lay it up against one of the desk legs in a spot where he wouldn't have been able to see it from where he'd sit behind the desk. About half of the rest I planned to just throw in the dumpster in the alley on the way out. I had plans for the remainder of them. I'd spotted a trash can over in the corner and it had a white liner in it, just a couple of scraps of paper in it. I gathered up the rest of the envelopes and tossed them into it, took the bag out of the can and twisted the top into a knot, then took the bag and stood it next to the back door. I'd put that in the dumpster when we left and maybe it'd still be there when the cops searched the place and maybe it wouldn't be. Didn't matter. They'd be sure to find the one on the floor. My guess was they'd be able to get a fingerprint or two off of it. Brewer's fingerprints. Or Sally Boxleiter's. Didn't much matter which, and maybe both would be on it.

Even if they weren't, I was sure they'd call Brewer in and he'd identify it as one of his packets.

My next move was to empty all of the display cases. Those items—altogether, the brooches, pins, rings, necklaces, gold and silver doodads and other stuff must have weighed seventy-eighty pounds—I loaded up into three triple-strength garbage bags I'd bought earlier at the same drugstore I'd picked up the rubber gloves at. Most of the diamonds I figured were Zircon or if they were real, knowing Spencer's sleazy way of doing business, were probably full of flaws, but some of them had to be real and of decent quality. I wanted it to look like Spencer'd decided to take it on the lam, probably because he was afraid he'd be connected to the Brewer robbery. At the least, all this "evidence" would confuse the cops and more importantly make them think that somehow he was mixed up with the robbery at Brewer's place.

One more bit of "evidence" to leave for the Dick Traceys to hook him up with Walker, just in case somebody didn't step up and put him and Spencer together. I picked up the phone on his desk and dialed Walker Joy's phone at his apartment. The answering machine picked up on the fourth ring. I replaced the receiver and winked at Spencer who was staring quizzically at me.

"You just called your partner, Spencer. That establishes a link between you. If the cops watch the same TV shows I do, they'll check out your phone records."

I went into my pocket and pulled out a piece of paper with a phone number on it. "Here's something you can do, fat boy, and if you do it right, I may not kill you. Or...I may." I told him what I wanted him to do. That I was going to phone his fence in Chicago and that he needed to tell him I'd be back up, that he'd given me the wrong amount for the diamonds. Some other instructions. "Do this and maybe I'll change my mind," I said. Spencer looked up at me and

I could tell he was considering his options. Finally, he said, "Okay. I'll do it."

I picked up the phone again, put it on speaker mode, and dialed the number.

On the second ring, a voice said, "Bill Bradley. How may I help you?"

For a second Spencer hesitated and then he did as I said. "Bill? It's Spencer."

"Hello, Spencer. Did your man get there?"

Spencer hesitated, then said, "Yes. Yes, he did, Bill. He said you didn't give him the right price."

"Well, Spencer, you know how it is. The guy didn't seem to have the right bona fides."

Spencer assured him that I did. Told him I'd be back up, pick up the balance. That I might have some additional merchandise. Told him goodbye.

One last thing to do.

What I needed was Spencer's car keys. That was easy. I found his London Fog topcoat hung up neatly in the back closet, and in the right pocket I found his set of keys.

Finally, I picked up the diamonds I'd taken from the safe from where I'd put them on the floor and put them into the velvet bag the money'd been in. The first one in was that canary. That done, I went over to Spencer and grabbed him by his suit collar and yanked. "Come on. Time to boogie."

"You're going to kill me, aren't you?" The whine in his voice was repulsive.

"I'm going to do what I should have done first time we met."

"What if I don't cooperate? You don't want to shoot me here."

I laughed. "Go ahead. Resist. It'd be better if I killed you someplace else, but this'll work out. Cops'll just think Walker did it. Besides, I know your slimy little mind. You got to be thinking you'll be buying some time, can come up with some kind of plan. Who knows? Maybe you think you're so slick you can talk me out of this. Maybe I'm not really a killer, just like you thought. Maybe I'll get buck fever, something. Maybe God will intervene, save your ass."

I read him right. We got to his Mercedes with no trouble at all from him, going out the back door after I'd checked to make sure no one was out and about. I threw the garbage bag in the dumpster. I made Spencer climb into the trunk. He started to protest then shrugged and climbed in. It was comical to watch him. Reminded me of a whale trying to fit inside a sardine can.

"Tell me something, Spencer. Was it you who called Big Daddy, told him I was an ex-con?"

I watched his face, got my answer.

"It's going to be cold," he whined.

"No it isn't," I said, and shot him in the face.

Chapter 43

My luck was holding.

Spencer had a full tank of gas in his Mercedes.

The last thing I needed was to have to pull into some gas station and have some moron attendant remember I'd been driving his car.

After I shot him, I stood there a minute and looked up and down the alley. No doors opened, no inquisitive souls peeked out to see what caused the sudden noise of the gun report. Satisfied no one had heard the gunshot or if they had, hadn't bothered to investigate, I took the velvet bag with Spencer's gems and looked for a place to hide it. That was the hard part. I'd thought earlier I could just pull up a piece of the trunk's carpeting and stash it under that, but it was stitched too tightly. Then, I got an idea. I unzipped Spencer's trousers.

Luck!

He was wearing Jockeys. I would've bet the farm he was the sort to wear boxers, but he wasn't. Perfect! I stuffed the bag down inside them and zipped him back up.

Twenty minutes later, I was pulling into the South Bend airport. I drove to the short-term parking lot since it was unattended, unlike the long-term lot where you had to take a ticket from a guy at the gate. A guy who could identify me.

The last thing I did before leaving the car was wipe down the steering wheel and everything a driver could possibly touch and leave a print on. Not that I'd left any—I was still wearing my gloves—but to make it look as if whoever had driven the car had.

That driver—in the cops' mind—would be Walker Joy. I took his billfold and dropped it beside the seat where it wasn't visible. The detectives would think it had fallen out of his pocket and he hadn't noticed the loss.

Hopefully.

The next part was the dicey part.

I had to get back to my own car.

I walked across the lot to the terminal and pulled my collar up and tucked my chin down inside and climbed into the back seat of the first cab in line.

"The Football Hall of Fame," I said, sliding over to the far side where the cabbie couldn't see me easily. I made my voice a whisper, as if I had laryngitis.

The cabbie made a couple of efforts at conversation, but I mumbled incoherent monosyllables back at him until he gave up and we rode the rest of the way in silence, save for the crackling of the dispatcher's voice on his radio and the hiss of the tires on the snow-melt on the streets.

He let me off on the north entrance, and I had a ten-spot ready for the six-dollar fare. Not enough of a tip that he'd remember me, and not so little he would, either.

"Keep the change," I hissed in my faux-laryngitis voice, hopped out of the cab and began walking briskly to the entrance of the Hall of Fame, South Bend's monument to mostly Notre Dame players, a building visited by an average of maybe five-six people a day. On busy days. Surreptitiously, I kept the cab in view until he turned the corner and then I made a one-eighty and headed over the Museum of Art along the St. Joe River and waited for a southbound bus at the stop in front of it. Forty-five freezing minutes later, the third bus by rolled up with "S. Michigan St." displayed and I boarded it. No more than another fifteen minutes after that and I was stepping down off the bus, a block from where I'd parked my car.

The minute I switched on the ignition, I began shaking. Uncontrollably. It was like I had epilepsy or something, teeth chattering like those joke teeth you buy in novelty stores, the whole bit. I just sat there until it subsided, then took a deep breath and shifted into drive.

A couple of minutes later, I was on the phone with Paris, telling her something had come up and I might not be back until late. Maybe not until the morning. Don't worry, I said, everything's under control. Ten minutes after I hung up I was back on the toll road, heading back up to Chicago.

Chapter 44

I got to Bradley's place a lot quicker this time since I didn't have to hunt for it. The door was open and I walked in and there he was, behind his desk.

"So," he said, smiling. "You're the real deal, Mr. Bishop."

"Yes, I am," I said. I took out the .45.

He stared and then laughed. "You're going to rob me?"

"Yes."

He leaned back on his chair. "Do you know who I am?"

"Yes," I said. "You're Bill Bradley, the designer. Jewelry, I assume. Your sign doesn't say what you design. Not the basketball player. Although you went to school with him and even were in some of his classes. Your son's going to be a preacher. You'd even sell stolen John Deere tractors if the money was good. Anything I forgot?"

"You don't know who I am," he said. "If you rob me, there's no place on earth you can hide."

"So you're connected," I said. "That what you're trying to tell me."

He didn't answer, just narrowed his eyes. Then, "What's next?"

I motioned with the gun for him to get up. "Let's go," I said. "The safe." I paused. "Or wherever you keep the goodies."

Bradley didn't resist in the least, didn't even try to argue me out of what I was doing. I could almost read his mind.

This turkey doesn't know he's a dead man. I followed him into a back room.

Thing is, I did know that. It just didn't matter. Something had turned in me. I might have been a dead man, but I was going to leave my wife and kid with something. At least that was my motivation.

Bradley had the same Super Brown Fortress as Brewer and Spencer had. Jesus—these guys must all think alike.

He crouched and dialed the combination, then swung the door open. He started to reach inside. I could see stacks of white canvass bank bags.

"Hold it!" I said. "Get back."

He withdrew his arm and I motioned him to step back. I held the gun on him with one hand and reached in. Just as I thought. The first thing my fingers felt was cold metal. A gun. The twin to the one I held on him, a .45. I pulled it out.

"Sorry," I said. "I like a fair fight as much as the next man...except when I'm one of the participants." I looked up at him and he smiled. I reached back into the safe and grabbed one of the bank bags and brought it out. I didn't even have to look inside to see what it held. It was obvious from the feel of it. Stacks of money.

I looked back up again and he was still smiling. One thing was different. He had that revolver I'd seen on my first visit in his mitt. Holding it on me.

Chapter 45

"You should always search the person you're robbing," he said. "This is not very smart of you, Mr. Bishop."

"What now?" I said.

"Well, if you shoot me, I'll still have time to shoot you. It appears to me as if what we have here is a good, old-fashioned Mexican stand—"

I shot him in the middle of his sentence. He stood there a long second, his gun arm slumping a split second before he did, surprise in his already-dead eyes. He collapsed to the floor. I walked over, kicked his gun away from him, just like on any *Law and Order* episode.

"That's the trouble," I said, speaking to his body, "with Mexicans and their goddamned standoffs. All you need to do is just shoot the fucker. Nobody's reflexes are that good, they get hit in the right place. You've seen too many movies, Mr. Bradley. All you need to do is just shoot while the other fucker's selling you his wolf ticket. Guess they didn't teach you that at Princeton." I paused. "That's something you learn in another school. Pendleton."

I got busy on the safe. Besides the money, there were the diamonds I'd sold him. I left them. Before I left, I emptied out the rest of the manila packets from Calvin's safe and placed them in the safe along with the diamonds.

Some smart detective would be getting a promotion when he figured out that Bradley and Spencer were both connected to Calvin's robbery. I'd love to be a fly on the wall when they put two and two together and came up with five. As I was going out the door, I flipped Bradley's body a little salute.

Thanks, motherfucker, for telling me about the hot sheet.

I guess his little preacher son was going to get embarrassed when it turned out his dad was a criminal.

Chapter 46

The biggest thing on my mind on the drive back to South Bend was to stay within the speed limit. Poetic justice wouldn't be the right term to describe someone getting busted for a traffic violation with four million dollars in the trunk.

Four fucking million dollars!

I could hardly wait to see the look on Paris's face.

A few minutes after coming off the toll road, I was pulling to the curb in front of my house. It was just going on eleven o'clock at night.

The snow was melting. Weird—it was months too early for the spring thaw. I don't know how I knew that this warm spell was different from any others, but I knew it was. It was the way it smelled. Like a fevered wind, coming off a swamp.

I realized something. It was Christmas Eve. Unless Paris had gone out and got one, we'd forgotten to get a tree.

I stepped out of the car and into water streaming along the pavement. The way the streetlight hit the pavement, it looked black and like a stream. It was a creek, not a road, not Twynkenham Street. Spring runoff, come down from the mountains, except there were no mountains near South Bend. The grass along the curb was spongy and soft. I walked up our walk and water began running across in front of me in a rivulet. Like the lawn was bleeding; no, like it was pregnant and its water had just burst.

I felt my forehead going up the step and it was hot. A helluva time to be getting the flu, but that's what it was, most likely.

I felt strangely excited about entering my house. About what I'd find there. What I'd reveal to Paris. The bags in the trunk.

I looked forward with eagerness to tell her it was all over now. All we had to do now was just wait a bit and our future would be fine.

I knew what I was going to do. Convince her we had to get out of the country. Show her the money first. Let it dawn on her how rich we were. It wouldn't be easy, convincing her to leave, but she'd see the wisdom of it. Get her out of the country and make sure she understood we had to cut all ties—even with her parents—and she'd go along. Four million dollars plus the other money should seal the deal.

That's what I was thinking, anyway.

"Where've you been?"

Paris was sitting on the couch. Her posture—sprawled out, sitting on her spine, her stomach pushed out farther than I'd ever seen it—and the way she asked the question puzzled me. Her tone was like her posture—listless, desultory. As if she'd been popping downers or something. She had her white robe on and was clutching it around her like she was cold." You've been gone a long time." She inclined her head in the direction of the kitchen. "If you're hungry, there's hamburger patties in the refrigerator. I just put them there, so they're still warm." Her voice sounded funny, strained somehow.

"To Chicago again," I said, in answer to her first question. "I told you where I was going after I left Spencer's." I put down the garbage bag I was carrying on the floor. "You're going to see something on TV in the next couple of days. The police aren't going to say publicly, but they suspect Walker Joy." I told her briefly what had happened, starting with when I first walked into Spencer's store to when I'd left him at the airport. Told her about Bradley in Chicago. During the telling, I picked up the garbage bag, walked over and sat down in the easy chair facing her on the couch, placing the bag on the floor beside me. During my entire narrative she never said a word. Never nodded or made any other indication of interest. Just kept staring at me with unblinking eyes.

"I may get called in for questioning," I said when I was finished. "Being a known associate of him, you know. Don't worry if that happens. It's just routine. I doubt if they'll even suspect me—probably pull me in more to find out if I know where he is than anything. I think we're in the clear pretty much.

"We'll have to leave the country. There's just no way around it. This should make it easier for you." I flipped open the garbage bag to show her the sacks of money.

Nothing. She still gave no outward response to what I'd been saying. Just glanced at the bags like they were groceries. Just continued to stare at me, no expression whatsoever on her face. I couldn't tell if her lack of reaction was because she was in shock at what I'd done or not. That didn't make sense, seeing what I'd already done, but maybe it was some kind of delayed backlash or something.

"Look," I said, somewhat exasperated. I picked up the garbage bag and dumped the contents on the coffee table between us.

It made quite a pile.

Still no expression on her face. I picked up bundles of cash, began throwing them in the air. Everywhere.

"Bradley's nest egg," I said. I still had my coat on and I took that off, laid it across my lap. I began pulling out stacks of bills from one of the canvas bags and tossing them to her where they just fell to the floor. What the hell? "Four million dollars," I said. "We're rich, baby. And," I said, "there's more. Spencer's cash is out in the car." I felt excited. This was going to be better than any Christmas she'd ever had, even if we didn't have a tree.

When I finished emptying the bags, there was money lying everywhere. On the table, on the floor, on the couch. A blizzard of bills. I looked up, hoping to see approval, but instead her brow was creased, as if she was concentrating on something particularly knotty. She was breathing funny, too. Panting, like during sex. Excited, I guessed, at seeing all this money, hearing how it had all turned out good.

"We're rich, baby," I said.

She reached behind her, pulled out something.

Gloria's beret.

God.

"Would you like to tell me how my mother's hat got here?" Paris asked.

"She left it on her last visit?" That was dumb, but what else could I say? I felt nauseous.

"It was in the couch, Jake. But, then... you *knew* that, didn't you?"

This was a pure disaster. Why hadn't I gotten rid of the damn thing? I felt like a little kid, caught by his mother masturbating in the dark. Naturally, I did what that little kid would do. I feigned complete ignorance.

"I don't get what you're saying. You're saying your mom's hat was in the couch and that I knew it was there? Why would I know your mom's stupid hat was in the couch and why are you making a big deal over it if it was? She probably lost it there the last time she was here. You know your mother. She's always losing stuff. Just ask her next time you see her."

Not bad. A brief flicker of confusion passed over her face, making me feel like I was using the right tactic. I took a long breath and went on. "And who says that's your mother's hat? There's a million hats like this. It could have belonged to the previous owner for all we know. Didja think of that?"

We'd bought the couch at a yard sale.

"It could," she said, her eyes narrowing, "but it didn't. I clean this couch every month. It wasn't here the last time."

I thought quickly.

"Well, then, maybe it was buried deep and just now worked its way on up. Happens, you know."

I'd been pretending being wounded by her implied accusation, but all of a sudden, that's exactly what I felt.

Indignant.

Christ, I'd just killed for her! Driven out to the airport with a body in the trunk, a body that could have been discovered by a chance traffic stop. I'd driven back up to Chicago and iced another guy. I'd be sitting in a cell right now, I'd been caught. And protecting my wife. Doing everything in my power to keep her part out of it. I'd be on my way back to Pendleton or to Michigan City and she'd be in the clear. Not only in the clear, but pretty well set for life with what we already had. Everything I'd done, every move I'd taken, had been with her welfare in mind. I'd even had to kill her mother to protect her. If I'd let Gloria live, she would have gone straight to the police, and if that had happened, Paris would be sitting in a cell right now instead of sitting on our couch, holding that damned hat in her hand, giving me the third degree.

The more I considered everything I'd been through for her, the madder I got. Couldn't she see the four million bucks sitting right in front of her? What'd she think that was—confetti?

Beads of sweat popped out on her forehead.

"Something's . . . wrong. The baby . . . hurts . . . It hurts, Jake. It hurts so bad." Her voice cracked on the words, like an old woman's. Tears ran silently down her cheeks. For the briefest of seconds, I was confused. I thought she was babbling about what I'd just told her, and a split second later, I understood. She was in trouble. Pain so intense she probably hadn't heard half of what I'd said.

"Ohmygod!" I said. I ran to her, sat down beside her and pulled her to me.

She fell over into my lap, limply, and then her eyes rolled back and she began convulsing.

"Paris!" I was dimly aware I'd screamed. And was shaking her, in some imbecilic attempt to bring her out of her seizure. I stopped, realizing shaking someone to keep them from shaking wasn't the thing I should be doing. I gulped down a deep breath, another; tried to collect myself.

Just like that, the convulsions ceased and she opened her eyes wide and looked up at me. Oddly, her expression was calm, even lucid.

Relief flooded my body. "Paris! Are you all right, sweetheart? What was—"

Her voice was husky. "The baby's coming, Jake. Only it isn't... *right*. Something's really wrong. Oh God, it hurts so bad!" Her face twisted and darkened in agony and she closed her eyes against what must have been a new wave of pain.

Her robe fell open and I saw she was naked under it. And bleeding. *Really* bleeding. It wasn't coming in spurts, but was just flowing, like lava from a volcano.

"I'm calling an ambulance," I said, trying to keep my voice normal so she wouldn't panic.

"No time," she said, her voice barely a whisper. "No time—" She screamed and arched her back. Collapsed into unconsciousness.

God.

She came back, briefly, her entire body wet with perspiration.

"The baby's coming, Jake. You'll have to deliver it. *Now.*" To punctuate her words, she groaned and I hope I never hear another human being sound like she did then, especially a human being I loved. It tore my heart in two. It didn't sound like it came from Paris. It was the sound of a feral animal. One that had been badly hurt.

"I'm calling," I repeated.

And I did. I ran to the phone, dialed 911. Just as the operator came on, Paris screamed and slip-slid off the couch onto the floor. I dropped the phone and ran to her. Blood was gushing from between her legs and she began to shake violently in long shuddering convulsions.

The blood just kept pouring out from between her legs and her eyes rolled back and she went still. The blood just kept coming out. I put my hand on her vagina and pressed down hard in an attempt to staunch the flow, but it was like trying to stop a river. The sticky fluid just flowed over, around, and through my fingers.

I was sitting like that, on the floor beside my beautiful wife, my hand between her legs, watching helplessly as her lifeblood kept running out of her and through my hand like it was a sieve, pooling in a viscous puddle, when a furious knocking began at the front door, and someone shouted, "EMT! This where the emergency is?" I heard them twisting at the doorknob. It was locked.

What happened next changed everything. I jumped up to let them in and then I looked at the pile of diamonds on the table and money scattered everywhere and I realized what would happen if anyone saw that.

I had a choice to make.

Paris made a small sound and I looked at her. She looked at the table, then back at me, eyes widening, and the pounding at the door intensified. I read the question in her eyes perfectly.

And made my decision.

Chapter 47

I'm back inside.

They were going to send me up to Michigan City on account of my age—I passed my thirty-first birthday sitting in the St. Joe County Jail waiting to go to trial—but I made a deal with the prosecutor that if they'd send me to Pendleton, I'd tell them the whole story, leave nothing out. Take them to the bodies.

Paris died, so it doesn't look like I did the smart thing after all, only I was past thinking like that.

As you may have guessed, I opened that door, didn't take the time to gather up and hide the money and diamonds. I had it in my mind that the five minutes or so it'd take me to do that could mean the difference between them saving her or not.

Turns out, it didn't.

I'd like to report that she opened her eyes and looked at me in her last seconds and whispered, "I love you," and I said something like that in return to her, but that just didn't happen. She just bled to death, and quickly. It just ran out of her and she was dead. It all happened so fast. I wasn't sure until sometime later that it had really happened. When it came down to it—when push came to shove as they say—I chose saving Paris over saving me. That's the one decent thing I get to live with for the rest of my days.

There was some luck. Reason the EMT got there so quick

was the 911 operator had our address from her screen from my call, had sent an ambulance immediately, and, as it turned out, a unit from Memorial Hospital was just around the corner at the Linebacker, having just finished a run, and they were grabbing some lunch before going back to the hospital.

I stood there beside the emergency techs and watched helplessly as they performed what amounted to a caesarian. On a dead woman. All the while they kept looking at the money on the coffee table and giving me weird looks. They pulled a boy out of her and he lived all of three days.

"Preeclampsia," Dr. Grayson said at the hospital, later. That was the word I couldn't remember or pronounce. "It's not an uncommon condition for pregnant women. There was nothing you could have done, Mr. Bishop. It can happen very quickly. I'm sorry, sir."

He went on about some other stuff—medical stuff about swelling, blood pressure, what caused the convulsions, how many women had it, things like that. I was only half-listening by then.

When he walked away, the cops were standing there. Those EMT techs weren't dummies. Soon as they'd left Paris in the hands of the emergency team, they'd gotten hold of the Man. It seems they'd been there for a few minutes, but saw me talking to the doctor and waited until we were done.

I knew it was over when I turned around and saw the same detectives who'd taken Bobby in.

"Jacob Bishop," the big one said. "Assume the position."

And that was it.

While I was in lockup waiting for my trial, I read the news-paper account. In one part, it said the police had recovered "three and a half million in cash and a number of diamonds." Seems some things never changed. Whenever I got busted in the old days, the announced "take" was always about half of what the cops had grabbed. I wondered what beach those two detectives planned to vacation on.

I never had a chance to tell Paris I loved her. That she was the light of my life, of my very soul. That I was so sorry I'd gotten her mixed up in all this mess. That I wished I'd never thought I owed Walker Joy anything.

There are a lot of things that hurt.

I'd like to say it's not bad in here, but it is. It's a thousand times worse than the other two times I was here. I guess because I didn't give up anything the other two times. And I knew I was getting out. That's over. The judge did just about what I expected. Leaned over his podium, peering at me over his wire rims and sentenced me to life under the Bitch. Also, life under several other counts of murder. Oh, there's a possibility of parole after thirty years, but that's meaningless. I won't be around then.

Chapter 48

It happens tonight.

Toles's brother came up to me at noon chow today. I still didn't know his full name, so I asked him. It's Jerome. His number was easy. It was stitched on his left shirt pocket. I made a mental note of it—78663—and wrote it down later in a letter I wrote. I knew right then what I was going to do. I'm not going to spend the next thirty, forty years in here, even though I deserve to more than any man Jack in here. And, if I go, I intend to give a little payback for what Toles's brother did to me. That Hatfield-McCoy thing. Childish? I suppose…

Over and over in my mind, I keep going over a memory of a class I'd taken that semester I'd met Paris. Poly-sci. The memory that comes up, unbidden, is of an anecdote the prof told.

"Thurgood Marshall," he'd said, using the story to illustrate some vague point or other, "states it well, when he said that 'the problem with the sword of Damocles is that it *hangs*—not that it drops.'"

Exactly.

I'm just not going to play that game anymore.

I'm good to go.

"Here," I say to an old friend from my last bit, Dutch Teutch. I stopped by his cell when the cell doors opened for recreation. I hand him a cartoon of Camels and two bags of cookies. It reminds me of the day I left Walker Joy behind on my last parole.

"What's this?" he says.

"A going-away present," I say.

"I didn't know you made parole," he says. He gave me a look. "You just came back."

"I'm keeping it a secret," I say. "I decided I didn't want to do the time. I'm making a break. Fixing up my own parole."

"Yeah," he says. "Well, Jake, you're a good man. You need any help?"

"I don't think so," I say. "What I want is for you to do me a favor." I hand him an envelope. It is addressed to the superintendent. "Put this in the mail tomorrow, for me."

He takes the envelope, tosses it on the bunk behind him, gets up and holds up his hand for a high five. Most people don't realize that high fives didn't start with athletes. They came from the joint. An old con told me the story, which everybody in the joint pretty much knows. It came about from some guys in Sing-Sing, who started it, back in the fifties, spread around to other joints all over the country. You shake hands with a man in prison, he can grab you, pull you toward him and shank you in the gut. Since lots of black guys do time, it made its way out onto the street, where ballplayers picked it up. Most of the public think it's a jock thing, and now it is, I guess, but it didn't start out that way.

I hold out my hand. "I'd rather shake your hand, Dutch," I say. "Like we were regular guys. Humor me, huh?" I show him my other hand is empty.

Toles is waiting for me when I get to the gym. He motions for me to follow him and I do. We end up in a little alcove behind the far basketball hoop. All around us the sounds of guys shooting hoops, banging the boards, and trash-talking each other fill the air.

"You ready to drop you drawers, white boy?" he says. There is a smirk on his face.

"I don't think so," I say. "I've been thinking this over and it just doesn't sound like something I want to do. You're a lot like your brother, aren't you?"

"Well, shit," he says, and steps toward me. He brings his hand out from where he's been holding it behind his back, and sure enough, there is a shank.

Some surprise.

"How 'bout now?" he says.

"Naw. Let me ask you something. How much time you doing?"

He tilts his head to the side, considering my question. "One t' ten. Why?"

"Well," I say. "House creeper, eh? I hope you like it here."

"What you mean?"

"Nothing," I say. "Just think about what I said in a couple of days, okay? It'll make sense then."

I take a deep breath. Think of my dad. Realize I've been pointing toward this moment my whole life. I feel something like relief that it is finally here.

"I don't suppose you got some salt, do you? Or a glass of water?"

That stops him for a minute.

"What th' fuck you talking about?"

"Private joke," I say. "Fuck it. Let's get it on." I add, "You know, Toles, the only thing bothers me about this is I wish you were smarter."

"Where's your shank?" he says, circling toward me.

"It's in your hand. Bring it to me."

Then he comes.

CPSIA information can be obtained at www.ICGtesting.com
Printed in the USA
BVOW03s2046150114

341980BV00002B/11/P